The
Best of Friends

Also by Susan Mallery

SUSAN MALLERY

The Best of Friends

POCKET **STAR** BOOKS
New York   London   Toronto   Sydney

Pocket Star Books
A Division of Simon & Schuster, Inc.
1230 Avenue of the Americas
New York, NY 10020

First Pocket Star Books paperback edition October 2010

POCKET STAR BOOKS and colophon are registered
trademarks of Simon & Schuster, Inc.

ISBN-13: 978-1-61664-910-4

Designed by Jill Putorti
Cover design by Lisa Litwack. Illustration by Tom Hallman.

Manufactured in the United States of America

The
Best of Friends

One

"No gold-digging for me . . . I take diamonds! We may be off the gold standard someday."

—Mae West

THERE WERE TWO TYPES of people, Jayne Scott told herself as she hurried from the waiting car toward the international terminal at the Los Angeles airport. Those who skated through life never spilling coffee on themselves, or tripping, or showing up at the wrong time for the wrong event. And the rest of the world. As she dabbed at the growing damp spot on her shirt, left by her grande nonfat latte, Jayne knew exactly into which camp she fell.

She scanned the crowded arrivals area, ignoring the dozens of different languages, the happy families reuniting, the couples in love. Instead, she looked for a tall, beautiful blonde with an excessive amount of luggage and a half dozen or so minions. Seconds later she spotted two porters with overflowing luggage carts, a burly guy with a briefcase chained to his wrist, and a head-turning woman wearing leather pants and a leopard duster. Rebecca always did like to make an entrance.

Jayne waited until her friend spotted her, then waved. "I'm late," Rebecca called, then hurried forward and hugged her. "I got stuck in customs. They thought I was a jewel thief. Don't you love that?"

"Anyone offer to do a strip search?" Jayne asked, hugging her back and inhaling a custom-blended floral perfume.

Rebecca straightened and wrinkled her nose. "No, and I didn't want anyone to."

"No one cute enough?"

"Pretty much. Jayne, this is Hans, my bodyguard."

The burly guy barely made eye contact before returning to scanning the crowd.

Jayne glanced at the briefcase in his hand. "You couldn't use a courier service like everyone else?" she asked, leading the way to the waiting limo. "You had to bring them yourself?"

"That's what the customs people said. They lack imagination."

"Or maybe they were overwhelmed by seeing a couple million in loose gemstones."

"I'm a jewelry designer. It's what I do."

"If you were a ship builder, would you travel with a three-ton hull?"

"Of course not. Ships are so last year," Rebecca said, linking arms with Jayne. "Thanks for coming to meet me. I've missed you."

"I've missed you, too."

They walked out to the waiting limo that Jayne had arranged. She'd known better than to bring her own car. Not only did Rebecca prefer to travel in style, there was no way all the luggage would fit in Jayne's Jetta.

Rebecca stared at the vehicle with approval. "It's a stretch limo."

"I know you love them."

"Wait until you see the place I rented in Santa Monica! It has a view of the ocean and everything. I'll have to get a car, of course. Everyone needs a car in L.A."

"You could just hire the limo permanently. It could go with you everywhere."

Rebecca slid in the backseat, then looked up at her. "Now you're mocking me."

"I can't help myself." Jayne settled next to her. "Do you want to talk about your mother now or later?"

"How about never?"

"She's the reason you're back."

"I've returned to announce myself," Rebecca said, leaning back in the leather seat. "To reintroduce myself to society after a ten-year absence."

"You're here to be a pain in her ass."

"That, too."

"Rearranging your life to annoy your mother is expected at thirteen. At twenty-nine it's just kind of sad."

Rebecca turned to her. "Tragedy keeps my art fresh."

"I see you're still dramatic."

"I see you're still dressing badly."

Jayne glanced down at the faded magenta scrub

shirt she wore, now decorated by the latte stain. "I came straight from work."

"Maybe something more tailored?"

"I'm a nurse, Rebecca. This is what I wear."

Rebecca gave a little sniff, then pulled a bottle of water out of her carry-on.

She was the only person Jayne knew who could fly from Italy to L.A. and look ready to step into a photo shoot. Carefully highlighted blond hair hung past her shoulders in layered curls. Her skin was flawless, her lips full, and gold-and-diamond earrings, her own design, glittered as she moved.

Hans finished supervising the luggage being loaded into the trunk, then walked to the front passenger seat and slid in next to the driver.

"What about a workspace?" Jayne asked. "You're not going to be making jewelry at the condo you rented, are you?"

Rebecca laughed. "I think the landlord would object to me melting gold in my living room. I'm going to look at a place in an industrial park."

"You're not the industrial-park type."

"People grow and change, Jayne. I have."

Jayne ignored the smug smile. "Is this where I remind you that you're back in L.A. to piss off your mother?"

"Not if you love me. Speaking of the socially correct Mrs. Worden, how is Elizabeth?"

"Stuck in France."

Rebecca raised her eyebrows. "Seriously? Did the

private jet develop mechanical trouble? Are my parents being forced to fly commercial?"

"Nothing that dramatic. There's fog. She and Blaine are delayed a few hours." Jayne glanced at her watch. "Which means I asked the driver to drop me off at my place. I need to head to your parents' house."

"Why?"

"I have to open it up for David."

Jayne was careful to keep looking at Rebecca as she spoke. Her friend might be self-absorbed, but she wasn't stupid. Still, after nearly twelve years of keeping her secret, Jayne was an expert at making sure nothing ever showed.

It was foolish, really. One of those freak things that happen every now and then—like plane-grounding fog in France. Twelve years ago, at the age of sixteen, Jayne had gone on vacation with the Worden family. They'd spent the holidays at an exclusive resort in the Bahamas. The hotel had been fabulous, the weather perfect, but what Jayne remembered most was how she'd taken one look at David, Rebecca's older brother, and fallen madly and completely in love.

Well, as completely as a sixteen-year-old could.

Since then, she'd seen him every couple of years. The conversations had been casual and friendly. Siblinglike. Because that's how David saw her. As a sister.

Having him ignore her would have been better. At least then she could have held on to the fantasy that one day he would look up, finally notice her, and utter the classic, "Ms. Scott, you're beautiful." He didn't even need to think she was beautiful, although it would be a nice little bonus. But no, he thought of her as a sister.

She'd overheard the damning truth about eight years ago, at a lovely Worden Christmas celebration. The tasteful party had included a few hundred of Elizabeth and Blaine's closest friends. David had flown home, and Jayne had been all quivery at the thought of seeing him again.

She'd been supervising the catering staff, checking that everyone had enough stuffed puffs or caviar when she'd heard David's girlfriend du jour asking who Jayne was.

"A friend of the family," he said easily. "Has been for years. She's nice. Sort of a second sister, without being a pain in the ass."

And that had been that.

She'd consoled herself with the knowledge that at least he'd had good things to say about her. While "not a pain in the ass" wasn't anything she wanted on her tombstone, it was nice. In a dismissive, I've-barely-noticed-you kind of way.

Now in the back of the limo, she reminded herself it was better this way. It was one thing for her to be friends with Rebecca and an unpaid part-time assistant to Elizabeth. It was quite another to get involved with the heir . . . or, as Rebecca loved to call him, the "young prince."

Over time Jayne had accepted that her feelings were little more than an intense crush. But knowing they were irrational, and based on nothing but her personal vision of what she wanted David to be, didn't make her knees tremble any less when he was around.

"Carmine can do it," Rebecca said.

Carmine was the Wordens' housekeeper.

"Carmine is visiting her daughter in Chicago."

"Let me guess . . . Mother called and asked for your help."

"A few hours ago. She had planned to be back this morning, but fate intervened."

"You're choosing her over me?"

"On nearly a daily basis."

Rebecca pouted. "You're my best friend. You can't do what she says. You have to take my side."

"It's an hour," Jayne said calmly, used to Rebecca's tantrums and mostly immune to the guilt. "I'll be by later. Besides, if I don't do what Elizabeth asks, she'll want to know why. If she starts asking questions, she might find out you're back before you want her to."

"I hate it when you use logic on me."

"Yes, I know."

"Fine. Go be dutiful. One of us should be. It's a family thing."

Jayne didn't bother pointing out she wasn't family. Not in any way that mattered, at least from their perspective. From hers, the Wordens were the closest thing she had to relatives, which made her relationship with all of them complicated.

The driver pulled off the freeway. Rebecca looked out the window. "You still live in your condo?"

"We can't all have a villa in Milan."

"It wasn't a villa, exactly."

Jayne had seen Rebecca's Italian house a few times. It was pretty damned fabulous, with seventeenth-century tile and the original stained-glass windows. "It was amazing."

Rebecca shrugged. "I never did learn enough Italian to fit in with the locals. Your place is nice. Homey."

"I like it." The condo was close to work, affordable, and a safe haven from the craziness of the Worden world.

The limo pulled up in front of the multistory building. Before opening the door, Jayne hugged her friend. "I'll be by later."

Rebecca nodded. "You have the address?"

"You e-mailed it to me about forty times."

"We'll have dinner?"

"Yes, and drink wine and tell lies about boys. Here." Jayne pulled the current issue of *OK!* magazine out of her handbag. "I bought this for you."

Rebecca took it and hugged her. "You're so sweet. All I brought you is a pair of earrings I made."

Which was why, after all this time, they were still friends, Jayne thought, knowing that in Rebecca's mind, the cheap magazine and the no-doubt-fabulously-expensive earrings were on par. Because she and Rebecca were freakishly addicted to celebrity gossip, and the magazine showed Jayne cared.

"I'll see you later," Jayne said, hugging her. "Welcome home."

"Rearrange the pictures on the mantel," Rebecca called after her. "It will make my mother crazy."

"If I have time."

Jayne waved, then hurried to her condo in the back of the building. She had less than an hour to shower, change, and get over to the Worden house in Beverly Hills. While she'd been willing to pick up Rebecca in her scrubs, her crush was powerful enough that she wasn't willing to face David in shapeless hospital wear and no makeup.

She raced to unlock the front door and stepped inside. Bright light flooded the spacious room where her comfy IKEA sofa acted as a divider between the living and eating areas. There was a kitchen around the corner to the left and a hallway to the right, leading to the bedroom and bath.

What she liked best about the condo was the courtyard in back. It was nearly as big as the whole unit, with Mexican pavers and potted plants. She could sit out there in the morning and have her coffee. She often ate dinner at the glass-topped patio table. There was a small barbecue and a little fountain in the corner. It was her haven.

But there was no time to enjoy it now, she thought as she flew into the bedroom, tearing off clothes as she went. After plugging in her electric curlers, she brushed out her long brown hair and quickly rolled it on the curlers. She replaced her plain white bra with a lace one that pushed her breasts together and up in a way that made the most of what little she had, then washed her face and applied a tinted moisturizer. She used eye shadow, mascara, and blush.

She'd spent more time than she wanted to admit planning what she was going to wear. A dress seemed too fancy and obvious, while jeans were just . . . jeans. It was spring in L.A., which meant high seventies and clear skies. She pulled on a pair of tailored white pants and a fitted cotton shirt with a scoop neck. After taking out the curlers, she finger-combed her hair, sprayed the life out of it with hairspray—hoping the curls would last more than six minutes—then ran back toward the front door. She had less than thirty minutes to make it to Beverly Hills.

Blaine Worden's great-great-great-grandfather had established Worden's Jewelry back in the 1800s in New York. Blaine's grandfather, excited by the fledgling movie business, had moved the family and the company headquarters to Los Angeles in the 1920s. He'd bought in Beverly Hills when land was cheap and houses were built to be the size of airplane hangars. Over the years the mansion had been remodeled and some of the land had been sold off, but the estate was still one of the largest and most elegant in town.

Jayne hit the remote control on the passenger's-side visor, then waited for the big wrought-iron gates to swing open. She sped up to the main house, jumped out, and ran to the front door.

Her concern was silly—she knew that. Carmine would have taken care of everything before she left. It wasn't as if David was expecting a marching band and floats to announce his return to the family home. But Elizabeth had asked, and Jayne . . . well, Jayne didn't mind welcoming David home.

She'd seen him only a couple of times in the past few years. Before each meeting she'd desperately hoped he'd gotten old or fat or had grown an unattractive hump on his back. If that wasn't possible, she waited desperately for her crush to fade. She was twenty-eight—a crush on her best friend's brother was no longer cute.

But every time she saw him, her heart pounded, her knees went weak, and she found herself torn between wanting to bolt for cover and beg him to take her, just one time, up against the wall. Okay, she thought as she hurried up the steps and opened the front door. Against the wall would be tacky and was probably one of those positions that only looked sexy in movies. But she wouldn't turn down a nice, slow, private seduction.

Instead, David was charming, friendly, and so obviously uninterested in her that she was left feeling foolish. It was hard to hope in the face of constant reality, but Jayne did her best.

She punched in the alarm code, then checked her watch. David was due any minute. She scanned the foyer, with its marble floors, two-story ceiling, crystal chandelier, and custom furniture, then frowned when she saw that the large, round table in the middle of the department store–size space was empty. Elizabeth always put flowers there. Well, technically Elizabeth told Carmine, who always put flowers there, but still. Hadn't the flowers been delivered?

"No one was here," she said aloud. She dropped her purse onto the chair by the wall, then raced down the hallway, through the kitchen, past the utility room—

which was the size of her entire condo—to the back door.

Sure enough, a gorgeous spray of flowers sat on the wide rear step. It was done in Elizabeth's signature white—a combination of Casablanca lilies, calla lilies, dendrodium orchids, and roses.

Jayne bent down to grab it and nearly lost her balance. Not only was the glass vase wet from being overfilled with water, five or six hundred dollars' worth of flowers was damned heavy. She tried again and got the arrangement off the pavers, then stood. Her hands slipped a little. She swore. Dropping the vase wasn't an option.

She made her way through the house to the foyer, where a series of events conspired to ruin her day.

First, she heard someone put a key in the front door. Trying to get rid of the armful of flowers before David walked in, she started to run . . . only to catch the side of her right foot on the leg of a small, curved sofa. She was moving too fast to stop her forward momentum, and scrambling only caused her to skid like a cartoon character. Then her fingers slipped on the wet glass of the vase. She threw herself forward in an effort to keep it from falling.

The vase went up, the flowers rained down, and Jayne was caught in the middle. She stared helplessly at the soaring glass vase. Even as cold water and flowers drenched her, her only thought was to keep the vase from hitting the marble floor and shattering. She reached up and grabbed it. The unexpected weight caused her to stagger back, where her heel came down on a lily stem.

Her foot shot out from under her, and she fell, just as David walked into the house. She landed on her hip and her left wrist. The unfortunate cracking sound didn't come from the glass . . . it came from her.

David Worden, tall, handsome, blond, and blue-eyed, immediately rushed to her side. "Jayne? Is that you? Are you all right?"

She sat in a puddle of water, wet flowers and greenery hanging off her, the picture of humiliation. If only she could believe the pounding in her chest was a result of her fall and not his crouching next to her, looking all concerned and drool-worthy. Even the sharp pain in her wrist, regrettable proof that she'd probably snapped a bone, wasn't enough to jolt her out of her longing for up-against-the-wall sex.

So much for being over her crush, she thought sadly as he took the vase from her arms. So much for the sophisticated first impression she'd planned. She probably looked like a drowned rat.

"Where does it hurt?" he asked.

"My wrist. I think it's broken."

"Then we'd better get you to the hospital," he said, helping her to her feet. "Can you walk?"

"It's my arm, not my leg."

"You have wet flowers in your hair. Do you really think attitude plays well with that look?"

Despite her humiliation and the pain and the fact that she would never be able to look David in the eye again, she smiled. "Attitude is all I have going for me right now."

"Rebecca would tell you to work your strengths." He pulled a couple of flowers out of her hair, then put his arm around her. "Let's go get you X-rayed."

Rebecca waited while the limo driver carried in all the luggage she'd brought, but her attention was on Hans. The security expert had disappeared into the second bedroom of her rented space to check out the safe she'd purchased. Only after he'd declared it acceptable would she get possession of her little beauties.

The driver finished, and Rebecca walked down the short hall to the spacious spare bedroom.

As her landlord had promised, it was prepared for guests. A queen-size bed sat opposite a sliding-glass window with a view of the beach and ocean. There was a flat-screen TV on the wall, a private bath, and a big closet. And sitting right in the middle of that closet was a black 980-pound safe.

"It will survive two and half hours at over twelve hundred degrees," she said, leaning against the doorframe. "There are twenty-six locking bolts securing the door and a drill-proof steal plate."

"I know," Hans said in his lightly accented voice. "I read the specs." He closed the door and locked it. "Tell me the combination."

She smiled. "I might be a natural blonde, but I'm not stupid. No one knows that combination but me."

One dark eyebrow raised. "Very good. I give you your diamonds now."

"Lucky me."

He unlocked the briefcase from his wrist and set it on the bed. Rebecca moved closer as he opened the case and unfastened the protective covering. Inside, 387 diamonds glittered and winked in the afternoon light. Her cost—three million. Retail value once she set them in jewelry—about twelve million.

A few of the diamonds were white, but most of them were colored. They ranged from pale yellow to champagne to cognac to the rare dark pink stones.

"Very nice," Hans said.

"Thank you."

She pulled her inventory list and her triplet loupe out of her purse, then set the bag on the bed. Hans also had an inventory list and a loupe. Together they went over each diamond, confirming it was exactly the same as it had been before they'd left Italy. When they were finished, they signed each other's copy of the paperwork and she put the diamonds in the safe. Hans made a call to the insurance company, letting them know the diamonds were back in her possession.

"Great doing business with you," Rebecca said. "The limo driver will take you wherever you want to go."

Hans put his jeweler's loupe back into his jacket pocket, then smiled. "Or I could stay." He moved toward her. "Just for an hour."

He was big and handsome and probably knew what he was doing, and she couldn't have been less interested in an afternoon quickie with a stranger. Must be jet lag, she told herself. It couldn't be for any other reason.

"A thrilling offer," she said with a smile. "Tempting, but no."

"You're sure?"

"Yes."

He shrugged as if to say the decision was incredibly stupid on her part, then left. When she'd locked the front door behind him, she returned to explore the rest of the condo.

There was a master suite, with a balcony and west-facing view of the Pacific; a big living room with the same view as the master; and a kitchen she would use only to store leftovers. An envelope from the car rental company sat on the counter. She opened it and withdrew the keys. A note told her which underground parking space held her car, information she would need when she went out to get something to eat. Or maybe she and Jayne could walk down to one of the oceanfront restaurants for an early dinner.

Rebecca went into the master to deal with her luggage. Hans had carried the diamonds, because they were the most valuable, but she had the settings with her, and a little something Hans and the insurance company didn't know about.

She opened her carry-on and pulled out several boxes of platinum settings that she'd designed over the past year. One-of-a-kind pieces waiting for her beautiful diamonds to complete the looks. She removed her small laptop, a book, the *OK!* magazine Jayne had bought her, and a six-pack of Oreo cookies. When the bag was seemingly empty, she felt around at the bottom until she found a small plastic snap partially concealed by a fold in the lining. She pulled it free and removed her treasure from its hiding place.

Three layers of soft cloth protected the uncommon stone. She unwrapped it, letting it fall onto her palm where it winked in the afternoon light. Six carats of perfect blue diamond.

Blue diamonds were so rare, most jewelers never saw one. Rebecca remembered her father taking her to the Smithsonian years ago, where she'd seen the famous Hope diamond. But that stone, while large, had been a grayish-blue. This one was deep ocean blue. Flawless. Precious.

Nigel had given it to her six months ago, when he'd flown to Milan to tell her he was getting married. But not to her.

Despite her claims of independence, her need to go it alone, she had truly been defined by two people in her life—her mother and Nigel. She had loved others— her father, David, and, of course, Jayne. She'd hated her mother, and she'd lived through every emotion possible with Nigel. In the end, he'd chosen someone else.

She'd told herself that it didn't matter, that she was too powerful for him, too determined. That he had never respected her abilities, her intelligence, or her drive, and that he'd been threatened by her success. All of which was true, but didn't take away the ache inside. For ten years he'd been the center of her universe, and now, without him, the world was a darker place. He hadn't wanted her. Shades of the conversation she'd overheard when she'd been seven. Her mother complaining to her friends that Rebecca had been an accident—one she'd always regretted. At least Nigel's dismissal had been kind.

The diamond was a hell of a consolation prize. Natural blue diamonds were nearly impossible to value, and this one was perfect. A small, cold piece of rock she'd been given instead of a man's heart. Only time would tell if she'd gotten a good deal.

She rewrapped the diamond in the cloth and put it back in her carry-on bag. The bag went in the safe, where it would stay until she decided what she was going to do with it.

She'd barely closed the door and made sure it was secure when her cell phone rang. She recognized David's number on the small screen.

"Are you back?" she asked by way of greeting. "Did Mom arrange a band, or did you have to make do with a small plaque?"

"Nice. Very loving and supportive."

"The young prince returns home. All is well in the kingdom."

"I'm not the young prince anymore."

She grinned. "I know, but 'the rapidly aging prince' doesn't have the same ring to it."

He chuckled. "You're pushing thirty, kid."

"You got there first." She had planned to say more, then heard a loudspeaker in the background. "Where are you? Still at the airport?"

"No." He hesitated. "At the hospital."

Her humor faded. "What? Are you okay? What happened?"

"I'm fine. It's not me, it's Jayne. She had an accident."

Rebecca's stomach tightened as her whole body went cold. Panic surged. "Is she all right?"

"She's going to be fine. She broke her wrist. They're setting it now. She'll be released in a couple of hours. I know you two are tight, so I wanted to let you know."

"Broke her wrist? How?" she asked, then thought about Jayne's errand to her parents' house. "This is about you, isn't it? This has 'young prince' written all over it."

He winced. "It wasn't my fault. She was carrying a big vase of flowers. I wasn't there at the beginning, so I don't know how it started. Apparently she slipped, and when she fell, she broke her wrist."

Some of the panic eased. "I am so going to kill you. Jayne is my friend. How could you hurt her?"

"I didn't hurt her. It was an accident."

"It was your fault."

"Hey," he said, sounding both amused and frustrated. "I don't like this, either. And before you go off on me, I'll remind you that I have a pass for the rest of my life. Let's not forget that, little sister."

He was right—ten years ago she'd promised him she would never get mad at him again. "This is different. This is about Jayne." She walked to the master bedroom and dug a notepad out of her purse. "What hospital? I'm coming right over. And don't for a minute plan on leaving until I get there and say you can."

"You're turning into Mom. You know that, right?"

"Don't think you can distract me, David. You're in big trouble. Now stay with Jayne and make sure she's all right. I'll be there as fast as I can."

"I'll alert the media."

"You're trying to be funny, and it won't work." She put her purse over her shoulder and walked to the kitchen, where she grabbed her car keys.

"I'm trying to tell you everything is fine," he said. "Of course I'll stay with her until you get here. I've always liked Jayne."

"Oh, please. You've never even had a conversation with her." She walked out of the condo and locked the door behind her.

"Sure I have. She's funny."

"Don't for a moment think you can make time with my best friend. Just stay put and don't make trouble."

"Promise. Jayne and I will be here, waiting for you, planning our elopement."

"You're so not her type."

"There's a challenge."

"I'm hanging up now."

Two

"THE PAINKILLERS WON'T WORK tonight," the ER doctor said cheerfully. "Don't expect to sleep. You'll try. Everyone tries, but you'll be up. Tomorrow will be better."

"You need to work on your bedside manner," Jayne told him, nearly shifting on the bed, then remembering that any movement would send pain shooting through her arm. She'd already done it twice in the past three minutes and was determined not to face the searing wave again anytime soon.

"Just telling you what you need to know," the doctor said, patting her uninjured arm, then winking at David. "Give the nurses a few minutes to finish up with the paperwork, then you'll be free to go." The thirty-something doctor eyed David again, then left.

"You have a fan," Jayne said absently, staring at the pink cast that went from her knuckles to about an inch below her elbow. Talk about stupid. She couldn't even pretend it was just one of those things. It wasn't. It was just dumb. Idiotic, even. She'd sacrificed herself for a vase. Who did that?

"I get that a lot," David said.

She looked at him. "Excuse me?"

He shrugged. "I'm irresistible. You should see me around kids and dogs. They go crazy."

Had she hit her head, along with breaking her wrist? "What did you say?"

"Nothing." He moved closer to the bed as his smile was replaced by an expression of concern. "How are you feeling?"

"Wonderful. Practically perfect. Look, it was great of you to bring me to the hospital, but you don't have to stay. You said Rebecca would be here soon and . . ." She found herself getting lost in his dark blue eyes. "I'll be fine."

"Nice try, but no. Rebecca insisted I stand guard. She's worried about you. Actually, she blames me for the accident."

"You didn't have anything to do with it!" She'd been well on her way to tumbling before he'd walked into the house.

"You're going to have to tell her that," David said, pulling up a chair and sitting. "She's out for blood, and she can be vicious."

He was teasing. She heard it in the tone of his voice, saw it in the humor glinting in his eyes. He was big and muscled and so close to physically perfect that being around him nearly made breathing impossible. Of course that could also have been the throbbing pain in her arm.

"I'm not usually so uncoordinated," she said, plucking at her shirt, noting that the material was finally dry. There were very attractive stains on her white pants, however. So much for looking classy.

"It was spectacular," he said, lightly touching the cast. "Too bad you won't have a scar. Guys really go for scars."

"And tattoos." She smiled. "I actually have one of those already."

"Really?"

"No, not—"

"Are you okay? What happened? Is that a *cast*?"

Jayne managed to jerk her attention away from David's mesmerizing gaze to see her friend Katie hurrying into the room. Katie, a petite redhead who worked at the breast center with Jayne, came to a stop on the other side of the bed. The visit wasn't a surprise. All the radiology nurses knew one another, including the nurse who had taken Jayne's X-rays. No doubt she'd called the breast center to spread the word.

"What happened?" her friend demanded. "You take off for a couple of hours and now this?" Katie glanced at David. "Who are you?"

"Jayne's ex. We were married in high school. She didn't mention me?"

Katie's mouth dropped open. "Seriously?"

Jayne did her best not to laugh. "No. Don't be funny," she pleaded. "Movement of any kind will hurt. Katie, this is David. Rebecca's brother."

Katie looked at him, then raised her eyebrows. "Keeping it in the family? You never mentioned him before. He's *very* mentionable."

David leaned close. "See? If there was a dog here, you'd be really impressed."

Jayne accidentally chuckled, then wished she hadn't as it jiggled her arm. "Ow. Stop it. David doesn't visit very often. I don't really know him."

"But she's pined after me for years," David said. "It's a curse. It happens everywhere I go."

Jayne told herself he was kidding. The man had a sense of humor—something she hadn't noticed before. Probably because she'd been too busy gazing from afar to listen to actual words.

Katie crossed her arms over her chest. "You're not all that."

"You said I was mentionable. You can't have it both ways."

Katie grinned. "I like him." She glanced back at David. "You're not gay, are you?"

"No. Sorry."

"Don't apologize. It's not a bad thing. Usually the good-looking ones are gay." Katie picked up Jayne's injured wrist and clucked her tongue. "You're not coming to work with that."

"I know."

"I'd say four weeks off, at least. Then light duty. Lucky you."

Staying home by herself for a month wasn't Jayne's idea of a good time. No doubt Elizabeth would find plenty to keep her busy. Again, not good news. At least with Rebecca in town, she could do the lunch thing.

"I would rather take it all back and be whole," she said with a sigh.

"And you will be." Katie leaned over and hugged her gently. "I have to report back that you're doing okay, and I'm only on break, so I need to run." She glanced at David. "I can trust you, right?"

"No, but don't tell anyone."

Katie grinned.

"See," David said as Katie left. "She likes me." He leaned back in his chair. "Where do you work?"

"Across the parking lot at the breast center. I'm a radiology nurse. We do . . ." She narrowed her gaze as she saw he was no longer listening. "Stop it."

"What?"

"I said breast center, and you went somewhere else."

"I did not."

"Don't be gross."

"Define gross."

"You're picturing a bunch of topless women running around."

The corners of his mouth twitched. "Maybe."

"We do medical procedures. This is serious stuff."

"Do they need any part-time help?"

She eased her cast onto her belly, then closed her eyes. "You're such a guy."

"You sound surprised."

"I am. You're usually more proper. No, that's not the right word. Formal." She opened her eyes. "Serious."

He raised his arms and linked his fingers behind his

head. "Damn. Did Rebecca tell you about that stick up my ass? Because I got it taken out a while ago. There's barely a scar."

She laughed, then groaned when her wrist throbbed.

He dropped his arms and half came out of his seat. "I'm sorry. I'll stop talking."

"Probably a good idea."

"Because I can't help being funny. It's just the kind of guy I am."

She waved her free hand and focused on the pain for a second. That took care of any lingering need to chuckle.

Rebecca burst into the room. "Are you all right? Is that a cast? Dear God, what happened?" She rushed toward the bed and hugged Jayne, then jumped back. "Can I do that? Did I hurt you?" She flicked her fingers at David. "I need to sit there. I'm the friend."

"As my queen commands," he said, standing up and grinning at Jayne. "She's always been bossy."

"I know."

Rebecca perched on the edge of the chair, leaned forward, and took Jayne's uninjured hand in hers. "Talk to me. Are you all right?"

"I will be."

She turned to her brother. "This is all your fault."

"Me? What did I do?" He glanced at Jayne. "You gotta protect me, here, Jayne. Tell her I'm innocent. And suffering. There wasn't even a parade to welcome me. You're not the only one dealing with something bad."

"He can be punished later," Rebecca said. "I can't believe this."

"Me, either," Jayne said, hoping she could leave soon. She was ready to be out of the emergency room, not to mention away from both the Worden siblings. Together they were a little too intense for her.

"You can't be sick," Rebecca said earnestly. "I need you."

"I'm not sick. I'm broken. There's a difference."

Rebecca winced. "That sounds worse. What happens now?"

"They release me, and I get to go home."

"I'll take you." Rebecca squeezed her fingers. "We'll go to my place. I'll take care of you."

David snorted. "I'd pay money to see that."

"Ignore him," Rebecca said. "We'll go by your place and pick up a few things, then I'll take you to my condo. It's great. You'll love the view. We can watch people on the beach and mock them."

"Good times," Jayne said weakly, knowing Rebecca taking care of her would be anything but restful. "I'll actually be fine on my own. I'd prefer it. I just want to sleep. A good night's sleep will make everything better."

Behind Rebecca, David raised his eyebrows, as if remembering the cheerful doctor's claim that there was no sleep to be had. She stared at him, willing him to keep quiet.

"As for driving me, you don't have to," she continued, earnestly. "You're busy settling in. I don't want to get in the way of that. I'll take a cab home."

Rebecca sighed. "You're always thinking about other people. Stop it. This is why you get stuck doing so much crap for my mother. You've hurt yourself. You need to be fussed over. I know how to do that."

"Technically, you know how to have it done to you," David murmured.

"Do you hear a buzzing sound?" Rebecca asked. "It's annoying. I wonder if there's a way to make it stop."

"I'll be fine on my own," Jayne began again, but Rebecca shook her head. Blond curls tumbled artfully . . . like in a conditioner commercial.

"No way."

David put his hands on the back of the chair. "Jayne has a point," he began. "You're not even unpacked, sis. Do you have any food in the house?"

Rebecca frowned. "No, but—"

"Why don't we do this? I'll take Jayne to her place and get her stuff. We'll get her prescription filled, as well. Then I'll drop her at your house. By then you'll be ready to fuss over her. You can look up instructions on the Internet."

While Jayne appreciated the interference, she wasn't sure David would be much better than his sister in the caretaking department. Of course, just looking at him made her feel better, so there was that.

Rebecca nodded slowly. "You're right. There's no food, which we'll need. And maybe some movies. Okay." She released Jayne's hand and stood. "I'll go get things ready and see you two in a couple of hours."

"I'll be the one with the broken wrist," Jayne said.

Rebecca turned to her brother. "I'm trusting you with her. Don't screw up."

He raised both hands, palm up. "Hey," he said with a shrug. "It's me."

Just over an hour later, Jayne guided David to one of the guest parking spots at her condo complex. They'd stopped at a local drugstore to drop off her prescription.

She turned to him and forced a smile through the throbbing of her wrist. "You could wait here. I'll go faster if I don't have you . . ." Underfoot came to mind, but that didn't sound very nice.

"My plan is to help, not get in the way."

His BMW M3 might be sleek and expensive, but there wasn't much room between the two seats, and when he angled toward her, their arms nearly touched. She told herself she was aware of that contact because her whole left arm was tender, but she knew it was more than that.

She was close enough to see the various colors of blue that made up his irises and the tiny scar by the corner of his mouth. He smelled clean, but with a hint of guy. Even his shirt—a soft-looking white cotton tucked into worn jeans—was perfect, as was he.

"Jayne?"

"What? Oh, fine. You can help. Thanks."

"Next time, try sounding enthused. I'm a guy—it'll work on me."

"Good to know."

He got out on his side, then circled around, opened her car door, and closed it behind her. She led the way to her condo, pausing to pull the keys from her purse. He took them from her and unlocked the door, then motioned for her to go in first.

She set her purse on the small table by the front door, tried not to notice that her entire condo was smaller than the foyer at his parents' house, and said as she disappeared around the the corner, "I'll just be a minute."

"Not so fast." He appeared beside her, put his arm around her shoulders, and led her into the bedroom to the small wing chair in the corner. "Sit. I'll handle this. Do you want something? Water? Cheetos?"

Despite the steady throbbing in her wrist, she managed a smile. "No, but the Cheetos are an interesting choice."

"Tell me about it. Where's the suitcase?"

"Linen closet in the hall."

He left to get it, then returned and put the small wheeled bag on the bed.

"What next? Girl stuff? Makeup? Creams in bottles?"

She stood. "I'll do it."

"No. Just tell me. I can pack. I have skills. Yell out what you need." He pushed on her good shoulder until she sat. "Better."

She talked him through a few skin-care products, a blow dryer and brush, then told him where to find her cosmetics bag. When he walked back into the bedroom, he grinned.

"Now for the good stuff. Top drawer? It's always the top drawer."

She was on her feet in a flash. "You're not getting into my underwear drawer."

"But that's why I'm here."

He was funny, irreverent, and unlike anyone she could have imagined. In the past ten or so years, she'd probably talked to him less than a dozen times. They'd mostly chatted about the weather and whichever beautiful woman he had with him at that moment.

He reached for the drawer pull. "Please?"

"Get back."

"Fine." He sighed heavily, then sauntered to the chair and threw himself on the cushion. "But I protest."

"Duly noted."

She collected a couple of panties and bras and tossed them into the suitcase. T-shirts and a pair of jeans followed. By then the throbbing pain was all she could think about. David must have seen that in her face, because he took the jeans from her.

"I'll finish packing and load the car," he said. "You sit. I don't want you fainting. If you do, I'll panic, and let me just say, that's not pretty."

She hurt too much to smile, so she nodded and collapsed onto the chair.

David loaded the suitcase in the trunk and returned for Jayne. She was where he'd left her, the injured arm up against her chest, her good arm cradling the broken one. Her face had the pallor of pain rather than a good sunscreen. He crouched in front of her.

"I can carry you, if that would help," he offered. She was of average height, but pretty skinny. The car wasn't that far.

Her eyes opened. They were dark brown and large.

Pretty, he thought absently. He'd always thought Jayne was pretty.

Not that he'd done anything about it. She was his sister's friend and Elizabeth's protégé. He'd learned early to hone his skills of self-preservation, which meant avoiding complications.

"I'm supposed to be the one on drugs, not you," she said.

"Is that a no?"

She waved him back and stood. "I'm fine. Let's go."

He locked her condo, then got her in the car. "I'll take you to Rebecca's, then go get the prescription."

"Thanks," she murmured, and leaned back in the seat.

He reached around her for the seatbelt, then snapped it into place. He'd barely started the engine when his cell phone rang. Seconds later, it connected in his car. He pushed the button on his steering wheel.

"This is David," he said as he backed out of the parking space and started out of the complex.

"Are you at the house?" his mother asked. "Did you make it?"

"I made it," he said, and glanced at Jayne. She looked panicked, as if he was going to mention her. I won't, he mouthed.

Thanks, she mouthed back.

"The house looks great, Mom," he said. "I really liked the flowers."

Jayne covered her eyes with her free hand.

"What an odd thing to say," his mother told him.

"The virgins were a thoughtful touch, too. A dozen is a nice, round number."

Jayne's mouth twitched.

"Really, David." Elizabeth sounded exasperated. "Half the time I don't know what you're talking about. Jayne was there to welcome you?"

"Of course."

"Good. Tell her if you need anything, and she'll take care of it. Your father and I are finally out of France. Why the French can't do something about that hideous fog, I'll never know. And of course we had to stop for fuel. God forbid we should buy a plane that can get from France to Los Angeles without having to stop. It's like being on a commuter train. But you know your father. He thinks this is fine. We should be there in about six hours."

"I'll be waiting."

"Will it be late there? I can never keep track of the time change. Ask Jayne. She'll know. And eat something. You're such a bachelor. When was the last time you had a vegetable? Corn chips don't count."

"We seem to be having some trouble with the connection. There's static."

"I don't hear any static. You're hanging up, aren't you?"

"Yes, Mother."

"I'll see you later."

"I'll be counting the hours."

He disconnected the call.

"The flowers," Jayne said as soon as he hung up.

"Give me the name of the florist, and I'll order some more. She won't know what happened."

"She'll know. There's water everywhere and flowers."

"I can clean it up."

She looked at him, her expression doubtful.

"I'm very capable. Trust me."

Her eyes told him that wasn't likely to happen any-time soon, but she gave him the name of the florist.

He pushed another button on his steering wheel, spoke Rebecca's name, then listened as the call was connected.

"Very fancy," Jayne told him.

He grinned. "Hey," he said when his sister picked up. "We're coming over. Are you ready?"

"I'm here with food and movies."

"Great. Give us five minutes, then come out front."

"Okay. I'll be waiting."

He hung up. "Impressive. A few more days like this and you'll be as spoiled and demanding as my sister."

"Something to aspire to," she said with a laugh.

Something unlikely, he thought. Jayne was nothing like Rebecca. He wasn't sure why they were ever friends, although the relationship had lasted for years. They'd met in high school. He vaguely remembered Jayne's mother dying and Jayne coming to live with the family. He'd been long gone by then, though.

He glanced at her again, reminding himself he didn't do complications. Except Jayne was all grown up now, and he'd passed thirty a couple of years ago. He'd learned there weren't that many women who got him to thinking the way Jayne had. He had a gut feeling she was someone he could like.

He pulled up in front of a beachfront condo. Rebecca was waiting on the sidewalk, hopping from foot to foot.

As usual, his beautiful sister caused men all around to stop for a second look. Just as usual, Rebecca didn't notice any of them.

"You're here," she said, pulling open the passenger's-side door. "I'm going to take excellent care of you because I need you healthy and strong. Come on, Jayne. Can you do stairs?"

Jayne climbed out of the car. "If we go slow and sing camp songs, I'm sure I can make it."

David grinned. "I like her," he said.

Rebecca glared at him. "Don't for a moment think I've forgotten this is probably your fault. You hurt Jayne, just when I came back home."

David got the suitcase and followed them inside. He loved his sister, but he wasn't blind to her faults. She was the center of her universe, and little else mattered to her beyond her own comforts. Still, she seemed really to care about Jayne, which David thought said more about the friend than his sister.

He was back in L.A. to settle down. Find the right kind of woman, a house. Be normal. After a decade traveling the world, he was looking for home. Wouldn't it be funny if he found it in a place he'd never thought to look?

Three

JAYNE ALLOWED HERSELF TO be led into Rebecca's large condo with a view that practically stretched to Hawaii. But right now what interested her most was the cushy sofa. There were already several pillows in place, along with blankets. Even though she'd worked only half a day and then had done little more than snap a bone, she ached everywhere and was exhausted. As she settled onto the cushions, Rebecca took her luggage and hustled David out.

Jayne looked at the gorgeous stretch of the ocean, the sun heading for the horizon. Rich was a very nice way to live. Weird, but nice.

"How are you feeling?" Rebecca asked, hovering by the sofa. "Your poor wrist. What can I get you? There's food, and David's getting your prescription. Should you eat something so you can take it?"

"In a minute," Jayne said, not sure she could face food. Although she would have to. Otherwise, she would be barfing the pill nearly as soon as she took it.

"Do you want more pillows? A blanket?"

"How about if you sit?"

Rebecca sank onto the coffee table next to the sofa. "Am I being my mother?"

"She would send staff."

Rebecca smiled. "You're right. I just feel so bad that you're hurt."

"I'll heal. The body does."

Her friend had changed out of her leather pants and leopard duster into jeans and a cropped T-shirt. She still looked like a model prepping for an "at home" cover shoot, but Jayne had learned to deal with Rebecca's beauty a long time ago. She'd read an article once that said the difference between stunningly beautiful and ordinary could be measured in millimeters. An eye too narrow, a mouth too small. It was all in the numbers, and Rebecca's features were perfect, although right now she looked a little sad.

"I got *Pride and Prejudice*," Rebecca told her. "The long version with Colin Firth. We'll watch it tonight with lots of junk food and ice cream. You still like chocolate chip, right?"

"I'd like that. Are you all right?"

"I'm worried about you. This is me being caring. You should enjoy it while it lasts."

It was more than that. There was something else going on. Something that screamed handsome-man trouble. "Have you talked to Nigel?"

"No. Not for months. Since before the wedding. A friend sent me the write-up in the paper."

"Not a very good friend," Jayne said.

Rebecca rested her forearms on her knees. "It's better this way. I could never have trusted him. He doesn't care about anyone but himself."

"What does that have to do with anything? Love isn't sensible. If it was, there'd be a whole lot less heartache in the world. Love is impossible and foolish." Jayne knew that for a fact, although she told herself she wasn't in love. She had a crush. There was a difference.

Rebecca's blue eyes filled with tears. "I miss him. How stupid is that? I actually miss him. He came and told me to my face that he was marrying Ariel, and I still want to be with him. There's a hole where my heart used to be." She frowned. "Isn't that a song?"

"I think so. Probably from the eighties."

Rebecca sniffed, then straightened and pressed her index fingers to the inside corners of her eyes. "No tears. Not over Nigel. He was a blip on my emotional radar. Nothing more. He's not worth it."

"So few of them are."

Rebecca nodded. "It's just . . . I still remember what he was like the day I met him. I was young and foolish, and he was everything I could have wished for."

Stopping the tears was a whole lot easier than ignoring the past, Rebecca thought, trying not to recall how Nigel had looked the first time she'd seen him. It had been colder than she'd expected for July. But then, it had also been her first time in Australia and her first experience with the switch in seasons.

He'd been laughing in the sun, in shirtsleeves, when

everyone else had been in a coat or jacket. He'd turned and smiled at her, and she'd been in love with him ever since.

Nearly eleven years ago she'd run away, assuming one could call it that at eighteen. Tired of fighting with her mother, she'd taken off. Jayne had begged her to stay, had promised to help work things out between Rebecca and Elizabeth, but the chasm ran too deep. Like trying to cut a flawed stone. Eventually, it simply shattered.

So she'd left. She'd had a bit of money, but not enough to support herself in the style she'd grown up enjoying. Meaning a job was required. Jayne had doubted her friend's ability to make it in the real world, but Rebecca had surprised her—and maybe herself—by getting an office job at one of the large diamond mines in Australia. The Worden name had helped, as had David's willingness to vouch for his sister. She'd learned about the family business, literally from the ground up.

Nigel had taught her how to see diamonds hiding in what looked like worthless rock. She'd studied geology with the experts employed by the mine, had watched the diamond cutters work their magic. But drawn more by the finished product than by the lure of discovery, she'd left a few years later.

At twenty-one, she'd come into a large portion of her inheritance, enough for her to move to Europe. She settled in Milan to study jewelry making with a grumpy master craftsman who made her sweep floors for months before he would even speak to her. Eventually, he'd taught her his craft, and she'd discovered a talent for creating the perfect setting to make a diamond shine.

And as constant as the sun, there'd been Nigel. Like David, he had traveled the world, looking for the next perfect find. Unlike her brother, who brought his stones back to the family business, Nigel searched for the rare, the perfect, the unobtainable, and sold it to the highest bidder.

She often thought that was why they'd lasted so long. If she'd stayed in Australia, the relationship would have eventually burned itself out. But she'd left, and no mere woman left a man like Nigel. So he'd followed her, showing up when she least expected him, staying just long enough for her to remember how much she loved his hands, his laugh, his words. Then he disappeared, and all she had left was the work that filled her days and the memories that made her ache at night.

While their relationship had always been volatile, she'd never thought he would marry someone else. Right now, given the choice between him and the perfect blue diamond, she would choose the man. Hopefully, with time, that would change. Like Jayne, she would heal. Because right now she felt . . . broken.

"Have you considered that Nigel is all flash and no substance?" Jayne asked.

"A thousand times."

"And?"

"On my good days, I believe it."

Nigel hadn't been her first lover, but he'd been her

first love. Her only love. God knows she'd tried to fall for other guys, but so far she'd been spectacularly unsuccessful.

There was a knock on the front door. She answered it and collected the prescription from David. When she returned to the living room, she held out the pills to Jayne.

"I went to the Italian place on the corner. There's minestrone soup, bread, and gorgonzola-and-walnut ravioli with a butter garlic sauce. Is that all right?"

Jayne shook her head. "No spaghetti in a can for you."

"Is that what you want? It sounds disgusting."

"No. I'll start with the soup and bread. If I can keep that down, I'll eat more."

Rebecca went into the kitchen and pulled out the containers of soup. She dumped one in a bowl and put it in the microwave. A minute later, she carried it to Jayne, who'd sat up. She put the soup on the coffee table.

"Bread, right?" she asked, then sighed. "I'm not very good at this caretaking thing."

"You're doing fine. I'll talk you through it."

Rebecca collected a second bowl of soup for herself, along with bread and bottles of water. Then she sat on the floor on the other side of the coffee table.

"What happened at the house?" she asked. "I left you alone for all of an hour. This is about my mother, isn't it?"

Jayne groaned. "It's a mess. I went over to open up for David and realized no one had been there to let in the florist. The floral display for the foyer was waiting out back, but you know how big they are. I wrestled with the vase and lost."

Rebecca winced. "You didn't get cut by the glass?"

"Oh, I saved the vase. I'm the one who got smashed. It's fine."

"You've got to stop doing things for my mother."

"Tell me about it."

Elizabeth had always treated Jayne as an unpaid assistant. Jayne was smart, easy to be with, and efficient. Rebecca got why her mother liked the arrangement—what she couldn't figure out was why Jayne put up with it.

"Why are you nice to her?" she asked.

Jayne reached for a piece of bread. "Because I want to be. Your mother isn't the devil."

"I'm not so sure."

"She's always been good to me," Jayne said. "I owe her."

"At what point is the debt paid? At what point are you even? You've given back enough. Move on."

"If only I could," Jayne murmured.

"Meaning what? You've thought about leaving?"

Jayne sighed. "Everyone has a fantasy life. In a not-so-subtle change of subject, when are you going to tell your parents you're back?"

"I don't know. I was planning on showing them rather than telling them. I'll wait for the right opportunity." Something flashy that would ruin her mother's day.

"What about the jewelry? You have to tell them what you're doing. Elizabeth loves your work."

Rebecca grinned, delighted. "Wait until she finds out those wonderful designs she so admires are made by her own daughter. She'll be horrified."

"She'll be proud." Jayne hesitated. "In her heart."

Rebecca laughed. "You're being kinder that she deserves. Knowing that I'm Rivalsa will make her want to pound her head against the wall. It'll be a great show, and I plan to enjoy every minute of it."

Once Rebecca had started designing jewelry, she'd created a name to hide behind. Rivalsa, Italian for revenge, suited her. David had wanted an exclusive deal with her. She agreed, but only on the condition he keep her identity a secret. While he hadn't wanted to go along with that, she'd insisted, and in the end, they'd both made a lot of money. The first time she found out Elizabeth was wearing her pieces had thrilled her. She'd known then she was close to returning home—she just had to wait for the right moment.

"I know she's difficult," Jayne began.

"I swear, you're secretly a middle child," Rebecca complained. "No. You can't make this better. She never wanted me—she made that clear over and over again. When I left, she didn't bother getting in touch with me. At least my dad came out and made sure I was all right."

"You didn't get in touch with her, either."

"I'm not the parent," Rebecca said. "You know she was glad I'd left. I'd been nothing but trouble. You're the perfect daughter she never had."

"I'm not her daughter."

"I know, but she would have preferred you to me."

Jayne pressed her lips together but didn't speak. There was nothing to say.

Rebecca knew in her head she should let the whole mother thing go. She was an adult. But there was a part of her that had never accepted Elizabeth's indifference. A part that wanted to make her mother pay attention, and if she couldn't get her attention by being good, she was happy to earn it by being bad. That philosophy had bitten her in the ass plenty of times, but not enough for her to change.

"Do you think I need therapy?" she asked.

Jayne put down her spoon. "You're the most mentally healthy person I know." The corners of her mouth twitched as she spoke.

"Gee, thanks."

"Any time."

Rebecca reached for the DVD case and opened it. "Let's see what Mr. Darcy has to say about all of this. How does it go? Any man of good fortune must be in want of a wife?"

Elizabeth Worden walked into her house and breathed a sigh of relief. Home at last. While travel always sounded glamorous, the reality was, it was inconvenient and required one to go to foreign places. She'd never truly understood the thrill of the unknown. She had always preferred the comfortable rhythms of her perfect life. She walked through the foyer, only to pause and stare at the flower arrangement on the center table.

It was a haphazard mess of crumpled orchids and crooked lilies. The greenery was all bunched on one side, as if a five-year-old had put it together.

"I can't believe it," she murmured.

"Hello, Mother."

The voice of her son distracted her momentarily. She looked toward the stairs and saw David. He dressed like a street urchin, but she'd learned to ignore the worn jeans and casual shirts he liked so much. Instead, she took in the handsome face and the way he moved, and she felt a fierce surge of pride. No matter what else went wrong in her life, David had turned out exactly right.

"Welcome back," she said, crossing to him and cupping his face.

"Same to you. I'm sorry you had trouble with weather."

She studied him, noticed a new line or two. Not that lines were a problem for a handsome, rich man. Unlike women, men could age gracefully. After offering her cheek to be kissed, she set her handbag on a side table.

"Fortunately, we won't have to go back to that wretched country for the rest of the year. I refuse to even think about traveling anytime soon. I don't know how you did it, always moving around the world. It's so inconvenient." She turned back to the flowers and frowned.

"I must call the office in the morning and complain," she said. "I'm more than a little surprised Jayne would put out the display. She's normally more discerning than that."

David laughed. "You don't like the flowers?"

"They're horrible. Whoever arranged them has no training and the aesthetic sense of a five-year-old."

"That would be me. I bumped the vase when I was

bringing my things in. A few flowers fell out. I put them back, but apparently not well enough."

"Oh, that explains it. Good. I'm not in the mood to fire anyone." She linked arms with him and led the way into the living room. "Do you want something to drink? I'm exhausted. Blaine is helping the driver with the luggage. Sometimes your father is the oddest man."

She crossed to the antique buffet and opened the door on the right. "Scotch?" she asked, holding up the bottle.

"Sure."

She collected three glasses, then poured. After handing David his, she crossed to one of the sofas and took a seat.

This room was one of her favorites. Open and large, yet elegant, it had taken her nearly a year to get it right. But now everything was perfect. From the custom-mixed pale sage paint to the Italian silk she'd chosen for the draperies. Blaine had complained about the five-hundred-dollar-a-yard fabric, but she'd ignored him. Quality mattered. She wasn't about to have any of their friends talking about their cutting corners.

"So you're back," she said, then took a sip. "You said you were moving to L.A. Is that true?"

"Yes." He settled across from her. "I'm going to buy a house and settle here permanently."

While she wanted to believe him, he'd been living out of a suitcase for years. "You've never wanted to have a home base before."

"Dad and I have been talking about it for a couple of

years. I can do more for the business in the office. I'm ready to take on the responsibility."

He sounded so serious and mature, she thought, telling herself to focus on what was good and would make her happy rather than on the fact that David and his father were annoyingly close. Blaine had ridiculous ideas about things that didn't matter and a total disregard for one's place in society. He was the most frustrating man. The last thing she wanted was his influencing David when her son had *finally* returned to the fold, so to speak.

"I know several excellent real estate agents," she said. "Have you picked an area? My schedule is fairly full, but I can move a few things around and go with you. No man should buy a house on his own."

"I appreciate the offer, but I'll be fine. I promise not to buy any building that used to house a circus. Now, if I could find a former bordello, that would be interesting."

"Oh, David."

She knew he said those things just to upset her, but he could be so maddening.

"The luggage is upstairs," Blaine said, walking into the living room. "David. You made it."

David stood and approached his father. The two men greeted each other with a backslapping hug.

They were both tall—an inch over six feet—with thick hair and blue eyes. Blaine's hair had gone gray, which actually looked just as handsome as the blond. Elizabeth knew her friends envied her perfect family. They thought she had it all. If only that were true.

She took another sip of the scotch and waited as the

greeting continued with a stupidly complicated series of hand gestures and slaps.

"I poured you a drink," Elizabeth told her husband.

"Excellent." Blaine grabbed it and sat on a second sofa with David. "You think you can handle living in one place all the time? You ready for real life?"

"I'm ready to know where I am when I wake up in the morning."

"Good. Good. What did you bring me?"

Elizabeth sighed. "You're not going to talk business now, are you? It's late, and we're all exhausted."

David grinned. "I won't say a word except I found another designer."

"As good as Rivalsa?" she asked. "Those designs are excellent."

"Close," David said. "I'll show you in the morning."

"You said Jayne was here when you arrived," Elizabeth said, more to keep them from talking business than because she was interested.

"Yes. It was a greeting full of pomp, but not so much on the circumstance."

"She's a sensible girl. Smart." Loyal, which Elizabeth valued more than intelligence. Jayne could always be counted on to do the right thing. She eyed her son. "If you won't take me house hunting with you, then at least take Jayne." Jayne would keep him from buying something horrid or inappropriate.

"You're buying a house?" Blaine asked. "Not something a man should do on his own."

"That's what I said."

"Doesn't Jayne have a life?" David asked.

Elizabeth dismissed the idea with a flick of her fingers. "She has a job, but I'm sure she can rearrange her schedule. I'll call her." The best part of David's taking Jayne along was that Elizabeth would know everything he was doing.

"I can call her," David said slowly. "You'll be busy, getting settled."

So true. Running this house was a massive responsibility. There was also the matter of letting everyone know David was home.

"I want to host a welcome-back party," she said. "Nothing huge or formal. A brunch."

He shifted on the sofa. "Mother, that's not really my thing."

"Yes, I know. It's mine, which is why I'll take care of it. Come on, David. Let us show you off to our friends. Blaine, don't you want everyone to see how your son turned out?"

Blaine smiled. "Of course. As long as there are a lot of pretty girls for him."

"What would a party be without pretty girls?" Elizabeth had been working on a list of appropriate women ever since David had said he was returning to Los Angeles. If she could just get him married to one of them and get her pregnant with her first grandchild, she would be able to relax.

"I can get my own girl," David said.

"Your mother has excellent taste," Blaine reminded

him. "You might want to let her cull the herd, so to speak. It will save you time."

"I like the culling process."

"You're thirty-two," Elizabeth said. "It's time to settle down. If you don't get married in the next couple of years, people are going to think there's something wrong with you."

"We wouldn't want that," David mumbled, then nodded slowly. "I'm back to make changes, start working your end of the business, Dad. Buy a house, get a wife. Or is it get a house and buy a wife? I could always go on the Internet. Have someone sent next-day air."

"Oh, David." Elizabeth sighed.

Blaine grinned and clinked glasses with his son.

Men, Elizabeth thought grimly. Without a firm, controlling hand, they could muck up everything.

By eight the next morning, Jayne was exhausted. Despite her best efforts in Rebecca's airy guest room, she hadn't been able to sleep. The painkillers had only taken the edge off the throbbing. Every time she'd nearly drifted off, a new and uncomfortable twinge had jerked her back to consciousness. She was groggy, achy, and desperate to be back in her own place. Which meant waiting for Rebecca to wake up. Usually not a problem, although Jayne was desperate to be home sooner rather than later. She thought about calling a cab, but doubted she would be able to sneak out.

She walked into the living room and was surprised to find Rebecca standing in front of the sliding-glass doors leading to the balcony. It was another perfect L.A. day— clear, with blue skies and an endless view of the ocean. Rebecca wore a short nightshirt that was probably silk. The masculine tailoring suited her elegant beauty. Even mussed from sleep, wearing no makeup, Rebecca would stop traffic.

Ordinary people had no idea what life was like for the truly beautiful. How the world catered to them and shifted to make things more convenient. Jayne had been friends with Rebecca long enough to see how different things were. She'd been on plenty of shopping trips where clerks came running and nearly trampled her in their desire to be close to Rebecca. She'd had waiters pour water down her front rather than in her glass because they were so mesmerized by a smile or a glance from her friend. She'd watched men walk into walls, doors, and cars.

Rebecca turned. "You're up. Did you sleep at all?"

"No. You?"

"I fell asleep on the sofa. Sorry. I wanted to stay up and keep you company, but I guess the jet lag got me."

"I appreciate the effort."

"Did I snore?"

"Even if you had, you would have been elegant."

Rebecca laughed and pointed to the kitchen. "I made coffee. Oh, and there are those nasty frozen pastry things you like." She shuddered.

Jayne crossed to the kitchen and opened the freezer.

There was a box of toaster pastries—blueberry with extra icing. She laughed. "You sure you don't want one?"

"Positive."

Jayne put one in the toaster Rebecca had left out on the counter, then poured herself coffee. As she sipped it, she leaned against the counter.

Jayne had first met Rebecca on the second day of her sophomore year of high school. Jayne's mother had taken a job as a housekeeper to a very wealthy family living close to the Wordens. The job came with a steady paycheck, benefits, and a small cottage at the rear of the property. After years of living in cheap motels and some-times in shelters, the accommodations had been like a palace. Jayne's mother had found the work easy enough, and while Jayne appreciated not having to worry about things like having money for meals and being able to go to the same school, she'd dreaded having to deal with über-rich teenagers.

Complicating the situation were her clothes. Elizabeth Worden had donated three boxes of barely used clothes her daughter no longer wanted. Even Jayne had heard of the Wordens and their fancy jewelry stores. She had a feeling their daughter would be happy to inform the entire school that Jayne was wearing her castoffs. Not that she had any choice. There weren't other clothes to be had.

So Jayne had braced herself for taunts and ridicule. But when she'd come face-to-face with Rebecca Wor-den, the beautiful seventeen-year-old had only wrinkled her nose and said, "Thank God that skirt looks good on you. It looked hideous on me." Then Rebecca had invited Jayne to sit with her at lunch.

The previous year of partying and stealing her friends' boyfriends had come back to haunt Rebecca. The Worden princess had not only been forced to repeat her junior year, she'd found herself ostracized from her popular girl clique. Both alone and not able to fit in, they'd become friends, awkwardly at first, since they had little in common. Then Rebecca had discovered that beneath her quiet exterior, Jayne was funny and smart. Jayne figured out there was a heart behind Rebecca's perfect facade. They discovered they both loved gossip magazines and thought math was just as easy for girls as for boys. Jayne had talked Rebecca down during her frequent rants about her mother, and Rebecca had shown Jayne that every family had its problems.

"It's Elizabeth's loss," she said now, watching as Rebecca sat at the glass-topped dining table.

Rebecca shrugged. "Fuck her and the horse she rode in on. What do you want to do today?"

"Go home. I have to talk to my boss, and go fill out paperwork explaining why I'm on disability for the next few weeks. You probably have a million things to do. Why don't I call a cab so you don't have to bother?"

Rebecca stared at her. "What? This is L.A. Do we even have cabs? Don't be silly. I'll drive you."

"Okay. Thanks."

"Just give me a second to get dressed." She twirled in her nightshirt. "Unless you think I can wear this and convince everyone it's the next big thing."

"If anyone can, it's you."

Rebecca laughed.

Fifteen minutes later they were in the car, Jayne wishing she'd taken a pain pill instead of waiting until she got home. It was early—before seven—and they were in the thick of rush hour. Even so, they made good time, and Jayne found herself digging for her condo key a mere forty minutes later.

She found it and opened the door. Rebecca followed her inside.

"Do you have food?" her friend asked. "Should I have a grocery store deliver?"

"I'm fine," Jayne said, sinking onto the sofa and closing her eyes. "Plenty of food. I just want to sleep." Assuming the pain backed off enough that she could.

"I could get you a latte," Rebecca said, sounding doubtful. "Except you probably don't want coffee, right?"

Jayne shook her head, then forced her eyes open. Rebecca would need direction. Gently telling her to take off would give her friend permission to start her own day and leave Jayne blissfully alone.

"You don't have to—" she began, only to stop when someone knocked on the open door. She glanced up and saw Katie stepping into her condo. Her friend from the breast center carried two grocery bags.

"I called and said I was coming in a couple of hours late," Katie told Jayne. "I wanted to check on you." Katie looked at Rebecca. "Hi, I'm Katie. I work with Jayne."

Rebecca glanced between them. "I'm Rebecca."

"Right." Katie's smile was easy, but Jayne caught her

interested study of Rebecca's fabulously cut and colored hair, of her amazing designer jeans, Italian sandals, and a silk sweater that probably cost as much as a used car.

"Jayne's told me about you," Katie continued, walking into the kitchen and setting down the bags. "All great stuff. It's really nice to meet you."

"You, too," Rebecca said, but sounded doubtful. "You're a nurse, too?"

"Uh-huh."

Katie returned to Jayne's side and touched her forehead, as if checking for a fever, then placed Jayne's uninjured wrist in her hand and took her pulse.

"I'm fine," Jayne muttered.

"I'll be the judge of that," Katie told her. "Did you sleep?"

"I tried."

"Tonight will be better. I brought you food. Plenty of crackers and soup, a couple of premade sandwiches. You've got to keep food in your stomach if you want to keep down your painkillers."

"I know."

"Ginger cookies. They help the tummy. Popsicles." Katie smiled at Rebecca again. "We do digital imaging at the center, but we also work with cancer patients. Trust me, no one knows better than a chemo patient how to keep food down."

Rebecca looked both uncomfortable and nauseous. "Good to know," she said weakly. "So you're going to stay with Jayne?"

"For a couple of hours."

"I see. Then I should go. Let you two . . ." She waved vaguely. "I'll talk to you later."

"Are you okay?" Jayne asked.

Rebecca nodded, but she looked oddly lost. Jayne wanted to reassure her but didn't know what to say. Did Rebecca think she was Jayne's only friend? That while she was out of the country, living large in Italy, Jayne sat home alone, waiting desperately for her return?

Obviously yes, Jayne thought, too tired and sore to deal with the problem right now. Later, she thought, as Rebecca left.

The front door closed. Katie went into the kitchen and started putting away groceries.

"Wow," she called. "Impressive. She's even more beautiful than I imagined. And her clothes."

"Tell me about it."

Katie returned to the living room with a handful of crackers and a bottle of water. "I've never felt more ordinary in my life. It doesn't make you crazy?"

"I've been friends with her for years. I'm used to walking in her shadow."

Katie passed over the crackers and water. "Pain pills?"

Jayne pointed to her purse.

Katie got out the prescription bottle, checked the label, then shook one into her hand. Jayne took it.

"*He* was gorgeous," she said, just as Jayne was about to swallow.

Fortunately, Jayne managed to avoid choking. She gulped water, then nibbled on a cracker.

"David?" She hoped she sounded less interested than she felt.

"No. The male nurse on the third floor." Katie sat in the chair next to the sofa. "Yes, David. He gets a 'wow,' too. Pretty family."

"Yes, they are."

"You like him."

Like that mattered. "He thinks of me as a sister."

"Maybe," Katie said. "Maybe not."

"Trust me, he does. I heard him say the words."

"He wasn't looking at you like a sister last night. He was hovering. It was sexy."

Jayne winced, and this time it had nothing to do with her wrist. "Don't say that. Hope is the enemy when it comes to David Worden."

"You haven't been out with a man in ages. Months. When was the last time you got laid?"

Jayne laughed. "Don't you have to be at work soon? Shouldn't you be leaving?"

"I'm just saying, he looks like he knows what he's doing."

"Maybe, but he's not for me. He'll marry someone from a good family."

"Who said marriage?" Katie raised her eyebrows. "I'm talking a night or two of hot sex. You do have it bad."

"I know, but I'll figure out a way to get over it. Maybe I could get into a clinical trial or locate some experimental medication."

"Or maybe you could let him know you're interested and see how it plays out."

"Did you see ice in hell? Because that's what it would take."

Katie rose. "Fine. Be that way. Eat before you medicate and try to get some sleep. I'll call you later."

"Thanks."

"That's what friends are for."

Four

JAYNE'S DAY PASSED SLOWLY. After talking to her boss and arranging to come in later in the week to fill out the required paperwork, she spent most of her time waiting for her arm to stop hurting enough so she could sleep. Despite Katie's food delivery and advice, the pain-killers made Jayne uncomfortably queasy, so she settled on ibuprofen and hoped for the best.

There was even less on daytime television than she'd thought, which meant the afternoon crawled by. She called Rebecca, but her friend didn't pick up. Jayne wasn't sure if she was busy or if she was upset about Katie's appearance.

About six thirty someone knocked on her front door. Grateful for the interruption, she hurried to answer it.

She hadn't showered, had barely combed her hair. She had on sweats with baggy knees, a T-shirt with a rip in one sleeve, and absolutely no makeup. Which meant seeing David Worden on her tiny front porch was thrilling and horrifying in equal measures.

She tried to speak but couldn't. Not when his killer

blue eyes seemed to crinkle with pleasure and he smiled at her. He seemed taller, somehow, and broader through his shoulders. She half expected to hear movie theme music in the background.

"What are you doing here?" she asked, blurting out the words before she could come up with a slightly more gracious version.

"Delivering your car from my parents' house," he said. "Invite me in. I have food."

She glanced down at the bags he held and inhaled the scent of something delicious. Her stomach growled.

"Come in."

She closed the door behind him and followed him into her small living room.

"Great sofa," he said. "I've been to a lot of places where a family would give you their best goat for a sofa like that."

She cradled her cast in her other arm and stared at him. "What? Who would trade a goat for a sofa? A goat gives you milk and meat, although once you get the meat part, it's pretty much over. If it's female, you can get more goats. Who needs a sofa? You can make somewhere to sit out of dead leaves."

He laughed. "Someone's been watching a little too much National Geographic Channel. Are you hungry?"

"Starved," she admitted. "I'm sorry I'm crabby. Apparently I don't do the pain thing well. And as much as I hate to repeat myself, and I do say this hoping to sound really warm and friendly, but why are you here?"

"I'm checking up on you. I'm somewhat responsible for your breaking your wrist yesterday, so I wanted to stop by and see how you were doing. I don't have your number, so I couldn't call. The thought of asking my mother for the number sent me down a road I didn't want to go, and apparently you and Rebecca aren't talking."

Jayne stared at him. "We're not?"

David grimaced and swore. "Maybe I'm wrong."

"I doubt that. Rebecca said we're not talking?"

He hesitated. "She implied something had happened earlier today. She was muttering. I didn't push too hard."

Jayne's first reaction was guilt, quickly followed by annoyance. "I know she's your sister, and God knows I love her, but sometimes she's the most self-absorbed person on the planet."

"Just sometimes?"

Jayne managed a smile. "A friend of mine stopped by to check on me. Katie. You met her at the hospital."

"I remember."

"I think Rebecca was hurt that I had another friend." She shook her head. "Is that crazy?"

"With anyone but my sister." David led the way into the kitchen. "Rebecca doesn't share well. Especially not you."

"So I should feel special?" She motioned to the small dinette set in the corner by the window. "Have a seat."

He crossed the room in three long strides. "You'd probably go off on me again if I said anything about the table, right?"

"Are we talking more goats?"

"I was going to mention cattle, but you're pretty sensitive." He set the two bags on the table. "Chinese. I got one of everything because I didn't know what you like. So what we need now are plates."

Plates? As in something to put the food on? She was having trouble wrapping her mind around the fact that David was actually here . . . in her condo. Was he staying to eat with her? She couldn't figure out a way to ask without being rude, so she kept the question to herself and pointed to the cupboard with the plates. When he collected two, she had her answer.

She put out flatware and napkins. "I have wine," she said. "Either color."

"Very cosmopolitan. How about red?" He put cartons of takeout on the table. "Wine okay with your prescription?"

"No, but I'm not taking the painkillers anymore. They don't agree with me. I'll do the ibuprofen thing until the swelling goes down."

Five minutes later they were sitting across from each other at her small table. There was plenty of food, a nice merlot, and David Worden smiling at her. What was wrong with this picture?

"Need me to cut your food?" he asked. "Or feed you? I'm good at that sort of thing."

"It's egg rolls," she said. "I'm fine."

"If you change your mind, just let me know."

"You'll be the first."

Which apparently didn't impress him as he scooped food onto her plate.

"And if I don't want that much?" she asked, pointing to the large portion of chow mein noodles.

"Not my problem." He picked up his fork. "Don't sweat the thing with Rebecca."

Jayne wasn't sweating it, exactly. She felt . . . weird. "I wasn't trying to hurt her."

"It's more than that. Friendship works both ways. If she had a problem, she should have said something."

"You're using logic. This isn't a logical situation. This is female friendships."

"Words that sound scary, I'll admit. But the truth is, you get to have a life. She's been living on another continent for years. She can be pouty. Don't let her boss you around."

"You're taking my side."

He grinned. "Part of my charm. Admit it. I'm the highlight of your day."

He was, but she couldn't even joke about that. "I broke my wrist about thirty hours ago. It's a pretty low bar."

"A win's a win."

She laughed, enjoying her time with David. He was fun—something she'd always known. But until the last couple of days, she'd never had the full force of his charms focused on her. It made thinking with a clear mind impossible

Time for a change of subject, she told herself, searching for something safe. "Elizabeth mentioned you were moving to L.A. permanently. Is that true?"

"I'm ready to give up my traveling ways. I've seen the world, found plenty of exciting gemstones."

"You'll have cocktail party conversation for a lifetime."

"You don't think people will get tired of hearing about the time headhunters had me trapped?"

"Unlikely."

He leaned toward her. "I have a favor to ask."

Was it possible he wanted to see her naked? Because that would totally work for her.

"Which is?"

"You're not going to blindly say yes?" he asked.

"Do I look stupid?"

He grinned. "No. You look good."

She thought about her ratty clothes and messy hair, but decided to take the comment in the deranged spirit in which he must have meant it.

Their eyes locked. She felt and heard an actual click as they stared at each other. Jayne told herself to look away or at least blink. Somewhere in the complex, a door slammed. She jumped.

"The, ah, favor?" she asked, reaching for her wine.

"I'm buying a house."

"Okay."

"Apparently this isn't something a man should do on his own." He pointed at her wrist. "Based on what Katie said last night, you won't be going back to work for a while. Would you mind helping me? Looking at property with me and giving me your opinion?"

She said the only thing she could think of. "Why do you care what I think?"

He looked puzzled. "Why not? You're smart, you have good taste, and I think it would be fun."

How did he know this about her?

He sighed. "My mother wants me to have a woman along," he admitted. "She's not on my short list, but she trusts you."

Now this was making sense. "So you're using me to keep your mother at bay."

"I'm asking you to help me buy a house because I also trust your judgment, and I would enjoy spending the time with you."

She opened her mouth, then closed it. He was good. Better than good—he was a Worden.

"Sure," she said. "I have a few weeks off."

"Excellent." He flashed her another smile. Had she been standing, she would have been fighting weak knees.

"I have to go into work tomorrow morning to fill out paperwork," she said. "After that I would be happy to offer my opinion on the real estate front." She picked up her wine. "Do we know what I'm supposed to stop you from buying?"

"Not a clue."

"Okay, I'm sure Elizabeth will be in touch to let me know."

"I have no doubt." He grinned.

She smiled in return. "Have you picked an area you want to focus on?"

"Something close to a nude beach."

"There are places in the Valley where they film porn."

"That works, too."

* * *

Elizabeth poured tea into a thin china cup, then passed it to Jayne.

"How are you feeling?" she asked, eyeing the bright pink cast with only slightly concealed horror. "Weren't there any other choices in color?"

Jayne took the tea and did her best not to smile. "Several. I wanted something cheerful."

"I see. Perhaps something less obvious next time, dear," Elizabeth murmured. "Although you're still relatively young. I suppose it's better than plain white." She offered the plate of cookies, then leaned back in the cream-colored wingback chair in her office.

Three large windows allowed a view of the side yard, where roses bloomed. The desk was antique, having once belonged to Queen Victoria. The sideboard, where Elizabeth kept her office supplies, was Italian from the eighteenth century. Or seventeenth, Jayne could never remember.

"David is back," Elizabeth announced. "Permanently, or so he says. He's a man, so one can never be sure. Still, this is excellent news. He says he's interested in buying a house and getting married. I'd like you to help him with that."

Jayne knew Elizabeth meant for Jayne to help with the house hunting, but she had the brief, humorous thought of saying, "Yes, of course. I'll sacrifice myself and become David's wife." If only to be able to stare into those blue eyes every morning, she thought, remembering how nice the man had looked sitting across from her last night at dinner.

"I intend to influence him," Elizabeth continued. "The house hunting is frightening enough, but God knows what kind of woman he'll want to date. Men, as a rule, are idiots when it comes to picking the right kind of woman to marry. Especially the rich men. So I'll want you to tell me if he mentions anyone."

"I'm not going to spy on him," Jayne said.

Elizabeth's thin eyebrows raised slightly.

"I can't," she added, hoping she wasn't blushing. "If he knows I'm giving you information, he won't say anything. Besides, he's gone this long without making a mistake. I doubt he'll suddenly make a bad choice now."

"I suppose," Elizabeth said grudgingly. "I don't need details, but if he's about to propose to someone completely wrong, you have to tell me."

"I'll mention disasters, nothing else."

Elizabeth didn't look pleased, but she nodded anyway.

Jayne picked up her tea. The truth was, David was unlikely to tell her anything about his personal life. Too bad, in a way. Hearing about the amazing beauties who cluttered his bed might help with her peace of mind. Once she got over the heartache.

"Now about the house," Elizabeth said. "He hasn't given me any hints as to where he's thinking he wants to buy. You know what areas to avoid. Nothing too big. He can always trade up when he starts a family. Ignore the carpet and paint color. That can all be fixed. Go for large rooms that flow well. A decent kitchen. But location is key." She sighed. "I just wish he would take me along. But he's stubborn. He gets that from Blaine."

"And from you," Jayne said.

Elizabeth smiled. "I'm determined. There's a difference." She set down her tea and reached for a pad of paper on the small table next to her. "I'm going to host a brunch in the next few weeks. Invite the right people. Friends, associates. We're going to tell everyone this is about welcoming David home, but I also want to use this as a chance to let him meet some nice girls. I'll need your help with this."

"Of course," Jayne said automatically. Just how she wanted to spend her day—finding a nice girl for David.

Elizabeth spent the next half hour going over details until Jayne was finally able to excuse herself.

Once she was home, she collapsed on the sofa and wondered how she'd gotten into such a mess. She hadn't set out to become Elizabeth's lapdog. The situation had just sort of evolved. And the truth was, while Elizabeth could be a giant pain in the ass, she'd also been the one to take Jayne in when her mother had died.

Jayne had been in her senior year of high school, with no money, no family, just an aching emptiness and total terror. She remembered standing by her mother's side, staring down at her body, willing her to open her eyes again and say that everything would be all right. One of the nurses, she couldn't remember which, had led her into the hallway. Jayne had stood there shaking, too frightened and sad to cry.

Panicked thoughts had chased each other, one more desperate than the last. What would happen to her now? Where would she go? Foster care was the obvious solution, and that thought was nearly as horrifying as the death of her mother. She'd been cold down to her bones—cold in a way that had nothing to do with temperature.

Then she'd heard a familiar clicking sound. Expensive shoes on the hospital floor. Elizabeth had walked toward her, looking elegant and completely out of place in the medical setting. She'd put her arm around Jayne and led her to the closest waiting area.

"You'll come home with us," Elizabeth said. "Your things are being moved this afternoon. Rebecca needs your steadying influence, and you need a place to stay. It will work out for the best. We're practically family as it is."

Jayne had listened without responding. She'd been so afraid of saying or doing the wrong thing. Of speaking the words that would cause Elizabeth to change her mind. She'd been beyond grateful, but she had known better than to try to express it. Instead, she'd vowed to show Elizabeth by her actions.

Practically family. When the alternative was having nothing at all, practically family seemed like more than enough.

Despite the time that had passed, nothing had changed, she thought sadly. She was still on the fringes, her nose pressed against the window of the Wordens' world, looking in. Never quite belonging.

The phone rang. She grabbed it.

"Hello?"

"May I please speak to Jayne?"

"This is she."

"Hi, Jayne. My name is Paula Nichelson. I got your name and number from a mutual friend, Andie Raven. You used to work with her?"

Jayne sat up straighter. "I remember Andie." She'd left the breast center a couple of years ago when she'd gotten pregnant with her third child.

"Great. I'm a human resources director in Dallas. We're opening a new breast center here. Construction is well under way, and while we have a lot of staffing in place, we have a few key positions we're looking to fill. I'd like to talk to you about that."

Jayne heard the words but didn't quite understand what she was saying. "I have a job."

Paula laughed. "I'm hoping to offer you a better one. We're going to be a state-of-the-art facility. We have public and private funding, the best and newest equipment, and a mandate to make a difference. We're the reason you got into nursing."

Jayne smiled. "You're not, but I understand the sentiment."

"We're very interested in speaking with you. Let me tell you all we can offer. I'm hoping you'll be intrigued enough to want to come visit, at the very least."

Dallas. Jayne had never thought about leaving Los Angeles, let alone moving to Texas. She didn't know very much about that part of the country, beyond that the Dallas Cowboy cheerleaders were there, and that the area had big thunderstorms.

While she loved her job, it wasn't her world. Not completely. There was always a pull toward something else. The Wordens, she thought ruefully. Not that the family was especially good for her.

Moving that far away would mean being completely on her own. As she considered the possibility, she felt a little uncomfortable but also excited. Yes, she would have to start over and make new friends, but she would no longer be Elizabeth's unpaid assistant. She wouldn't have to deal with the sense of never being good enough. And she wouldn't watch David fall in love and marry someone else.

She would always have Rebecca, she told herself. Which was both good and bad.

Moving would mean starting over, and maybe, just maybe, that was the best thing she could do.

"Tell me more about the facility," she said.

Rebecca wandered through the Century City Bloomingdale's, trying to work up a little interest in a handbag or scarf. She'd already wasted an hour trying on shoes she had no intention of buying. She was pissed and sad and upset and couldn't seem to shake her mood.

In her head, she knew she was being stupid. Of course Jayne had other friends. Rebecca had left ten years ago. While she and Jayne stayed in touch through phone calls and e-mails, and they saw each other a couple of times a year, it wasn't the same as being able to go to lunch or get drinks on a regular basis. She had friends in Italy.

But that wasn't the same, the angry, whiny voice inside

complained. *She* was allowed to have friends, and Jayne wasn't. Jayne was supposed to be waiting for her, living a boring little life until she arrived to make it better.

Which made Rebecca feel like the most selfish person on the planet.

She hated feeling bad about herself, which explained why she was now out shopping, hoping to distract herself until the mood passed.

She left the scarves and found herself by the jewelry counter. There were necklaces and earrings. Bracelets and a couple of pins. She studied the designs, scoping out the competition. A pink-pearl-and-diamond necklace caught her eye—the pearls were perfect. She was about to ask the saleswoman to take it out of the case when she heard someone talking behind her. She couldn't place the voice, but it was oddly familiar. As if she *should* know who was speaking.

She turned and saw a tall man looking at a pair of earrings. He was fit, with graying dark hair. She moved closer, then stopped when she recognized Jonathan Mooney, a friend of her parents.

Jonathan was younger than the Wordens by eight or ten years, but still much older than she. She'd had a crush on him when she was twelve. Not that she'd ever told anyone. She vaguely recalled that he had two daughters and that his wife was an avid gardener.

She approached the counter. "Jonathan?"

He looked up, then raised his eyebrows. "Rebecca? Rebecca Worden?"

"Hi."

"Hello." He smiled. "I haven't seen you in years. Did I know you were back in Los Angeles?"

"No, and neither does my mother. You won't tell anyone you saw me, will you?"

"Of course not. How are you? You look great."

His gaze traveled her face, lingering on her mouth. The attention surprised her. Jonathan had never noticed her before. She glanced at the display of earrings on the counter and the saleswoman patiently waiting.

"Buying something for your lovely wife?" she asked. Male attention was fine, but married men annoyed her. They should either stick with what they have or leave. There shouldn't be middle ground.

"No. Liz and I are divorced. It's been a couple of years now. I'm looking for something for my oldest daughter. Her twenty-first."

Better, she thought, finding the attention more interesting. "That's a big birthday. What have you picked out so far?"

He pointed to the diamond earrings, some with pearls. She leaned over the selection and studied them.

"Not pearls," she said. "They're traditional and might be too old for a woman her age. These diamonds are nice enough." She fingered a design of three twisted circles, then asked for a loupe from the clerk.

After studying the small stones through the loupe, she put the earrings back. "Not really what you want," she said, linking her arm through his and leading him away. "Why don't you go to the Worden's store in Beverly Hills?"

"I should," he said. "I was in Century City visiting my attorney and thought I'd stop by to see what they have here."

She pulled a piece of paper out of her purse and wrote down two numbers. "Go and ask to see these. They're by a new designer they're carrying. Her work is brilliant. These earrings are young and fresh, and the stones are excellent quality. Canadian, actually, so they are conflict-free. You'll pay about the same, but she'll love you a whole lot more."

"Wonderful. How can I thank you?"

They walked out of the store, and she pointed to the coffee stand a few feet away. "You can buy me a latte."

"Is that all?"

"I'm low maintenance."

Jonathan laughed. "I know that isn't true. You're a Worden."

"What does that have to do with anything? I've been on my own for a long time."

"Fair enough."

They stopped by the coffee cart and placed their orders. After Jonathan paid, they moved aside to wait for the lattes.

"Where have you been all this time?" he asked.

"Here and there. Australia. Asia. For the past few years, I've been living in Milan."

"Doing what?"

His dark eyes flashed with interest. He leaned toward her as he spoke. All the signs were there. The question was, did she care?

The only thing wrong with Jonathan Mooney was that he wasn't Nigel. Other than that, he was successful, intelligent—and based on how much he was spending on his daughter's birthday present, still wealthy. More important, he was a distraction when she needed one, and any contact with him would seriously annoy her mother. No, annoy wasn't the right word. It would crash around her like a meteor and drive Elizabeth crazy.

All the better, Rebecca thought.

"Can you keep a secret?" she asked.

"Certainly. Who are we keeping it from?"

"Everyone, but most especially, my parents."

"Intriguing." He took the finished lattes and handed her one. They started walking.

"I design jewelry. The pieces I recommended are mine."

"That's the family business," he said. "Why don't Blaine and Elizabeth know?"

"For a lot of reasons that aren't particularly interesting. You won't say anything?"

"Of course not."

"Thank you. I'm sorry to hear about your divorce."

He shrugged. "It happens. I was too busy with work; she was too busy with her garden and charity work. We grew apart."

"Did you remarry?"

"No. I've dated some. That was interesting, after over twenty years with the same woman. The rules have changed."

"Not all that much."

He laughed. "They have for me. Women have changed as well. They're much more powerful and interested in their careers."

She glanced at him. "Does that intimidate you?"

"Actually, I like it. I dated the obligatory inappropriate young women for a while before realizing that I enjoy conversation with my eye candy."

"Who are you seeing now?"

"No one."

She leaned in and linked arms with him again. "I find that very hard to believe."

"The last woman I was with worked more hours than I, which I could understand, but when she was home, she was still at work."

"Kind of like dating yourself?"

He laughed. "Almost, although she was much prettier."

"And now?" she asked.

"Now, I'm looking."

She stopped and faced him. He was nice enough. Not a challenge, and her heart certainly didn't beat any faster when he was around. Maybe that was a good thing—it had been working plenty hard all those years with Nigel.

Rebecca gave an expert head toss, then flashed Jonathan her best smile. "This is where you ask me to lunch."

"Is it?" He dropped his latte cup into a nearby trash can and pointed toward a sign for the parking garage. "My car is that way."

Five

REBECCA SIPPED HER MARTINI, then leaned toward David. "You'll never guess who I ran into today."

David reached for the bread basket and tore off a piece for himself. He knew he could take it all, if he wanted. Rebecca rarely ate carbs. She also wasn't big on red meat, but as he'd invited her to dinner, he got to pick the place and he'd gone for steaks.

"Who?"

"Jonathan Mooney."

He shook his head. "Don't know the guy."

She wrinkled her nose. "Of course you do. He's friends with Mom and Dad, although he's quite a bit younger. Tall, graying, handsome."

"Like that will help me place him."

"Fine. Pretend you know him."

"Sure."

She looked annoyed. "He visited several times when we were growing up. Not that you were there. You were away at prep school or college. Lucky you."

Even as a kid, he'd known escaping home was the best

way to get along with everyone. "You should have thought of it, too," he said. "Asked to go to boarding school."

She shuddered. "No, thanks. You should have stayed around to protect me."

"When you were a kid, you hated me."

She shifted in her seat. "Hate is strong. I found you incredibly annoying. You were so damned perfect."

He'd been far from perfect, but he'd learned how to play the game. He reached for a second chunk of bread. "Why fight all the time?"

"To make a point."

"No, thanks. I'd rather go do something."

"Well, I'd rather be right."

He chuckled. "There's a surprise."

She grabbed a small slice of bread, tore it into a half dozen pieces the size of sand grains, and carefully ate each one.

"I supposed I should be grateful you don't hold a grudge," she said with a sigh. "Or you wouldn't have taken me in when I ran away."

"I'm a great guy," he said, leaning back in their booth. "You're lucky to have me as your brother."

She tilted her head. Her long blond hair fell over one shoulder. "Maybe I am."

A man walking by glanced at her, did a double take, and nearly stumbled. Then he saw David watching and gave a quick shrug of an apology.

"You didn't have to be so nice to me when I showed up in Australia," she said. "You could have sent me away."

"Not my style," he said.

She'd arrived at two in the morning, exhausted, crying, and talking so fast he had no idea what she was saying. Something about hating Elizabeth and needing to get away and running out of money and a guy downstairs offering to pay her for sex.

He'd brought her into his room, told her to go to sleep and that they would figure it out in the morning. They had. He'd gotten her a job at the diamond mine, then stuck around for a couple of months to make sure she would be all right on her own.

"Why *were* you so nice to me?" she asked, pushing the bread more to his side of the table.

"You're my sister."

"And?"

"And what? That's it."

"You're an incredibly simple person."

"That's not a bad thing."

The waiter appeared with the salads, offered ground pepper, and left. Rebecca sniffed the dressing on the side but didn't actually put any on her lettuce.

"Why here?" she asked. "I know a lot of great restaurants on the west side."

"I'm sure you do, but I was in the mood for a good steak, and as I did the asking—"

"What is it with men and meat?"

"It's a primal force you'll never understand."

"Have you seen Mom?"

"I'm living at the house. It's hard to avoid her." He scooped up more lettuce and a chunk of blue cheese.

"Well, how is she?"

"You could go see for yourself," he said.

"No, thanks. Have you told her you're back permanently?"

"Uh-huh."

She stared at him.

"What?" he asked.

"How did that go?"

"She was happy."

"I'll bet. You're making a huge mistake."

"No, I'm not." He put down his fork. "I've seen the world a dozen times over. I don't need to keep traveling just to prove a point. I'm ready for a change."

"Most people have to move away to get a change."

"I'm moving back. You know how I like to swim against the tide. It's more interesting that way."

"You'd better be careful," she told him. "She'll try to run your life."

"You've been trying for years and it hasn't worked."

She stabbed a piece of lettuce. "I'm an amateur when compared to her. Besides, you're the young prince. She'll want to keep you in line."

He knew he could handle Elizabeth. If only Rebecca could just accept her for what she was and let the rest of it go. But his sister was complicated and angry. She'd never forgiven her mother for not wanting her.

If asked the question specifically, Elizabeth would say she loved her children equally, but the truth had come out dozens of times over the course of his life. And Rebecca's. Especially when they'd been younger and Rebecca had been a challenge.

Like most men, David had a mental list of what he wanted in a wife. While his friends often talked about long legs or big boobs, David was more interested in finding someone who wasn't anything like his mother.

He didn't pretend to understand the complicated relationships women had with each other. The mother-daughter bond was beyond anything he could begin to grasp. What he did know was that nearly every decision Rebecca made in her life was determined by how much it would screw with Elizabeth. Rebecca might claim to loathe their mother, but she'd also never truly walked away from her.

"Elizabeth's sense of control is all an illusion," he said.

"For you, maybe. Not for me. I wish I was adopted. In case you were wondering, that's what I want for Christmas."

"You're not adopted. You're too much like her."

Rebecca's blue eyes turned icy. "Excuse me?"

"You heard me."

"How can you say that?"

"It's true. You manipulate people around you to get what you want. Your entire reason for coming back to L.A. is to screw with your mother. You want what you want when you want it. You assume everyone else's life comes to a stop if you're not in the room." He speared more salad. "I love you, kid, but you're not easy."

"I should leave right now," she said, obviously hurt and angry. "Dammit, David."

"I'm telling you the truth, and you know it. I understand you want Mom punished, but how long are you

going to live your life this way? You're trapped in a relationship with someone you claim to hate. But doing
everything because it will fuck with her is just as twisted
as doing everything she wants."

Rebecca leaned back in the booth and glared at him. "I
hate you when you're insightful."

"It doesn't make me comfortable, either."

David's blue BMW still had that delicious new-car smell.
Jayne hadn't noticed it the previous two times she'd been
beside him, but now she inhaled the scent and promised
herself that when her Jetta finally went to car heaven, she
would buy something shiny and new. And red.

It was a pretty distraction. Something to keep her
from staring at the man sitting next to her. He smelled
nearly as good as the car, and their arms almost touched
in the close quarters. She held in a smile. Touching arms
being a thrill? Was she still in high school?

"What?" David asked. "You have the strangest smile."

"Strange scary?"

"No. More intriguing. A man?"

"There are no men. I was thinking about buying a new
car." Which was sort of the truth.

"Are you planning to?"

"Not for a while. I was enjoying the new-car smell.
I don't care that they say it's bad for us. It's wonderful."

"What do you want to buy?"

"I have no idea."

"I could loan you my back issues of *Car and Driver*. But you'd have to promise to return them."

She laughed. "No, thanks. I doubt you have any old magazines lying around, but even if you did, I'll pass. It could be years before I get a new car, but it's fun to think about."

He glanced at her cast before returning his attention to the road. "You feeling better?"

She waved it. "Much. It only hurts a little, and I can use the cast as a weapon if I need to."

"I'll be on my best behavior. How are you enjoying your forced time off?"

"It's not my favorite," she admitted. "I'm restless and bored. I've spent three days reading nonstop, so that's getting old. I guess I'll go rent some movies." Of the other plans in her future, she said nothing.

"I would think anticipating the time you'll spend with me would fill your day."

She laughed. "It does. More than it should." She glanced at him, then drew in a breath. "If I tell you something, will you keep it to yourself? What I mean is, you can't mention it to your parents or Rebecca. I know they're family and I'm asking a lot, so it's probably best if I don't say anything."

He raised his eyebrows. "Intriguing. Now I have to know." He made an *X* on his chest. "I will take your secret to my grave. You have my word."

"I doubt you'll need to keep it that long." She shifted in her seat. "I'm going to Dallas next week."

"Okay," he said slowly. "Is there a warrant for your arrest in Texas? Is that the reason you don't want anyone to know?"

She laughed again. "No. I'm . . ." She cleared her throat. "It's a job interview. I got a call a couple of days ago. I've been recommended by a friend. There's a new breast center opening. It sounds amazing. They're staffing now, with the idea that we'd all start in a couple of months. I'd be in charge of several nurses, which is exciting but scary. I've never lived anywhere but here, so there's that to consider."

David nodded slowly. "You'd also be getting away from my mother."

"Oh. Well, that would be an unfortunate result of my move. Of course your family has been nothing but wonderful to me and I—"

David shook his head. "Don't worry. I'm very clear on the thrill of being around Elizabeth Worden. She's scary and difficult. Which could also describe my sister. Every baby bird has to leave the nest. Sounds like it's your time to fly south. Or in this case, east."

While she would never say that getting free of the Wordens was her primary motivation, she appreciated his understanding.

He smiled at her. "I think it's a great idea. If it's what you want, don't let either of them talk you out of going."

"I won't."

"Have you told Rebecca?"

"Not yet." So far Rebecca hadn't returned her call.

"She can be difficult," he said.

"I know, but she's also been really good to me." She shifted so she was angled toward him. His profile was perfect. "My senior year of high school, I was a mess. I'd lost my mom—she died of breast cancer. I had no family, and I didn't have anywhere to go. Elizabeth said I could stay with them. Honestly, I think it was Rebecca's idea. Regardless, I moved into the bedroom across from hers. She was like the sister I'd never had."

"She's not a saint."

"I know. I'm sure she appreciated me running interference. I understand that." She hesitated. "Sometime in early April, I started to freak. I was missing my mom and worried about my future and college and being totally alone in the world." If she thought about it too much, she could feel the panic growing inside of her. Instead, she looked past it to that day.

"One Saturday morning, Rebecca and I went shopping. Well, she went shopping, and I kept her company. We ended up in Worden's. The salespeople were always nervous when she was around because she could be difficult."

"My sister? Seriously?"

She smiled. "Amazing, but true. She insisted on trying on every necklace. They kept bringing out these stunningly beautiful diamond pieces. I had no idea how much they cost, but I remember how they sparkled. Somehow, one of them slipped onto the floor."

She didn't have to close her eyes to see the glittering diamonds winking up at her.

"While Rebecca was being demanding, I picked it

up. I meant to put it on the counter, but I didn't." She swallowed. "And I probably shouldn't be telling you this."

He glanced at her. "You can't stop now."

"I know, but this isn't a good story about me."

"You took it."

She nodded. "Yeah. I didn't think—I just acted. One second it was in my hand; the next it was in my jacket pocket. I've tried to figure out what I was thinking. Was it about attention? Did I think if I was bad enough, my mom would come back to life and yell at me? Was I trying to steal something for financial security? Was it a mini-breakdown? I don't know. I've never done anything like that before or since."

She shifted so she was facing front again. "When we got home, I showed Rebecca the necklace. About thirty seconds later, the house phone rang. A few seconds after that, Elizabeth was screaming. Obviously someone at the store had called. Rebecca was still holding the necklace in her hand. She walked out onto the landing and tossed it to her mother. She said that she took it and that she was tired of all of the stupid rules. They had a huge fight. The next day, Rebecca took off."

She stared at her cast. "She saved me. She could have told the truth. Elizabeth would have thrown me out onto the street. Or in my case, into the foster care system. Rebecca took the blame."

"Good for her," he said, sounding surprised. "I'm impressed my sister was so nice."

"She has her moments. And I've never forgotten what

she did for me. I don't know why I did what I did. It was the strangest thing. I never took anything again."

"She'd been looking for a reason to run, and you gave it to her."

"I know. That's the irony. She took the fall, but I was punished anyway. My best friend left."

"That had to be hard."

"You have no idea. I already felt alone, and that got only worse. When Elizabeth started asking me to help her with her parties and stuff, I was so grateful to feel as if I still had a place to be. It was like belonging. But no matter how much I do, I can't make them family. I tell myself they are—I pretend. We all pretend, but it's not real. The truth is, I'm Elizabeth's unpaid assistant. She parades me out when she wants to show the world what a good person she is."

Somewhere in the telling, she'd forgotten who she was talking to. But as the echo of her words lingered in the car, Jayne realized what she'd just said to Rebecca's brother and Elizabeth's son.

She covered her mouth with her fingers and stared at him. "I'm sorry," she whispered, dropping her hand back to her lap. "Oh, God. I can't believe I said that. It was very thoughtless and—"

"It's okay."

"It's not, David. I don't know how to apologize."

"You don't have to. I'm aware of my mother's faults. And Rebecca's. There's a reason I've spent the past ten years traveling the world. It was a whole lot easier than going home."

"You're being very nice, but—"

"Hey." He looked at her, looking more amused than annoyed. "Don't call me nice. I'm a guy. We don't want nice. Nice doesn't get us the girl."

"You don't have any trouble getting the girl."

"That's true." His smile returned. "As to what you said, I'm pretty damned impressed you've figured it all out. Most people go their whole lives without having a clue as to why they're not happy."

"I have more than a clue, but whoever said knowing the problem is half the battle was an idiot. Knowing the problem doesn't help at all. I still have to solve it."

"You're thinking of moving to Dallas. That's something."

"Yee-haw."

"I've never been to Texas."

"Me, either. I'll let you know what I think."

They turned down a long driveway that curved twice before ending at a four-car garage and a large house. They were at the top of a hill, with what looked like miles of undeveloped land around them.

David parked the car and pulled a folder off the backseat. "Four bedrooms, three and a half baths, sixty-seven hundred square feet. Ten acres and a view." He shook his head. "Five point five million."

Dollars. He meant dollars, she thought, hoping she didn't looked stunned by the amount. The Wordens were rich—she knew that. But every now and again, they managed to surprise her.

"It's really all about location," she said as she got out

of the car. "You can always redo a room, although good bones are important. But the one thing you can't change is location."

He climbed out as well, then rested his folded arms on the roof of his car. "You've been talking with my mother."

"She made me take notes."

He laughed. "Are you planning to influence me?"

If only she could, she thought, unable to look away. Tiny shivers tiptoed down her spine. Then she remembered her big confession and wanted to crawl back in the car.

"I doubt I could."

"You'd be surprised," he said. "Come on. I see the Realtor's car. When she's done giving us the tour, we'll ditch her and go jump on the beds."

"You do know how to have fun."

"Tell me about it."

They moved toward the house. On the path to the front door, she stopped.

"About Rebecca, and the necklace . . ."

He grabbed her free hand and held it in his. "I get it, Jayne. I know why you did it, I know why she took the fall, and I know why you've kept it a secret all these years. I get it."

It was a perfect moment, she thought hazily. With the sun shining down and the ocean in the distance. There was a light breeze. When she was eighty, she would remember everything about the first time David Worden held her hand. She would bore her roommate at the nursing home as she told the story over and over again.

He was nothing like she'd thought—mostly because she'd never imagined him as a real person. He'd been a fantasy. The good news was that reality was even better than her best fantasy. The bad news was, getting over her crush now would be practically impossible.

Elizabeth moved through the crowd in the solarium. Ten years ago she'd insisted it be added. The slate flooring and elegant pillars made it seem more like an extension of the house rather than an outdoor space. The weather in Beverly Hills meant they could use it nearly ten months out of the year. There were built-in heaters, fans and air-conditioning vents, room for two hundred standing and seventy-five seated.

Blaine had balked at the expense, but she'd insisted, and eventually he'd admitted she'd been right. As she usually was.

Now she greeted her guests and chatted with them, all the while keeping her eye on David. Her handsome son stood in the middle of a group of women, making them laugh at whatever he was saying. He was very much in demand. She'd been fielding phone calls from anxious mothers ever since the invitations had gone out for the brunch.

According to her master list, there were nine single women at the party. Two lawyers, one medical student, one pediatric resident, two models, a teacher, a social worker and—she wrinkled her nose—an actress. The latter had been a mistake, but she hadn't realized Tiffany had left college until a few minutes ago when she'd talked to her mother. The models were questionable enough, but an actress? Not in *her* family. She would wait to see if David showed any interest before getting involved.

She returned to the kitchen for a last-minute check of the food, then spotted Jayne and called to her.

Jayne spoke to one of the servers before walking over to join Elizabeth.

"The champagne is at the right temperature," Jayne said. "The shrimp quesadillas aren't moving at all. I think it's the presentation. They're difficult to pick up. I asked the caterer to put them on those tiny plates. It's more work, but otherwise, people won't eat them."

"Excellent." Elizabeth didn't mind paying for expensive food, but she loathed having too much left over. It wasn't as if she and Blaine would eat it, and Jayne could be counted on to take only a few containers home.

"The Jacksons are fighting," Jayne continued. "I think he's drunk already. I've moved them to the table by the fan. They'll be harder to hear there. But I was wondering . . . did you want me to separate them completely?"

"Yes. That's a good idea. Why she doesn't just leave him, I'll never know."

"I think it has something to do with the 'B' word." Jayne said with a grin. "Billions and billions. With her prenup, she won't get much."

Elizabeth nodded. "A word to the wise, Jayne. Never sign a prenup unless *you* have the money."

"Not really an issue for me, although I do appreciate the advice."

Elizabeth patted her upper arm. "You're a lovely girl, and you'll find someone. I'm sure of it. Blaine mentioned something about hiring a new accounting firm. I could ask if he knows of any single young men for you."

"I'm single," David said, coming up. "Who's looking?"

Elizabeth sighed. "No one interested in you."

"How is that possible?" he asked. "Have you met me?"

"Yes," she said, wishing he was still small enough that she could hug him and have him sit on her lap. Most women couldn't wait for their children to grow up, but she'd loved David's being small. Those had been the best years of her life. "Now tell me about those lovely women I saw you talking to. Melissa is very pretty, although that laugh . . . I'm not sure I could stand it."

David kissed her forehead. "Lucky for us, she's not interested in you."

"I'll go make sure the tables are set," Jayne said. "Excuse me."

Elizabeth watched her go. "I don't know what I'd do without her," she said. "Jayne is always so capable and smart. She takes care of things."

"Do you pay her?" David asked.

"What? Pay Jayne? What on earth for?"

"Isn't she your assistant?"

"She helps me. There's a difference. She's practically part of the family."

"So I've heard. But what does she get out of the arrangement?"

She dismissed the question. "We have a history with Jayne. You were gone for much of it, but she's been close to us for years. She moved in after her mother died. We've been very generous to her. We paid for most of her college."

A four-year college that Blaine had insisted on, Elizabeth thought grimly. She'd felt that community college was enough, but Blaine said Jayne was to get a four-year degree. At least she'd been practical. Nursing might not be glamorous, but she would always be able to make a living.

"What do you think of Tiffany?" she asked.

"Not my type."

Pleasure made her smile. "I didn't think so, either. But have you met Tara? She's a lawyer. Very pretty. I'll introduce you."

Jayne passed by the tables. As they'd been set up since the previous afternoon, there wasn't much to check. The caterers had worked Elizabeth's parties before and knew what to do. She went by the three bars and made sure they had plenty of supplies, then ordered a club soda for herself and headed back to the kitchen.

"You look busy," Blaine said, stepping into her path.

She smiled at him, then raised herself on tiptoes and kissed his cheek. "Welcome back. I heard the French have a problem with fog."

He chuckled. "Only in Elizabeth's eyes."

"How was Paris?"

"Familiar." He pointed to her cast. "How are you? Should you be here, working?"

"I'm scrutinizing appetizers and checking out the champagne. It's hardly work. I'm fine."

"I like the cast. Very bright."

"It's a fashion statement."

Blaine had always been kind to Jayne. He was traditionally aloof, keeping long hours at his office and disappearing into his study after dinner. After her mother had died and Jayne had moved into the house, she'd kept her distance from Blaine, partly because she didn't know him and partly because she hoped he wouldn't notice she was around. She'd been a little afraid he might spot her and ask her to leave.

One Sunday afternoon when everyone else had been gone, Blaine had seen her skulking down the stairs and invited her to play chess with him. She knew the basics, but little else. He'd been patient as she stumbled through the game. The next Sunday, the same thing had happened. Over time, their weekly afternoon session had become a tradition.

Blaine had been the one who'd encouraged her to think about college and her future. He'd read her English term papers and offered suggestions. And when she'd graduated from college, he'd quietly given her a check that had covered the down payment on her small condo. While they'd never discussed it, she had a feeling that Elizabeth didn't know about that particular gift.

"Oh, Jayne. That looks painful."

They were joined by Marjorie Danes, a middle-aged widow who had been an acquaintance of the family for years. Elizabeth had never liked her, claiming Marjorie lacked style, imagination, and anything close to a brain, but Jayne had always thought she was kind and generous. Unfortunately for Elizabeth, snubbing Marjorie wasn't an option. She'd gained her fortune the old-fashioned way, inheriting it along with everything her very rich husband had left her. She might not be the center of the Beverly Hills social scene, but her name meant something, as did her presence.

"I fell," Jayne said, holding up the cast. "Apparently, I'm breakable."

"We all are, and it only gets worse as one gets older." Marjorie smiled at Blaine. "How are things in the jewelry business? Smuggle in any fabulous jewels lately?"

"I leave the smuggling to others."

"You should ask me to smuggle for you. Ever since I turned fifty, I've become completely harmless. I pass through customs without anyone even noticing. Total strangers offer to help me with my shopping bags, as if I'm too feeble to manage on my own." She touched her graying light brown hair. "I think I look like everyone's grandmother."

"That's not true," Jayne said quickly, although the truth was Marjorie cared a lot more about comfort than fashion. Not that Jayne blamed her, but in the world of the superrich, it was an unusual trait.

Marjorie might be aging gracefully, but she was still aging, with lines around her eyes and mouth and a faint but noticeable sag to her neck. In a community where every woman over the age of thirty had had a little something done, Marjorie stood out. Jayne was sure her tweed jacket had cost plenty, but it wasn't new or particularly stylish, and her handbag looked like something the queen might carry.

"A very beautiful grandmother," Blaine said gallantly.

What Jayne wanted to tell her was that she was the most approachable person in the room, but she wasn't sure Marjorie would take that as a compliment.

"If only that were true," Marjorie said. "I prefer to think I wear my beauty on the inside. It's much cheaper that way—I don't have to spend nearly as much on night cream."

Jayne laughed, but before she could speak, there was a strange sound from inside the house.

She turned and saw through to the living room, where a very late guest entered. Make that two guests. Then Jayne recognized the couple and went absolutely still.

Her mind raced in a thousand directions at once. Even as she told herself this wasn't happening, she knew it was. There was Rebecca, crashing Elizabeth's carefully crafted welcome-home party for her son. Worse—so much worse—was Rebecca's escort. Jonathan Mooney, Elizabeth's former lover.

Six

JAYNE DIDN'T KNOW WHAT to do. Running away seemed the best option, but there were nearly sixty well-dressed people between her and the front door.

She searched the crowd and saw Elizabeth standing by one of the pillars. She'd gone completely white, although Jayne didn't know if that was from the shock of seeing Rebecca after all this time or the shock of seeing her daughter with her own ex-lover.

"What's going on?" Blaine asked, then followed her gaze and spotted Rebecca.

"Look at that," he said, sounding pleased. "My baby girl is home."

He headed for the couple, Marjorie trailing after him. David joined Jayne.

"From the look on your face, you didn't know she was showing up," he said.

"I haven't talked to her in days." She watched Blaine hug and kiss Rebecca, then shake hands with Jonathan.

"So that's the old guy Rebecca's seeing," David said, grabbing a handful of appetizers from a passing server. "I guess he's okay, although his kids must be her age. Am I the only one who thinks that's weird?"

Jayne stared at him. "That's not the biggest problem," she said before she could stop herself, then glanced around to make sure no one was within earshot.

"Tell me."

"No. I can't. It's . . ." She shook her head. "Elizabeth is going to have a heart attack. Do you think people have noticed?"

"The prodigal daughter returning during my welcome-home party? They're going to notice, but don't sweat it. Entertainment always makes these things better." He looked from Rebecca to Jonathan to Elizabeth, then frowned.

"No way," he said. "Are you telling me my mother and that guy had an affair?"

"Shh." Jayne waved her right hand at him. "Don't say it. Don't even think it. No one can know."

"Does Rebecca know?"

"Of course. I'm sure that's most of Jonathan's appeal." Rebecca dating Jonathan? Talk about a nightmare.

"I've never understood the female experience, but isn't there an unwritten rule about not sleeping with the same guy as your mother?"

"You'd think so," Jayne said, glancing around at the guests. Most of them had gone back to talking to each other and were paying less attention to Rebecca's entrance. A few hearty souls had actually gone over and were speaking with her. "Not to mention the giant ick factor."

"Dad doesn't know, right?" David asked.

"I don't think so. I like Blaine. I'd never want to hurt him."

"Me, either." He finished his appetizers. "I'm going in," he said. "Wish me luck. And remember—we never leave bodies of the fallen behind, so no matter what, you have to come get me."

She didn't know if she should laugh or run screaming from the room. "You're possibly the strangest person on the planet."

"You're not the first one to tell me that."

He walked toward his sister. Jayne hovered for a second, not sure what to do, then went over to stand by Elizabeth.

"So she's back," the other woman said.

"Apparently."

"You didn't know—I could tell by the look on your face."

Jayne ignored the flicker of guilt. Technically, she knew that Rebecca was back in town, but she hadn't had a hint about her showing up at the party. Talk about a ballsy move.

"We're going to be eating soon," Elizabeth said. "Naturally I don't have a place setting for them. I'll have to do some fast rearranging and figure out who would be safe next to her. And what she's doing with Jonathan . . ." Elizabeth cleared her throat. "I suppose that's the least of my problems."

"I can take care of the seating arrangements."

"No, I'll do it. Just please keep my daughter from ruining this any more than she already has."

Jayne nodded. Acting as go-between was a familiar role. She'd done it until the day Rebecca had left, taking messages between the women, trying to keep peace and to point out that while they didn't seem to get along, they were still family. None of which ever made any difference.

Jayne moved toward the crowd that had gathered around the couple. Rebecca looked stunning in a fitted dress and high heels, both in pale blue. Jayne knew she should probably be able to place the designer, but unless there were obvious signs, she usually got it wrong.

David and Blaine were talking to Jonathan, while Rebecca was surrounded by several of her mother's friends. As Jayne approached, Rebecca gave her an impish smile, then excused herself from the women.

"Jayne," she said, raising her eyebrows. "What a surprise to see you here. Oh, I suppose it's not a surprise after all. You would be needed to help things run smoothly. Whatever would my mother do without you?"

"Are you insane?" Jayne asked in a low voice. "Bringing him here?"

Rebecca laughed. "It's delicious. You have to admit I know how to make an entrance." She signaled a passing server and took two glasses of champagne from the tray. She handed the second one to Jayne.

Jayne took it, then leaned in closer. "He slept with your mother."

"I know. That makes it so much better."

Jonathan joined them. Rebecca leaned into him. "Jonathan, this is my friend Jayne."

"We've met," Jayne said, then desperately wished she could call back the words. "Years ago. I'm sure you don't remember. You were . . ." Sleeping with Elizabeth? Scratch that. "We were just teenagers and not of much interest."

Rebecca looked at her quizzically. "Nearly finished?"

"God, I hope so."

"Nice to meet you again, Jayne," Jonathan said, shaking her hand. "Nice cast. What happened?"

"I thought I had superhuman powers."

"You don't?" David walked up and put his hand on the small of her back. "Damn. Someone somewhere has to have them, and I'm going to find that person." He glanced at Rebecca. "Nice entrance. Very smooth and low key."

"Thanks. That's exactly what I was going for."

Jayne was glad they were talking, because she wasn't up for speech. Not while she could feel every cell of his skin touching hers. Well, touching through a couple of layers of fabric. Still, it was thrilling.

"You're staying for brunch, aren't you?" he asked Rebecca. "Mom arranged to have every single appropriate female in a fifty-mile radius brought here. There's going to be a talent competition later."

"Who would want to miss that?" Rebecca asked.

Oh, right. The other women. Some of the thrill left, and Jayne casually stepped to the right. David's hand fell away. No matter how she wanted things to be different, the truth was David would never be interested in someone like her. The young prince had a destiny. He would marry the "right kind of girl." Someone from a wealthy family, someone with social status and a closet full of designer handbags.

Rebecca looked at Jayne. "She wants you to keep me in line, doesn't she?"

"Oh, yeah."

"Are we taking odds?"

"I'm hoping you'll be merciful and behave."

Rebecca tossed her blond hair and laughed. "You've always had a delicious sense of humor, Jayne. It's one of your best qualities."

Rebecca's work space was little more than two hundred square feet in an industrial building. There were all kinds of artists working on different projects, but in her section were the jewelry designers. While she had her own tools for setting stones and finishing her pieces, she didn't like working in the condo. Something wasn't right. Maybe the feng shui was off or the view was too good. Maybe it was the silence. In Italy, she worked with other jewelers, so she was used to the conversations, the sound of grinding and polishing. Regardless, the second she sat down on the beat-up stool in her workspace and flipped on the intense light that flooded her battered desk, she felt wildly creative.

She'd just unpacked three diamonds and a bracelet setting when Jayne climbed the stairs and joined her.

"This is where you're working?" her friend asked by way of greeting. "Seriously?"

"Isn't it great?" Rebecca looked around at the paint-spattered cement walls. A guy at the far end of the huge space got out a blowtorch and prepared to climb up a twenty-foot-tall sculpture. "Can't you feel the energy?"

"Mostly I'm worried about the building burning down, but if you like it, that's what matters."

"I love it. No one knows who I am, and if they did, I doubt they'd care. I pay rent just like everyone else."

"You drive a Mercedes. It's so new, you don't have actual plates yet."

"The rental wasn't working for me."

"Welcome to the world of the little people."

"Don't mock me." Rebecca pointed to a stool in the corner. "You can watch me work my magic, then we'll talk about how brilliant I am."

"Lucky me." Jayne sat down and reached for one of the diamonds. "Ballpark it for me."

"Loose? Three. Three-fifty. But with these and in a bracelet designed by moi? A couple million."

Jayne carefully returned the stone to the table. "Not even if I made payments for the rest of my life."

Rebecca grinned. "I could give it to you for cost."

"Even so." She covered a yawn. "Sorry. I'm still recovering from the brunch."

"Did my mother make you stay late and scrub floors?"

"Nothing that dramatic. I did stay until the last guest left, and then I supervised the cleanup. That was the easy part. Listening to your mother rant about your return was painful."

"She was upset?" Rebecca asked, already knowing the answer. Her goal had been to stun Elizabeth. It seems she'd succeeded in spades.

"Upset doesn't come close."

Rebecca laughed and leaned her elbows on the table. "Good. By the way, you also looked a little shocked. I probably should have warned you, but maybe it's better that I didn't. Elizabeth won't think you were in on the secret."

"Thank you," Jayne said. "Was it everything you wanted? That entrance, making your mother squirm?"

"No. I always want more. But it was nice that she was unhappy. That makes it a good day."

Jayne shifted on the stool, then started to speak, only to stop. As if she were choosing her words carefully.

"Where's the win?" she asked. "At what point is toying with her enough?"

"I don't know. There's a whole lifetime of injuries that require payback."

"You've been gone ten years. Aren't you over it?"

Rebecca straightened. "Over not being wanted by my own mother? Over being told that I wasn't good enough, that I was a constant disappointment? Over the nagging, complaining, and not-so-subtle comments that life would have been better if they'd stopped with a single child?"

Jayne set her cast-covered arm on the table. "So 'over' is the wrong word. At what point do you move on? You're still defining yourself on Elizabeth's terms. You're still making what *she* thinks the most important thing."

Rebecca didn't like that. She picked up one of the diamonds, then put it down. "That's not true. I've been living my own life, without even thinking about her. I'm focused because I'm back."

"Really? Then why did you name your company Rivalsa? Isn't the revenge about her? Why won't you tell her you're the one behind the jewelry?"

"I don't want her to know. Not yet."

Jayne simply looked at her.

Rebecca picked up one of the diamonds, then tossed it back on the table. "Fine. I have mother issues. That's hardly unique."

"Yours drag you down. You spend so much time and energy hating Elizabeth. That can't be good for you."

Rebecca shrugged. Hating her mother was a whole lot easier than facing the pain inside. The emptiness. The fact that the only time she felt whole was with Nigel.

"Enough about me," she said. "How's the wrist?"

"Better. Healing. At least that's what I tell myself when it aches." She rubbed the cast. "I miss work. My friends, the patients."

Rebecca didn't want to talk about Jayne's other friends. "What did you think of Jonathan?"

Jayne grimaced. "I didn't get a chance to talk to him. I'm sure he's very nice."

"I'll admit he's not my fantasy guy," Rebecca said. "But he's reasonably intelligent and funny. Uncomplicated. I think I need uncomplicated."

"You'll get over Nigel."

"Could you give me a date? Even one month in the

future. It would give me something to look forward to."
Imagine closing her eyes at night and not hearing his
voice or picturing him in her mind. What on earth would
she do with her day when she didn't have missing Nigel
to fill up the time?

"You won't be in love with him forever," Jayne said.

"Is that a promise?"

Jayne looked uncomfortable. "No. It's not."

Because loving one man for the rest of her life, while
old-fashioned and depressing, was entirely possible.

"Why did I have to fall for him?" she asked, picking up
the smallest of the three diamonds and turning it over
in her hands. "Don't worry. I don't expect an answer. No
one knows why we love the people we love. If only love
were sensible."

"Like me," Jayne said. "That's how everyone sees me.
Not pretty or funny or charming. I'm sensible and reliable. Like a used compact car. Nothing flashy, but you
know it will start in the morning."

Rebecca stared at her. "That's not really what you
think, is it?"

"Sure. I'm the sensible friend, the person Elizabeth
can count on to do the right thing. I can be trusted to
know where the good china is and not steal it. I'm a para-
gon of incredibly boring virtues. You get to be all beautiful and fiery and dangerous."

"I'm hardly dangerous."

"You had your mother sweating yesterday at the
brunch. And then she sent me to make sure you stayed

in line. I'm like those placid dogs a family buys when the dog they chose first is too high strung. I'm the pet's pet."

"Which makes me the high-strung dog?" Rebecca asked, trying not to smile.

"Do not make this about you," Jayne snapped. "I'm serious here. Your mother asked me to help David house hunt. Apparently, men aren't capable of buying a house on their own. How lucky for all of us that I broke my wrist and am available. Although I'm sure if I was still working, she would explain to me why helping her son was more important than my job."

"Isn't everything?"

"Yes." Jayne covered her face with her hands. "She asked me to tell her any information I may pick up about who he's dating." She dropped her hands. "I told her no, but that's not the point. She asked. She expected I would be her spy. I'm an unpaid family retainer."

"Is that better or worse than being a reliable used car or a Labrador?"

Jayne's mouth twitched at the corners. "There are mean-looking tools all over this place. Don't make me use one on you."

"Are you threatening me?"

"Absolutely. It could get ugly."

"You can't take me."

Jayne stood. "Want to bet? I have years of resentful bitterness on my side."

Rebecca rose and walked around the table. "I have four-inch heels."

Jayne's expression softened. "Thanks for being my friend."

Rebecca stepped close and hugged her. "Always. I love you."

"I love you, too."

They held on to each other for several seconds.

"It would make me really happy if you told David to buy a house that would piss off my mother."

Jayne laughed. "I'm sure it would, but I thought you liked David."

"I do. You're saying any house that would annoy Elizabeth would be bad for him?"

"It's a possibility."

"Oh, sure. Think of everyone but me." She returned to her side of the table and sank onto her stool. "What's he seen so far?"

"A place in Malibu. It was lovely, if you're in to floor-to-ceiling views and forty-seven fireplaces."

"Forty-seven?"

"Okay. Three or four. It was huge and beautifully done. Ten acres. What does anyone need with ten acres unless you're keeping livestock?"

"It's for privacy."

"I didn't realize David was being stalked."

Rebecca laughed. "He's not, but land means wealth."

"I guess, but I think it's silly. And way too expensive. My entire condo is smaller than the master suite."

"What did he think of it?"

"He said it was nice, but he wants to keep looking."

"Did he say why he's looking in Malibu?"

Jayne rolled her eyes. "No, and if he did, I wouldn't tell you. If you want to know, ask him yourself. You sound like your mother."

"Hey, there's no need to be mean. I'm nothing like—"

Her cell phone rang. Rebecca walked to her purse and grabbed it, then stared at the small screen. There was a single word there.

Nigel.

"What?" Jayne asked, hurrying to her side. "Oh. What are you going to do?"

"Nothing."

She listened to three more rings, then there was silence. A few seconds later, the message envelope popped onto the screen.

"He's doing this on purpose," she whispered. "He doesn't want me, but he doesn't want me to forget him, either."

"Does he know you left Milan?"

"I don't know." Part of her wondered if he'd gone to see her, only to find out she was gone. Or was that wishful thinking on her part?

"Are you going to listen to the message?"

Rebecca nodded, then pushed the speakerphone button before dialing her voice mail. Seconds later, she heard Nigel's voice.

"Becca Blue," he said, that familiar, low voice making her stomach hurt. "Where are you? I can't get you anywhere. Are you hiding? I have to go to New York in a couple of weeks. Want to meet me there? The usual place? I promise days and nights of fun. Call me."

Anger replaced longing. She glared at her phone. "That bastard. I'm good enough to fuck, but not good enough to marry?" She pushed the button to delete the message. If only it were so easy to erase it from her memory.

"I'm sorry," Jayne told her.

"I know. Me, too."

"Are you going to New York?"

"No. Not even to annoy my mother."

"Well," Jayne said sympathetically, "that's progress."

If only it were enough, Rebecca thought. She looked back at her phone. She hadn't heard from Nigel in weeks. Not since he'd gotten married. She was cynical enough to think he wasn't missing her all that much. She would guess he might be having second thoughts about the blue diamond he'd given her. Was greed more powerful than guilt? She had a feeling she was about to find out.

Seven

AT ONE O'CLOCK, DAVID took the elevator down to the Worden of Beverly Hills boutique. The company offices were on the three floors above the store. His new office was next to his father's. After nearly two weeks, he was enjoying the transition from the excitement of searching for rare gemstones to a more structured day, complete with meetings and an assistant. He stuck his finger between his neck and his collar. The tie was tougher to accept.

He walked through the back room and into the quiet elegance of the retail store. Recessed lighting illuminated the brilliance of the stones, while polished glass protected millions of dollars worth of inventory. The salespeople were well dressed, knowledgeable, and charming; the carpet was plush; the two security guards by the door were huge and armed.

He glanced around until he saw Jayne leaning over a display of earrings. Her long brown hair fell onto the case. She pulled it away, holding it in one hand, the way women with long hair do. It was one of those unconscious gestures that drove men wild. At least it drove *him* wild.

There was something about Jayne. Something quiet and unassuming. She didn't demand attention or expect to be in the middle of everything. Yet whenever she spoke, he found himself wanting to listen.

She turned and saw him, smiled and gave him a little wave. Unexpected anticipation coursed through him. As if he'd been waiting for her to show up so his day could start.

"So you brought me back to the scene of the crime," she said quietly as she approached. "Do I look guilty? I feel guilty."

"Guilty about what?"

She poked him in the chest with her index finger. "My felony. I stole a necklace from here."

"No one cares."

"Ha. That sounds great, but wait until the police find out."

"I won't tell them."

"You say that now, but we'll see."

Laughter brightened her eyes. She wasn't wearing much makeup, so he could see the freckles on her nose. There was something glossy on her lips, something he wanted to wipe away so he could—

"David?"

"What? I'm fine."

"Are you sure? You look . . . I don't know. Strange. Are you feeling all right?"

"Great. I'm great. Come on. The elevator is this way."

He hurried her through the store to the doors at the rear. "This is our workroom. We replace watch batteries, do minor repairs, that kind of thing. Anything big is sent upstairs, where we have two full-time jewelers."

Jayne hadn't asked for an explanation, but he felt the need to keep talking. Mostly because, for one brief second, he'd been thinking that he wanted to kiss her. Kiss Jayne.

Talk about trouble. She was his sister's best friend, his mother's . . . he didn't know how to define her relationship with Elizabeth, but it was a complication. She wasn't his type. She wasn't . . .

He stopped by the elevator and looked at her. She looked back.

"Do you need a glass of water or something?" she asked. "Did you hit your head?"

"No."

Why not Jayne? She was smart, funny, easy to be with. The only difference between her and the women his mother had wanted him to meet at the brunch was a trust fund and family connections. Neither of which had ever mattered to him. He wasn't saying he was ready to propose, but there was no reason not to explore the possibilities. Assuming she was interested.

He pushed the up button.

She eyed him cautiously. "I have professional medical training, so if you need help, just say so."

"What I want is your opinion. That's why I asked you to come by."

"You said something about meeting a new designer.

Does Rivalsa know you're cheating on her with someone new?"

"We have multiple designers working for us," he said as the elevator doors opened and they stepped inside.

"Uh-huh. Just promise me I'll be in the room when you explain that to you know who."

He pushed the button for the fourth floor. "I have another house viewing scheduled in a couple of days. Want to come with me?"

"Sure. Maybe something nicer this time. You know, with a real view. And that kitchen? I doubt you could serve more than seventy or eighty people."

He laughed. "You're saying it was too much?"

"I'm saying you're going to need a series of 'you are here' maps to find your way around."

They walked out onto the fourth floor.

"The conference room is over there," he said, pointing toward the glass doors.

"I thought there'd be more security," Jayne said, her voice quiet. "A metal detector and one of those things you have to put your palm on. This is very disappointing."

"We don't keep the actual jewelry up here."

"Damn. And I brought my cat burglar suit and everything."

"Next time," he promised.

Jayne looked at him and raised her eyebrows. "You say that now, but I'm not sure I can trust you."

"What does that mean?"

"Apparently, you're the kind of guy who says one thing

and does another." She smiled. "You moved out of your mother's house."

He shuddered. "I had to. She was . . ."

"Too close?"

"Oh, yeah. She called you?"

"Uh-huh. She's not a happy camper. I'd get her something small but tasteful, if I were you. But she's pleased with your choice of hotel. If you have to leave the safe confines of her home, at least you're suffering at the Four Seasons."

There was something about the way she said the name. "You have a problem with the hotel?"

She glanced at him out of the corner of her eye. "I'm sure it's lovely."

"It's a place to sleep."

"Oh, please. Do you even know what a room there costs a night?"

He didn't have a room . . . he had a suite. "No. Do you?"

"I know if one has to ask, one probably can't afford it. I'll be fine."

He held open the door to the conference room. "The Four Seasons is really close to the office."

"You don't have to justify yourself to me. I've heard they have the best turn-down service." Her eyes sparkled as she spoke.

"Now you're just mocking me."

"Uh-huh."

They entered the conference room. Peter, their marketing director, was there with the designer.

David took care of introductions. "Jayne is a friend of mine. I wanted her thoughts on the pieces." He waited until Jayne took a seat across from the two men. "I discovered Élan's work while I was in Spain last year. I asked him to submit a few pieces for us to consider for the stores. They would be exclusive, of course."

Peter grinned. "Part of the Worden appeal. You can't get our beautiful jewelry anywhere else."

Élan put a small black case on the table and opened it. Inside were three rings, two necklaces, and two bracelets. Élan spread them out on a black velvet cloth, then slid the cloth toward David.

While Rebecca's work was all about lush curves and the female shape, Élan preferred geometry. There was a sharpness to his pieces, a sophistication. He used only white diamonds with platinum, which added to the modernist feel.

David had already studied the diamonds and knew their quality. What he was most interested in was Jayne's reaction to the collection.

She looked from the jewelry back to him. "What am I doing here?" she asked in a whisper.

"Telling me what you think. You're our target market."

She shook her head. "Not if these are real." She touched the necklace. "Do you have a price point yet?"

Peter waved his hands. "Nothing's been decided. We're thinking we want a more mass appeal with this collection. A younger consumer, which will be reflected in the price. Maybe twenty or thirty thousand for the rings.

Close to a hundred for the bracelets. Maybe one-fifty or two for the necklaces."

"I will have earrings, yes?" Élan said. "There was a problem with the mold, and they are not ready."

Jayne pressed her lips together. "Good to know."

Élan spent several minutes explaining his vision, where he saw the line going, and what other materials interested him. David listened carefully while trying to figure out what Jayne was thinking. He couldn't be sure, but she didn't seem to love the work.

Forty minutes later Élan packed up his samples and left. David promised Peter he would stop by later and angled toward Jayne.

"What were you thinking?" he asked.

"They're lovely. A little cold for my taste, but I can see a lot of women thinking they're perfect."

"And?"

"And . . . it's been very interesting getting to see this side of the business. I've never been up in the offices or at a meeting like this. I wonder if it's how companies decide on a new toilet paper."

He stared at her, not speaking.

She rubbed her cast, tucked her hair behind her ears, then spun in her chair toward him. "What?"

"You're not telling me what you think. There's more. I know there is."

She opened her mouth, then closed it. "Call me crazy, but does the world really need another hundred-and fifty-*thousand*-dollar necklace? On what planet does a twenty-thousand-dollar price tag on a ring indicate that it's more accessible to a younger buyer? Who has that kind of money—not counting your family and all the people you know? Conventional wisdom says that a guy should spend two months' salary on an engagement ring. Let's say he makes sixty thousand a year, which is pretty average. That's ten thousand dollars, pretax. You're talking twenty, and it's not even an engagement ring. This may be your world, but it's not mine, and it's not normal."

"The Worden brand is upscale."

"Everyone in this room is really clear on that." She pushed to her feet. "I don't know what you want me to say, David. They're lovely. And I'll never be able to afford them. Why can't you find someone to make jewelry for the rest of us? Don't we deserve something nice, too? I'm not saying we'll get the same quality of metal or stones or diamonds the size of small dogs. But something pretty. And affordable. Isn't that good business, too?"

He rose. "We've never gone in that direction."

"You could try it. Have you heard of Tacori?"

"Sure. Great jewelry."

"They sell it on QVC."

"What's QVC?"

Her expression turned pitying. "It's a television shopping channel. Everything from vacuums to cookware to jewelry. Tacori does a line for them. It's exclusive and pretty and affordable in a huge way. I have some earrings, and I always get compliments when I wear them. There are only a handful of people who will ever be able to afford Worden jewelry. What about the rest of us?"

When she said it, the idea sounded simple and obvious. "I'll look into it," David said.

"I hope so. Just don't tell Elizabeth it was my idea."

"Seven-point-five million," Jayne breathed as she read the flyer David handed her. "I went online and found a mortgage calculator. That's over forty thousand dollars a month, assuming twenty percent down. A month!"

"I'll put more down," David said.

"Sure, because of the payments." She looked up at the long driveway. "I like the palm trees. Very L.A. Six bedrooms, five baths. That means someone has to share. I don't get it. Why would anyone be willing to share? Of course, there's a separate apartment for the maid. That's important. You don't want the help living in."

"You're babbling."

"I know. I'm overwhelmed."

She was also having second thoughts about helping David with his house hunting. After her little rant earlier in the week, she'd expected him to cancel their appointment. But he hadn't, and she wasn't sure why. Nor did she know what she'd been thinking when she told him the Worden jewelry cost too much. Had she really talked about QVC?

The family was rich at a level she couldn't comprehend, and she'd known them for years. The house in front of them was proof of David's net worth.

"There's private beach access," she said, "but it's going

to be a hike down. And you'll be dealing with fire danger when the winds come."

"You're a worrier."

"Sometimes. I'm just saying, you'll want to test out the sprinkler system."

They walked toward the front door. It was large, with etched glass on either side. The real estate agent opened the door.

"There are so many amazing features to this house," she said, leading them inside where the two-story entry-way stretched for what seemed like miles. "As you can see, this has more of a rustic feel to it, with many natural and green touches. There are solar panels to generate electricity, extra-thick walls to keep the temperature even, and renewable products used wherever possible. The wood beams were recovered from a sixteenth-century cathedral in Germany."

"Where all good wood comes from," Jayne whispered.

David nodded but didn't say anything. He seemed distracted. Maybe he was pissed about what she'd said about the jewelry. Or thought she was being critical about the house. Or judgmental. Which brought her back to wondering why she was here. She should have told him no, that she couldn't go house hunting with him. Only that would require a level of self-control she simply didn't have.

The agent led them into a beautiful kitchen the size of an airport terminal. There were three ovens, an eight-burner stove, separate stainless refrigerator and freezer, either of which could have held a couple of bodies, and cupboard space for twenty. There were hand-painted tiles for a backsplash and a huge bay window above the sink.

"I'll leave you to explore it on your own," the agent said. "Then meet you by the stairs."

When she'd left, David ran his hands across the counter. "It's kinda big."

"Everything is lovely."

"But?"

"But nothing."

"You're not going to tell me we could store tanks here if the military has a surplus, or an orchestra? That whatever resources were saved by using the restored beams were wasted getting them here?"

She winced. "I don't mean any of that in a bad way."

"I know."

"I guess I talk too much. Some of it is nerves. I don't want to make a mistake. Some of it is you seem different today. Are you mad at me?"

He circled the car-size island to move in front of her. "Why would I be mad?"

"Because of what I said the other day. I wasn't being critical."

"I didn't think you were." He gestured to the house. "This isn't me. I don't want a place this big. I just want something by the beach, with good light and a room for a big-screen TV. But now I'm thinking land and property." He shoved his hands into the front pockets of his jeans. "I'm not a jerk."

"What?"

"I'm not a jerk. I'm not that guy who can't think about anyone but himself."

Now she was more confused. "I never thought you were. What does this have to do with the house? Or the business? And why do you care what I think of you?"

"What kind of question is that? Why wouldn't your opinion matter?"

"Because you don't know me very well. I'm your sister's friend and Elizabeth's . . . well, let's not go there."

He seemed angry and uncomfortable, which made her feel bad. She touched his arm. "I know you're not a jerk. You're really a nice guy. Funny and caring and supportive and a good brother. You're practically gay. Is that better?"

His eyes narrowed. "Sure. Kick me when I'm down."

"I don't know what else to do."

"I do."

He put both hands on her shoulders, which was stunning enough, but then he leaned in and kissed her.

She felt his warm mouth on hers, the pressure of his lips, and the tingles. They were everywhere. Not just where they touched, but zipping through her body, making her feel as if she'd gone all bubbly.

She couldn't breathe, couldn't react, couldn't do anything but feel skin on skin and wish that it would last forever. It took every ounce of self-control not to whimper when he stepped back.

"You kissed me," she whispered.

His mouth curved into a very satisfied male kind of smile. "I know."

"Was it because I said you were practically gay?"

"Partially."

So he was making a point. She could understand that. It wasn't as if he was actually interested in *her*. She had to keep telling herself that, or she would go down a very dangerous road.

"I won't say it again," she promised.

"What did you think?" the real estate agent asked as she came back into the kitchen. "Ready to see the rest of the house?"

"Sure," David said, taking Jayne's hand in his. "Let's see it all."

"Rebecca was difficult enough as a teenager," Elizabeth said, pacing the length of her office. "Now she's impossible. Bad enough she didn't warn me she was coming home, but to show up like that. I'm *still* getting calls. And has she been in touch since? Of course not."

Her frustration was increased by the fact that she'd actually called her daughter herself and Rebecca hadn't picked up. Or phoned back. Which made it all the more impossible to know what her next move would be. First showing up at the brunch. Anything could be next, including a nude billboard on Sunset Boulevard. She wouldn't put anything past Rebecca.

"Why can't she be more like her brother?" she asked. "David is cooperative. Driven. Successful. What does she have to show for her life? And speaking of David, she completely ruined his party. The brunch was supposed to be about him, not her. But that is so like Rebecca. Stealing the spotlight for herself."

Jayne sat in the chair by the fireplace, holding her coffee, looking trapped. Elizabeth supposed she should take pity on her, but she had to talk to someone, and she couldn't complain to Blaine. He would simply take Rebecca's side, as he always had. And her friends couldn't be trusted with information as sensitive as this.

"Plus, to have her show up with Jonathan," Elizabeth said, then pressed her lips together.

Jayne nodded sympathetically. "I know he's a friend of yours and Blaine's, and he's too old for her."

Elizabeth watched closely, but Jayne only sipped her coffee, looking as calm and patient as usual. Perhaps Rebecca hadn't told Jayne about Elizabeth's affair. It had been years ago, and while Elizabeth had denied everything, she had a feeling her daughter hadn't believed her. Blaine didn't know—Elizabeth was sure of that. And he could never find out. He was oddly old-fashioned in many ways. Yet another frustration for her to deal with. Sometimes it seemed as if the world conspired to keep her in pain.

"You didn't know they were dating?" Elizabeth asked.

"Not at all."

"But you did know she was back in Los Angeles."

Jayne hesitated, then nodded slowly. "I knew."

"I see." Elizabeth let the two words hang in the air. "I'm extremely disappointed in you, Jayne. I expected better."

Jayne flinched slightly. "Rebecca is my friend."

"As am I, and let me remind you, I've been a much

better friend. While Rebecca took off without a thought to anyone she was leaving behind, I have looked after you. Have you forgotten how I brought you into this house and made you feel at home? We came to your high school graduation, Jayne, and paid for your college. We saw you through the troubling time when a girl becomes a woman. I have always been here for you, available for advice, worrying about you. Blaine has considered you a second daughter. In return, we've asked for so little."

Elizabeth was good, Jayne thought, trying not to writhe on the uncomfortable chair. She felt like a very ungrateful bug.

"I would have warned you if I'd known she was coming to the party," she said at last. "But I couldn't tell you she was coming home."

Elizabeth's stern expression tightened. "So there are limits on our relationship. That is very unfortunate."

"I would think you'd be pleased that Rebecca has a good friend watching out for her."

"Rebecca hardly needs anyone on her side. She's a force of nature on her own." She pressed her lips together. "What's done is done. We'll move on now. How is the house hunting going? Or does some misplaced loyalty prevent you from discussing David, too?"

Jayne felt trapped and angry, though she knew she'd done nothing wrong. This was what it was like dealing with Elizabeth. A constant dance to maintain her footing. "It's not that I don't appreciate all that you've done for me. I do. I am grateful for your kindness. I don't know anyone else who would have taken me in."

Some of Elizabeth's tension eased. "I'm glad you realize that."

"I do. As for David, he's seen a couple of houses in Malibu. I'm not sure he's serious about either of them. They were large, maybe too large." Guilt was a powerful weapon, she thought grimly, wishing she were better equipped to fight it.

"It's so inconvenient that David moved out," Elizabeth said, then took a seat opposite Jayne. "I remember when he was little—he wanted to tell me everything. Now he keeps to himself. I don't suppose he's mentioned if he's seeing anyone?"

Jayne nearly dropped her cup. "Um, no. He hasn't said anything." David dating? Of course he would, and wasn't that exactly what she needed to make her day all sparkly.

He'd kissed her, but Elizabeth hadn't asked about that, and Jayne sure wasn't going to volunteer the information. She still didn't know why he'd done it. To prove a point? Because, like the tall mountain, she was there? Boredom? Maybe he'd slipped, and it had all been an accident. A delicious, yummy, bone-melting accident. If he could make her all quivery inside with a chaste three-second kiss, imagine what he could do if he really put some effort into it. She sighed. Her luck was not that good.

Wait. Stop that thought. She was trying to disconnect from the Wordens, not get more involved.

"Jayne," Elizabeth said in a tone that hinted she'd spoken her name before.

"Sorry. What?"

"You'll let me know if he brings someone else along to see one of the houses?"

"Yes," Jayne said. "That would mean he was getting serious and wanted her opinion on the house."

Would he do that—kiss Jayne while he was dating someone else? Stupid question. Men like him did what they wanted.

"Very good." Elizabeth smiled. "You're so sensible. Blaine and I were discussing that just the other night. How we've always been able to depend on you."

Jayne put down her coffee and stood. She didn't feel sensible. She felt confused and cornered and out of place. No matter how old she got and how much time passed, she still felt like that sixteen-year-old watching her mother die and knowing she had nowhere to go and no one to care about her. She felt desperately alone and willing to do anything just to pretend to belong. Even be Elizabeth's bitch.

This might be the only family she had, but it was a seriously dysfunctional one, and if she wanted to survive, she had to escape.

The good news was, she would be getting on a plane first thing tomorrow.

The flight to Dallas was uneventful. Jayne had been checking the weather all week, and the last of the spring thunderstorms seemed to have blown through a few days before. Now the skies were clear and blue, and there wasn't a hint of a cloud.

She collected her luggage and made her way to the taxi stand, where she took a cab into the city. There was an impressive skyline that reminded her a little of L.A. When they exited the freeway, they drove through a beautiful tree-lined residential area.

She'd been booked into the Rosewood Mansion on Turtle Creek. The Web site had been impressive, but the hotel was even more so. The elegant and spacious lobby screamed luxury. The Wordens would have been right at home.

After registering, she went up to her room—a quiet, pretty space with a small balcony. There was a marble bath, a huge tub with a separate shower, and a big basket filled with fruit and candy, along with a card welcoming her.

"We can't wait to meet you in person," the card read, and it had been signed by Paula.

Jayne had never been courted before. Neither by a man nor a company. Talk about nice, she thought with a laugh as she threw herself on the bed. For the first time in a decade, her future was completely in her hands. She knew in her gut that the job was hers to lose. And she very much planned on winning.

Eight

WHEN SOMEONE RANG THE bell at her condo door, Jayne practically danced across the living room to open it. She was flying. Beyond flying . . . she was empowered, excited, and still having trouble believing that everything about her life was about to change.

Rebecca stood there, looking chicly casual in a white gauzy dress and sandals, her hair hanging in loose curls, her eyebrows slightly raised.

"What's gotten into you?" her friend asked.

Jayne held out her arms and spun in a circle. "I have a job."

"Yes, you're a nurse. Although if they see you acting like this, they might want to talk drug testing."

Jayne waited until Rebecca stepped into her condo, then closed her door. "I have a new job!"

"What? When did this happen?"

"Yesterday. I just got back this morning."

"Back from where?"

"Dallas." Jayne flopped down on the sofa and explained about the call from Paula and the invitation to fly out for an interview. "They really want me. It's a great offer. A big raise, a week more vacation, assigned parking. I toured the facility, and it's amazing. Everything is new and well designed. The exam rooms are perfect, and there's a huge waiting area. They really thought this through. They're looking to fill a few more positions, so I told them about Katie, and they're going to call her." She sat up and grinned. "I have a job."

Rebecca stood behind the chair, staring, not looking the least bit pleased. "I see," she said. "When were you planning on telling me you were moving?"

Jayne felt her perfect mood slip a little. "I'm telling you now."

"Wow. Lucky me. But you didn't bother to tell me about the interview. You didn't bother to call at all. You made a huge decision like this without talking to anyone?"

Jayne stood and cradled her cast in her good hand. "Why are you being like this? I have a great opportunity. You should be happy for me."

Rebecca's expression tightened. "You called Katie, didn't you? You talked to her about it, told her they wanted her as well. Right?"

Jayne had. She and Katie had talked for hours after the interview. Jayne had raved about the job, and Katie had gone online, checking out the price of houses and condos. They'd been thrilled to realize the Dallas real estate market was significantly less expensive than any neighborhood in L.A.

"Rebecca," she said slowly, knowing it was too late. That she'd hurt her friend. "I was going to tell you."

"That you were leaving? Did you plan to let me know in person, or would I just get one of those change-of-address cards?" Rebecca's eyes flashed with pain. "You didn't even tell me you were thinking of leaving."

"I wasn't. I got a call about the job. It seemed interesting, so I went for the interview. It just happened." She sighed. "Can't you be happy for me?"

"Oh, sure. I'm blissful that my best friend wants to move thousands of miles away and didn't bother to let me know." Rebecca put her hands on her slender hips. "I just got home. Doesn't that matter?"

"You just got home from being gone," Jayne said gently. "You left me for over a decade. You went off and had a life while I was here dealing with your mother."

"Is that what this is about?" Rebecca asked, obviously annoyed. "My mother?"

"In part," Jayne admitted. "Look, I'm sorry I hurt you. That wasn't the point. I wasn't . . ." She couldn't find the word.

"Thinking," Rebecca said. "You weren't thinking about anyone but yourself."

Jayne's happy bubble burst. "Something that only you get to do?" she asked coolly. "It's okay for everyone else, but not for me, right? I'm the faithful family retainer. Always steady, always available."

She stepped toward Rebecca. "You're right. I didn't think to tell you. In part because it happened so quickly, but also because I didn't want to be talked out of a once-in-a-lifetime opportunity."

Rebecca's eyes widened. "I would never do that. How can you think that of me? I've always cared about you."

Maybe, Jayne thought sadly. But if Rebecca thought Jayne's leaving would inconvenience her in any way, she would be the first one to try to talk Jayne out of it.

Not that there was any point in having the conversation. Rebecca wouldn't admit it, and all they would do was fight.

"I just wanted to go see what they were offering," Jayne said slowly. "It's really going to be good for me." She drew in a breath. "I have to go. This isn't about you—it's about your mother and David and everything."

"What about David?"

Jayne knew she had to tread carefully so Rebecca didn't guess the truth. "I'm helping him buy a house, which is great. I like David. But what's next? Elizabeth asking me to quit my job so I can work with the wedding planner?"

"Probably," Rebecca said with a sigh.

"I need to escape. I'll never have my own life if I stay here. You know that better than anyone."

Rebecca pressed her lips together. "You should have told me. You should have trusted me to be happy for you."

"I know." Jayne didn't actually believe that, but saying it made things easier.

"You're my best friend," Rebecca told her.

"You're mine."

Her friend stared at her for a long time. "No, I don't think so."

"Rebecca, don't."

Rebecca shrugged. "You have any ice cream?"

Jayne smiled. "Every flavor you love, including Cherry Garcia and pistachio. Want some?"

Rebecca nodded.

They collected ice cream, spoons, and Diet Coke, then headed out onto the patio. Jayne settled into her chair. She reached for the pistachio, took off the top, and dug in her spoon.

Rebecca picked up the Cherry Garcia. "Have you told my mother?"

"No." Jayne didn't even want to think about the explosion that would cause. "She's not going to be happy."

Rebecca brightened at the thought. "Can I be there when you tell her?"

"I don't think that's a good idea."

"But it would make me happy."

Jayne laughed. "This isn't about you. This is about me. And your mother. I'm her lapdog. Do my ears look floppy? Because they feel floppy to me. She's all pissy because I didn't tell her you were coming back, and when I pointed out it's because we're friends, she said that she and I were friends, too." Technically, Elizabeth said she was a better friend, but Jayne didn't think sharing that would help anything. "I came home and got the call about the job. It was timing. Maybe a sign from God. The worst part is, I feel guilty and I haven't done anything wrong. How does she do that? How does she make me feel so small? Or do I let her?"

"I think it's because you let her, but asaying that isn't very helpful."

"No, it's not." Jayne scooped up the cool, creamy ice cream, then chewed the nuts. "I don't exactly hate her, but I wouldn't mind not running into her for another forty or fifty years. Why can't she be more gracious? I know what she and Blaine did for me, and I'm very grateful. But I'm getting damned tired of having it shoved in my face all the time."

Rebecca's expression turned speculative. "The reason she's so good at making you feel like crap is because she's been there."

"Oppressed and taken advantage of?"

"Poor."

Jayne nearly dropped the carton. "Excuse me? Elizabeth Worden, poor? I don't believe it."

"She wasn't always Elizabeth Worden. In fact, my snobby mother used to be a . . ."

Jayne found herself leaning forward. "What?"

"A secretary. She was Blaine's secretary. Based on what I know about David's birthday and their anniversary, I would say my mother was putting out before the wedding. In fact, I think the young prince is the reason they got married."

"She was pregnant?" Jayne tried to imagine Blaine and Elizabeth having sex, then wished she hadn't. "But I don't understand. If she was a regular person then, why is she such a bitch now?"

"It happens. People who don't grow up with money either get it or they don't. My mother doesn't. It's all about status and fitting in with her. I think she's afraid to even think about who and what she was. If she's nice to anyone less well off, she's afraid people will think she's like them." She took a big bite of the ice cream. "Kinda makes you look at everything differently, huh?"

"Yes. It makes me want a do-over on some of our conversations." Especially the one a few days ago, where Elizabeth had done her best to make Jayne feel guilty. Even more frustrating, Jayne had let her. "I wonder if she signed a prenup."

"No idea." Rebecca scooped up more ice cream. "She was pregnant, so I doubt Dad would have pushed, but wouldn't that be fun."

Jayne considered the options. "Do you think she would have risked it all with an affair if she had?"

"Ah, yes. Jonathan. Did she have a cow?"

"There was no actual mooing, but she wasn't happy. Did you have to pick him?"

"Pretty much." Rebecca tilted her head. "Did I say I was sorry for tossing you in the middle of that?"

"Of course not. You never apologize. The fact that Elizabeth doesn't know that I know about the affair helped."

Rebecca paused in midlick of her spoon. "What do you mean I never apologize? Of course I do."

"Uh-huh? Any examples?"

"No, but that doesn't mean I'm not sincere."

"Then it's okay."

"This would be you being bitchy," Rebecca said cheerfully, and dug back into the ice cream.

"I'm still dealing with everything happening. Considering I'm not even working, there's way too much going on in my life. Things are complicated."

"Like what things?"

Jayne hesitated. She wasn't sure how Rebecca would react, which made her not want to say anything. But she really needed to talk to someone, and Katie wouldn't get the problem.

"You have to promise not to tell anyone or discuss this with the person involved."

Rebecca put her carton on the table and set her spoon next to it. "Now I have to know. Tell me. And yes, I promise."

Jayne hesitated. "It's David. He, um, well . . . He kissed me."

Rebecca's eyes widened. "What?"

"I'm sure it was an accident. He slipped or something. It wasn't a big romantic kiss. It was just casual and meaningless, I'm sure."

Rebecca started to laugh. "This is great! *Beyond* great. Do you know how pissed my mother is going to be when she finds out you're dating David?"

"Ouch, and stop right there. I'm not dating him. We're not dating. We just sort of lightly kissed. It was barely a kiss. More of a greeting."

"Was he saying hello?"

"No, but I mentioned he was practically gay, so he had something to prove."

"Now you have to tell me everything. Start at the beginning and speak slowly."

Jayne swallowed another bite of ice cream, then explained how she and David had been talking about the house and what he'd said and what she'd said. "And then he kissed me."

"This is great." Rebecca's smile faded a little as she leaned forward. "It *is* fabulous and fun, but you have to be careful. David doesn't get serious, and I don't want you to get hurt."

"Because while I could easily fall for him, he could never fall for someone like me." Jayne put the top on her carton. The ice cream she'd eaten sat like a big cold rock in her stomach. "Great, yeah. Thanks for sharing. Although I'd already figured that part out myself."

"Don't get mad."

"For telling me I'm not good enough for your brother? I'm not mad. I really enjoy being put in my place."

"No." Rebecca stretched out her hands toward Jayne. "That's not what I said, and you know it. David is funny and charming, and women fall for him. All women. You're my friend, and I care about you. I don't want you falling for a guy I'm not sure will ever fall for anyone."

"Okay," Jayne said slowly. "In theory, he's back to get married."

"Men have married without love before. Especially men like him. I have no doubt he's interested in a relationship, but I'm less sure about how long it would last or if you'd like how it ends. Because with David, it always ends." She wiggled her fingers. "I'm telling the truth."

"Okay. I believe you."

"I think you're better than he deserves."

"That's true."

"I won't tell my mother. And you have to promise that if you have sex with him, we won't discuss details. The ick factor is way too big."

Jayne laughed. "It's a deal."

"I spoke with Jayne today," Elizabeth said that evening over dinner. "Apparently, she knew Rebecca was back and didn't bother to tell me."

Blaine served himself from the vegetable bowl before passing it to her. "Jayne is Rebecca's friend."

"Meaning she's not mine? Her complete lack of loyalty is appalling. I told her I was very disappointed."

"Leave her alone. Jayne's a good girl."

His attitude was so annoying, Elizabeth thought. And just so typical. "You take everyone's side but mine," she said. "I'm your wife."

"Therefore you're always right?"

She wanted to say yes, but didn't. "Meaning it would be nice if you supported me from time to time. I depend on Jayne. She's a great help to me, but now I don't know if I can trust her."

"She's not going to run off with the silver."

"That's not what I mean, Blaine. Honestly, you can be obtuse."

He smiled. "You used to like that I was obtuse. You told me I was a simple man and that was one of my best qualities."

"It's not now," she snapped, cutting through her

chicken breast. "I worry that I don't know Jayne anymore. Maybe she's not who I thought."

"Leave her alone. She's been more loyal than any of us deserve."

Elizabeth glared at him. "How can you say that? Have you forgotten all that we did for her? It was your idea to have her come live here after her mother died. You said she would be a good influence for Rebecca, and look how that turned out."

"I enjoy having Jayne around."

"Well, you'd better get over it. I don't know how much longer I'm going to have her helping me." She paused, waiting for Blaine to react.

He reached for a roll. "Good. She needs a break from you."

"What?" Elizabeth prided herself on always staying calm, but the single word came out as a screech.

"She needs her own life. She'll never get that if she's constantly at your beck and call."

"And my needs don't matter?" Elizabeth asked tartly. "Of course not. Everyone is more important than me, right? I depend on her. I can trust her with all sorts of details. Who would take her place? Who would help me? I don't want to have to train someone else. You'd think she'd be more grateful, but she isn't. No good deed goes unpunished. We should never have taken her in. I knew I'd regret being so generous."

"Did you?" Blaine asked. "You'll replace her with no problem. Hire an assistant. Someone to work full time. You were always saying that Jayne's work made it difficult for you. You'll have to train the new person, but you're good at that. It will be better with someone with regular hours."

"Maybe," she murmured, thinking that there was more to Jayne than just what she did to help. There was being able to talk about her. Every now and then Elizabeth liked to remind people how generous she and Blaine had been, taking in Rebecca's poor friend, raising her like their own child. It played well. Now the entire effort had been wasted.

No matter how many times David tried to forget what Jayne had said about Élan's jewelry, he couldn't. "Does the world really need another hundred-and-fifty-thousand-dollar necklace?" echoed in his mind. It was worse than getting a bad song stuck, because he couldn't get rid of the memory by humming "It's a Small World," which he'd already tried. Twice.

Which was why he found himself driving to the nearest completely normal mall, parking, and walking inside. If she wanted to have a conversation about jewelry for the masses, then he was going to become an expert.

He walked to the closest directory and noted the names and locations of the jewelry stores. He planned to visit them all.

He'd spent the previous evening online, looking at jewelry on QVC and other Web sites. The Tacori pieces were beautiful and looked well made. The price point was unbelievable.

He took the escalator upstairs and headed for the first jewelry store. As he walked he studied the women around him, looking at their jewelry, trying to see what their watches were like. A couple in their twenties, hands linked, bodies touching, hovered by a counter.

"But it's so expensive," she whispered as David walked past.

"I love you. I'm going to marry you. I want you to have the best engagement ring there is."

David stepped into the store and saw the salesclerk putting away a collection of solitaires. The stones were around a quarter of a carat. He circled the counters, stopping to look at a collection of pearls, then hovering over a tray of chains.

"May I help you?" asked a middle-aged woman. "Are you buying a gift?"

"Yes," he said with a smile. "Maybe you can help me."

Nine

"I'M GOING TO START charging admission," Jayne said, pretending annoyance as she opened her front door and let in David. "Or the going rate for therapy. Your family is here constantly."

Which wasn't exactly true. It was mostly him and Rebecca. Elizabeth was the type to summon rather than visit, and Blaine didn't get involved in anything emotional or messy.

"Is this a bad time?" David asked, stepping into her condo. "I need to talk to you."

He looked stressed, with his golden blond hair mussed and stubble darkening his jaw. It was a new level of sexy that made her knees go a little weak. Not a good thing—she couldn't risk falling and breaking something else.

"I'm delightfully available," she told him, then noticed the shopping bags in his hand. "You've been to the mall? There's a surprise."

"Tell me about it." He looked around her living room, then walked toward the small table in the kitchen. "You have to see what I have. I went to all the stores and bought samples. Have you seen this stuff?"

He started pulling out smaller bags and boxes and emptying them onto her table. There were rings and necklaces, bracelets and earrings. Mostly gold, a few silver pieces. Diamonds glittered, chains tangled, and a couple of charms slid to the floor.

It was like looking at the contents of a pirate's chest, Jayne thought, unable to believe how much he'd purchased.

"You're going to return all this, aren't you?" she asked, picking up a tennis bracelet. "There has to be thousands of dollars' worth of jewelry here."

David dismissed the question with a shake of his head. "Look at this." He picked up a slim gold chain and wrapped it around his finger. It immediately bent and crimped. "There's no quality. You can't tell me people want something this cheap. It'll break in a few weeks."

He reached for a diamond ring. After pulling a loupe out of his jacket, he handed both to her. "Look at it. Disgusting."

She looked through the loupe, and even her untrained eye saw the flaws. A few cracks that looked like feathers, dark spots. "They're not perfect," she said.

"There's an understatement. These are worse," he said, tossing a tennis bracelet toward her. He picked up a pair of earrings that were dangling circles. The circles were uneven and not completely attached to the stud. "And these are just plain badly made." He shook his head. "I don't get it. Why would anyone buy this stuff? Sure, these earrings only cost a hundred and twenty dollars, but they won't last or be wearable. I understand what you meant about making jewelry for everyone else. If this is all they have to choose from, then there's a big problem."

He looked angry and confused, and it was so completely adorable, she just wanted to grab hold of him and never let go. Which would only lead to trouble.

"I have those earrings," she said, mostly to distract herself.

David held them up and flushed. "No way. You don't. Tell me you don't actually own these." He swore. "I'm sorry."

She risked touching his arm, ignoring the heat as her fingers brushed against his skin. "Don't be. I'm kidding. They are really terrible." She sat down at the table and picked up an engagement ring with a tiny stone she had a feeling was seriously flawed. "I know this isn't the same as what someone could buy at the Worden boutique, but isn't there a middle ground? Nice pieces, reasonably priced? I refuse to believe the only choices are spending a hundred and fifty thousand dollars, or getting this."

He sat across from her. "What do women want?"

She laughed. "A question for the ages."

He grinned. "Fair enough. What do women want from their jewelry? I've spent the past twelve years finding perfect gemstones, but someone else makes the jewelry. I can look at reports that tell me what sells, but that's just data. What makes you buy or not buy something?"

"A lot of it is about price," she admitted. "A good sale helps. Jewelry is difficult, because we don't want all of it to be expensive. There are fashion pieces that are fun because we can buy new ones every season. Wait here."

She walked to her bedroom and grabbed her jewelry box. For a second, she hesitated. There wasn't anything in there to impress David, but that wasn't the point. She was helping him. In a way, it was kind of sweet that he'd been so affected by her freak-out at the Worden offices.

She returned to the table and sat down.

"We'll ignore the pieces Rebecca gave me," she said, setting a couple of pairs of earrings and a necklace aside. "They would never be in my price range."

He grabbed an earring that swirled and curved. The thick gold twisted, catching the light. They were substantial, beautiful, and very wearable.

"If we made these in sterling," he murmured, rubbing them. "No stones. We usually get our casting work done in Italy, but if I found a cheaper supplier . . ." He shook his head. "Okay, show me what you've got."

"Obligatory gold chain," she said, setting that in front of him. "I have no idea why I bought it, because I never wear it. It's too skinny to stand out, and I wouldn't know what kind of pendant to buy. Earrings are easiest. These are gold. I have one bangle."

She reached for the fashion jewelry. There were colored-bead necklaces, a couple of faux-pearl necklaces, different dangling earrings in various colors.

"Changing out a wardrobe every season is impossible," she said. "But a new pair of earrings or a chunky necklace makes me feel like I'm keeping up without spending a fortune. Most regular women don't want to spend a fortune. We want fun and easy. Pieces that go with nearly everything in our wardrobe." She showed him a sterling necklace with fake diamonds. "I love this one. If you hate it, I don't want to know."

He picked it up and studied it. "So you want choices and classic pieces with a sense of style."

"Maybe. Everyone is different."

He grinned. "So asking you for the definitive woman's opinion isn't going to work?"

As always, she found herself wanting to get lost in his dark blue eyes. He was so damned good looking. Some quirk of fate gave godlike status to a few and left the rest of the world wandering around wondering what life was like for greater mortals. A quirk with a sense of humor.

"I couldn't stand the pressure," she said, hoping she wasn't drooling.

"We work with an ad agency. I could ask them about a focus group."

"You're serious about pursuing this?"

"Sure."

"Then don't go to an ad agency. I have friends I can invite over. Katie and a few others, if you want. They can bring their favorites and what didn't work, and you can ask all the questions you want." Assuming he was interested in her friends' opinions, she thought, wondering if she'd just made a mistake. Maybe an ad agency would be better.

"That would be great. I could bring some inventory and get their opinions."

"Okay, then. I'll call them and get some dates." Her friends and David in the same room. It would be interesting. Scary, but interesting. "Now, what about everything you bought? You're not keeping it all."

He shrugged. "I might. It gives me a place to start."

"You're seriously thinking about selling jewelry that doesn't cost more than a house?"

"Why not? It makes good business sense to expand. Some companies worry about tarnishing the brand name with inexpensive products, but that won't hurt us. We're already the best. Everyone knows that. We'll have to run the numbers. There's a financial break-even point, and we need to stay on the side of profit. One of the reasons I'm back is to start taking over the business. I'm not interested in more of the same. To grow the market, we have to expand it. You had a good idea. Did I thank you for it?"

"No."

He stood and then pulled her to her feet. Still holding on to that hand, he tugged her close, then cupped her face, and stared into her eyes.

"Thank you," he murmured, right before he kissed her.

His mouth was warm and tender, yet firm against her own. Even as she absorbed the sensation of his lips on hers, his fingers lightly stroking her cheeks and the heat of his body engulfing hers, the rational side of her brain told her that this time she couldn't blame the kiss on his slipping. He'd been pretty damned deliberate about the whole thing.

She raised her arms, then dropped them, not sure what she was supposed to be doing. This wasn't a *real* boy-girl kind of kiss. She wasn't going to react. Except it was very difficult not to lean in when he kept his lips against hers, moving slightly, sending those tingles racing through her body.

When he dropped his hands, she prepared for him to pull back. She wasn't going to whimper or beg. She would be a total adult and—

Both his arms came around her and drew her against him. Suddenly, they were touching from shoulder to knee, and her hands were on his shoulders—lightly, so she didn't bang him with her cast. Involuntarily, before she could even stop herself, she tilted her head, as if this was a real, honest-to-God kiss. Then his mouth was moving against hers. She felt the light stroke of his tongue against her bottom lip. Her lips parted because that's what was supposed to happen next.

Then they were kissing like in the movies, and she felt herself slipping into passion. David was solid and safe in a world that was melting from the inside out. She hung on because she was afraid of falling, although she was careful not to clunk him on the head with her cast. He slid one hand to her hips, then down to her butt. Instinctively she arched against him, shifting her belly closer. She brushed against something hard and thick.

It was him.

Pleasure filled her. Not just liquid need, but satisfaction. No mercy kiss ended with an erection. He wanted her. David Worden wanted *her*.

Later she would tell herself it was just a guy thing. Pavlovian and meaningless. But for this moment in time, it was magic.

She gave in to the kiss, losing herself in the tingles and desire surging through her. When he finally stepped back, they were both breathing hard.

"Nice," he said.

She smiled. "I'd say the same, but the last time I said you were nice, you got all hysterical on me. You were practically shrieking."

The corners of his mouth turned up. "You've got attitude."

"Yes, I do."

"Want dinner?"

What she wanted was sex, but apparently that wasn't going to be offered. He was sensible, as well as nice. Who knew?

"Dinner sounds good," she said.

Time in his company, she thought happily. She would take as much as was available, enjoying every moment, until she left for good.

Jonathan pushed in deeper. "Are you close, baby?" His eyes were wide and slightly glazed, his mouth open.

Rebecca could feel his hot breath on her face. She squeezed hard, hoping to force him over the edge and get finished already.

"I'm there now," she breathed, forcing herself to pant slightly, then moaned. She squeezed again, pulsing in what she hoped was a good imitation of an orgasm.

Apparently it worked. Jonathan thrust one more time, then collapsed on top of her. She endured the dead weight for about ten seconds, then pressed on his shoulders. He rolled off her.

"God, that was great," he said, stretching out next to her, then reaching for her hand. "You're amazing."

It was all she could do not to snort. Amazing? At faking it, maybe.

It wasn't that she didn't like sex—she did. And Jonathan, while not the best in the world, was perfectly adequate. The problem was her. Or, more precisely, Nigel. Ever since he'd walked away, choosing Ariel over her, she hadn't been interested in anything close to intimacy. Something else Nigel had to answer for.

She had a feeling that if she closed her eyes and pretended she was with him, she could get over the top. But thinking about him while doing it with someone else seemed too much like letting Nigel win.

Jonathan released her hand, but before she could get out of bed, he pulled her close and began stroking her arm like she was a cat.

"Where do you want to go out to dinner?" he asked. "Somewhere around here? Or we could go to your place and order in."

"I'm not that hungry," she said, forcing a smile. "You've exhausted me. I think I'm going to go home and make it an early night."

He smiled at her, then bent down and sucked on her nipple. "I could change your mind."

Not in a million years, she thought grimly. "You could," she said instead. "But I am really tired."

"Sure." He stared into her eyes. "We should go away. Fiji's great this time of year. Or Hong Kong. You'd love the shopping. I could buy you a new wardrobe." He touched her throat. "Diamonds that sparkle like your eyes."

Gag and double gag, she thought, sitting up. "While I appreciate the offer, travel isn't on my agenda right now." She angled away from him, ignoring the fact that he was hard again. "Jonathan, you know this is just for fun, right? You and I? There's no relationship."

His face registered shock, which he covered, but not quickly enough. "Sex and fun," he said, the erection fading.

Her instinct was to run as hard and fast as she could, but she wasn't ready to be done with him. Being with Jonathan made her mother crazy, and where was the bad in that? Unless he got to be too much of a pain in her ass, in which case it was over.

"I was involved before," she said, thinking how strange it was that the truth was now her friend. "It ended badly, and I'm still dealing. This isn't about you."

He managed a smile. "I went through a divorce. I know about breakups."

"Including the fact that they take time to get over." She bent over and kissed him, putting as much passion into her thrusting tongue as possible. Then she nipped his lower lip and ran her hand over his penis. "I just need a little time."

He got hard again. "Sure. I'll be here. Waiting."

A needy man. That was attractive. She stood and collected her clothes. He got up and pulled on his monogrammed robe, then followed her into the bathroom.

"If you need more than time, I'm here for you," he said.

"Thanks."

She dressed quickly and let herself out. Once she was in twilight, she inhaled deeply and wondered if Jonathan had been a mistake. Life always exacted a price. Dealing with him might become more trouble than annoying Elizabeth was worth. Which meant she would have to get the most out of ending things.

Interesting possibilities, she thought as she got into her car and started the engine. There were always interesting possibilities.

Three days later Jayne found herself crawling through traffic. The café was by the Beverly Center in a trendy, crowded, and expensive part of town. Parking was impossible, so Jayne pulled in front of the valet sign, then groaned when she saw the price—there went twenty dollars she would never see again.

She got out and made her way past the crowd of people waiting. Inside, the hostess eyed her with a combination of indifference and superiority.

"The wait for lunch is over an hour," she said, looking over Jayne's shoulder, as if hoping to see Jennifer Aniston or Madonna come strolling in.

"I'm meeting someone," Jayne said, used to being dismissed in places like this. She didn't have that air of polished wealth or cutting-edge fashion. She was a regular person. This was not a regular-person part of town. "Elizabeth Worden."

The hostess immediately came to attention and smiled warmly. "Of course. She's here and expecting you. Right this way."

She led Jayne through a maze of tables, each covered with organic cotton tablecloths and matching napkins. The wallpaper was probably hemp or bamboo; the overhead light fixtures proudly displayed their low-energy lightbulbs. The scent of cinnamon and ginger hovered in the air.

Elizabeth's table was in a quiet alcove. It was larger than most. There was no bread basket—the truly rich and thin didn't do carbs—although a martini glass sat in front of the older woman.

Jayne hadn't wanted to "do lunch." She was still recovering from her last meeting with Elizabeth. But saying no was difficult, so she'd made a couple of feeble excuses and then had accepted. Plus, she needed to tell Elizabeth about her new job. Her only concession to self-preservation was a promise to herself that if Elizabeth started getting mean, she would walk away—avoiding a scene be damned.

"Jayne," Elizabeth said with a welcoming smile. "Thank you so much for joining me. Please, sit. Timothy has already told me about the specials, and there's a ravioli you are going to love."

"Thanks." Jayne sank into the chair opposite Elizabeth's.

"It's gorgonzola and walnut with a sweet curry sauce. But you'll want to look over the menu first. How are you feeling? Is your arm better?"

The friendly questions and concern were almost unnerving, but Jayne knew Elizabeth could be charming when it suited her. She did it just enough to lull people into a false sense of relaxation, then pounced.

"I'm great," she said.

Timothy appeared with bottled water and a menu. He listed the specials, which included the famous ravioli. Jayne refused an offer of a cocktail or wine and chose the ravioli. Elizabeth got the salmon salad, no dressing, no cheese.

When they were alone, Elizabeth leaned forward. "I've been thinking," she said. "I want to plan another party for David. The brunch was a disaster. Rebecca completely stole all the attention, and he barely had a chance to talk to the young women I'd invited. So I'm thinking of a dinner."

"Your dinner parties are always events," Jayne said.

"Yes, and you know I prefer elegant. But to give David a chance to talk with as many people as possible, I'm considering a buffet."

Jayne couldn't hide her surprise.

Elizabeth chuckled, then sipped on her martini. "I know, I know. Not my style, but sacrifices must be made. He swears he's back to settle down and get married. I need to make sure he finds the right sort of woman. If

I leave him to do that on his own, disaster will follow."

"The ladies do like him," Jayne said, thinking how much she had enjoyed their last encounter. The man knew how to kiss. Probably from years of practice. Dinner had been amazing, too. Three hours of great conversation. In fact, she wasn't sure which she enjoyed more—the kissing or the talking. She would need a lot more of both before she could decide.

She reached for her water, then paused. Wait a minute. If he was home to find the perfect someone and get married, what was he doing kissing her? She wasn't his type. And even if he had a fleeting thought that she might be fun to get to know, he had to be aware that his parents wouldn't consider her appropriate.

Issues for another time, she told herself.

"You'll help with the party?" Elizabeth asked. "I want your thoughts on the guest list and what we should serve. It will be so much work, but worth it."

"You can count on me," Jayne said automatically.

The smile returned. "I knew I could. At the party itself, you can help me watch him and figure out who has caught his attention. I already spoke to David, and he's looking forward to the dinner. We'll pick a day and then get going on the details."

"Does he know you're helping him find a wife?" she asked.

"Why on earth would I mention that? He's aware of the ultimate goal but little else. He's a man—he's not interested in the details. Besides, there will be a houseful of beautiful, well-connected, successful women keeping him company. That's hardly bad for him."

Timothy appeared with their lunches. Although the pasta smelled heavenly, Jayne found she wasn't as hungry as she had thought. She was also very clear on the reason. Elizabeth's description of the party had provided her with a visual of David in a sea of perfect women. Women who weren't her.

It wasn't that she wanted to be them, either. She was happy with herself and her life. It was just the stupid crush. Having David kiss her didn't help with the whole getting-over-him process. Maybe she should talk to him about that. Explain her goal and remind him of his and his mother's. Although admitting to her crush wasn't something she would likely have the nerve to do. Which left her feeling uncomfortable and annoyed.

"Did he bring anyone to see the last house?" Elizabeth asked.

"No. It was just the real estate agent and me."

"Good. Then he hasn't found anyone yet. I can narrow the choices down to two or three and guide him in that direction. We'll have him engaged before he knows what happened."

Jayne pushed the ravioli around on her plate and wished she'd ordered wine. "Lucky us."

Elizabeth said something else about the party, but Jayne wasn't listening. She was already feeling crappy, so she might as well get it all over at once. "Elizabeth, I was in Dallas last week."

"What? Why on earth would you go there?"

Jayne explained about the phone call and the job offer.

Elizabeth's eyes widened. "You can't seriously be considering moving."

"I've already accepted. I start in two months. I met with a real estate agent, and my condo is going up for sale at the end of the week."

Color bled from Elizabeth's face. "No. I forbid it. With David just home and getting him settled, this is the worst time imaginable. No." She gripped her martini. "Talk about selfish! After all I've done for you." She leaned over the table. "You will pick up your cell phone right now and call that place and tell them you've changed your mind."

Jayne stared at the woman across from her. Elizabeth had been a huge part of her life for over a decade. The selfish demands, the accusations were new but not surprising. It was Elizabeth's way. Jayne had no idea what life without the Wordens would be like, but it was time to find out.

She collected her purse and stood.

"You've always been good me," she said softly. "And I've paid you back a thousandfold. If you want my help until I leave, I'm happy to give it. If not, then I wish you the best. Good-bye, Elizabeth."

Jayne turned and left.

Ten

"I'M NOT MYSELF," REBECCA said dramatically, draped across the sofa, her eyes closed, her perfect face flushed.

"Then who are you?" Jayne asked.

Rebecca opened her eyes. "You know what I mean, and don't pretend you don't. I'm desperately depressed. Nothing about coming home is the way I thought it would be. I haven't even been fighting with my mother, and you know how I was looking forward to that."

"Then go see her. I'm sure the two of you could get into it. Then you'll upset her and feel better yourself."

"I'm not going to be the one to blink first. If I go there, she wins. I want to win." She sat up and sighed. "But it's not just that. You're leaving."

A topic that was bound to come up sooner or later. "Yes, I am."

"You're leaving me. We're supposed to be friends."

If Jayne didn't know Rebecca better, she would swear that actual tears had filled her eyes and that her lower lip had quivered. But she did know her, and she understood every one of Rebecca's self-absorbed tendencies, not to mention her tricks.

"I love you like a sister," Jayne said calmly, "but no. My leaving is not up for negotiation. You went halfway around the world ten years ago, and I didn't try to make you feel guilty. You stayed gone, and I was warm and supportive. I expect the same from you."

"But this is different. I'm back, and I want you here."

"Want some cheese with that whine?"

"You're not being very sympathetic," Rebecca complained.

Jayne leaned back in the club chair. "Probably because I'm not feeling sympathetic. There's nothing wrong with your life. You're young, beautiful, successful, and rich. You have a family who loves you, a best friend with the devotion of a search-and-rescue dog, and all the potential in the world." She raised her left hand. "I, on the other hand, have a broken wrist and had to face telling your mother I was leaving."

Rebecca grinned. "That was the best story ever. Tell me again."

"I've already told you three times."

"It gets better with every telling." She sighed. "You're very difficult these days. Very sure of yourself. Worse, you have a shiny new love interest, and all I have is an old, boring man."

Jayne desperately wanted to squirm. "David isn't a love interest. He's a . . . complication."

"A nice one."

"Definitely." A complication that kissed like the devil

and charmed her and made her laugh. David was the best kind of trouble.

Rebecca sat up, her eyes wide, her mouth open. "Oh, no. There's a party, for David. Now don't get upset, but my mother plans to—"

"Have several perfect women over so he can pick the right wife. I know. We had lunch to discuss the details. Then I announced I was leaving, so I don't know if I'll be helping or not."

"You can't be serious."

Jayne wasn't sure. "I'll do it if she asks."

"But you're dating David."

"We're not dating. We've been to dinner once. We talk and house hunt. We've kissed. It was no big deal." At least not to him, which was what she would be reminding herself over and over again. "I'm offering my advice, such as it is, on the houses he's looking at, and I think he's asking me along only because the alternative is his mother. It's nothing."

"That bad a kisser, huh?" Rebecca asked, her voice teasing.

"I'm not discussing him with you because, hey, he's your brother. Do you really want to know?"

Rebecca wrinkled her nose. "Right. I don't. But this has to bother you. You don't just go around kissing guys for the fun of it."

"Only because they're not asking." Jayne wasn't about to admit the truth. The crush made it beyond difficult to think about David falling for some rich, connected, beautiful woman. Not that his going after someone who wasn't rich, connected, or beautiful was any better. The more she got to know him, the more she liked him. The crush had been fueled by what she thought he *should* be. The liking was based on who he actually was, and that was the problem.

"David's great," she said. "But so what? Are we going to get involved? Am I 'the One'? You warned me yourself, he doesn't do relationships."

"Okay, but you're wonderful. He could fall for you. You're smart and funny and loving and pretty."

"Not as pretty as you."

Rebecca sighed. "So few are."

"We both know the type David will marry. It's not me, and I'm okay with that." Mostly. "Besides, I'm trying to get away from your family. I'm relocating to another state to escape the stress of the Worden clan. Getting serious with David would make a real mess."

"But if you like him . . ." Rebecca began.

"No, it's not going to happen. This is nice. Fun. Nothing more." She couldn't let it be. For all her daydreams about the man, she understood reality. The rich really were different, and she was okay with that.

"And while we're on the subject of men," Jayne said deliberately. "How are things with Jonathan?"

Rebecca groaned, then rested her head on the back of the sofa. "Can you spell disaster?"

"What's wrong with Jonathan?"

"He likes me."

"The bastard."

"You're not taking me seriously."

"I know. Part of my charm."

Rebecca drew in a breath. "He likes me too much. I want a fling. He wants more."

"You want to piss off Elizabeth."

"That, too. He's clingy and annoying. The sex is awful, but that's more about me than him." She slumped down into the corner of the sofa and folded her arms across her chest. "I miss Nigel."

Which was the heart of the problem. "More or less than you did?"

"Less," she admitted, "but not a whole lot less."

"Still, it's progress."

"I guess. I just thought . . ." She sat up. Her expression turned fierce. "I can't believe he chose someone else over me. I know he loves me. Our relationship was amazing. He won't have that with anyone else. What does she have that I don't?"

"Controlling interest in Australia's second largest diamond mine."

Rebecca slumped back against the cushions. "It's not just the money. Obviously the diamonds were a big appeal, but there's something else. I can't figure out if I was too much for him, or if I wanted too much or demanded too much."

"Why does it have to be you?" Jayne asked, annoyed. "This really pisses me off. Why do we, as women, assume it's our fault? I do it, too. Take the blame. Try to fix things. Maybe it's not you. Maybe you're the ideal combination of exciting and sexy and fun. Maybe it's him. He could have married her for the money or access to the diamonds he loves so much. Or maybe because she was easier or safer. Maybe he has a brain tumor that's interfering with his frontal lobe. I'm not saying you're perfect, I'm saying don't assume it's just you."

"That was quite the rant."

"I am passionate about a few subjects. I hate how women subjugate themselves to men, emotionally. Sometimes the woman is the problem, but sometimes she isn't. Sometimes it's both of them."

"Are you projecting?"

"A little, which is my right." Jayne leaned forward. "It's not you. It's Nigel."

"I'm not sure knowing that will make it hurt less."

"Maybe not, but eventually the information will help."

"Maybe. I think I'm going to have to dump Jonathan. He's not worth the effort."

"You could consider finding a guy you want to be with because of how he makes you feel rather than how it will piss off your mother," Jayne said.

"Where's the fun in that?"

"Are you sorry you came home?"

"Not yet."

Jayne considered her words carefully. "Is it possible revenge isn't as much fun as you'd hoped?"

"I'm not even going to consider that. Elizabeth and I have just begun our game. I still plan to win."

"Great."

There were casualties in any battle. Jayne just hoped she could stay out of the cross fire.

*   *   *

Rebecca did her best to work through her bout of self-pity with a Pilates class and a double-shot energy drink. When that didn't work, she curled up with a bottle of wine and all three Bourne movies. Matt Damon went a long way to making her feel better about herself, and she woke the following morning feeling ready to take on the world. She showered, put on makeup, and dressed, but before she could leave, someone rang her doorbell.

Immediately her heart jumped in her chest. She desperately wanted her visitor to be Nigel, coming to beg her forgiveness. He would tell her that he'd made a huge mistake marrying Ariel, that he was sorry and would spend the rest of his life making it up to her. If only, she thought as she crossed to the door and pulled it open.

It wasn't Nigel, or Jayne, or even David. Instead, her mother stood in the hallway, looking as well groomed as ever, her mouth slightly pinched, as if she had a painful rash somewhere that chafed.

"Rebecca," Elizabeth said, pushing past her and walking into the condo. She stopped in the middle of the living room. "This is nice. A little more public than I would like, but the view works." She set her Louis Vuitton bag on the table by the sofa and crossed to the sliding-glass doors. "You're renting?"

Rebecca closed the door. "Yes. I don't know how long I'll be in Los Angeles."

"Long enough to be an annoyance to me, I'm sure."

The harsh words created a slight twinge of pain, but Rebecca ignored it. "I look for my happiness where I can find it. What brings you here, Mother?"

Elizabeth turned to face her. "I thought you would have come to see me by now."

"Why?"

"Because you're my daughter, and you're back in town. It was the least you could have done after ruining my brunch. But you were never one to apologize."

Rebecca squared her shoulders. "I didn't realize an apology was required for visiting my family. My mistake. I assumed you would be happy to see me after all this time. It's been what? Ten years? I guess a 'Welcome home' is too much to ask for."

"Oh, please." Elizabeth crossed to the sofa and sat. "Is that really what you want? You left without saying a word, without an explanation. Why would you care what we think after all this time?"

"I don't," Rebecca told her. "But to clarify your memory, I didn't leave without an explanation. We had a fight. You were horrible. I ran away."

Elizabeth sighed. "You were eighteen. One runs away when one is five or six. And the fight was because you had taken a very expensive necklace from the store. A willful bid for attention. You were always flashy, Rebecca. So low class."

"Something I get from you?"

Elizabeth stiffened, then visibly relaxed. "I see time away hasn't changed you at all."

"Did you expect it to?"

"Honestly? Yes."

Rebecca knew she was different, but not in ways that would matter to her mother.

She started to say that she hadn't taken the necklace, but after all this time, what was the point? She would have, if she'd thought of it. Instead, taking the fall for Jayne had suited her. She'd used that fight as an excuse to leave.

"I am different, Mother, but I doubt you'll believe me."

"What are your plans, now that you're back? Make more trouble? Is this about your brother? You've always resented him."

The unfairness of the statement burned. David was the favorite, the wanted child. Rebecca had been angry and hurt, but she'd never resented her brother. She just wanted the same kind of treatment.

"You mean will I get in the way of your marrying him off?"

Elizabeth looked startled. "What are you talking about?"

Rebecca relaxed a little. "David tells me everything. We're close. We have been for years. Didn't he mention that? When I left, he's the one I went to. Your precious son has been watching out for me. Someone had to. I knew nothing about being on my own. Not that you worried. Or bothered to get in touch." Even Blaine had come to check on her, but not Elizabeth. "You must have been relieved to have me gone."

Elizabeth stood. "I refuse to rehash our past. You may find it interesting, but I don't."

"That's it? You don't have an explanation? One of your children disappears and you're fine with that?"

"What do you want from me?"

A little caring, Rebecca thought bitterly. A hint of maternal feeling. "Nothing," she said. "Which is what you've been doing, so it will feel very familiar."

Elizabeth pressed her lips together. "I see it's still all about you. Very well. Tell me why you're back."

"No."

Elizabeth crossed to the table and picked up her purse. "Very mature. Impressive. How proud we all are of you."

"Jonathan doesn't have any complaints."

To her credit, Elizabeth's calm facade didn't even crack. "He's been a good and loyal friend to your father and me. I hope you'll treat him with the respect he deserves."

"Did you? Did you like having sex with him, Mom? Did you talk to Dad about it?"

"I have no idea what you're talking about. As to your reasons for returning, keep them secret if you like. My concern is your brother. David is ready to settle down. I want him to be happy."

"With the right sort of girl."

"Do you think he could be happy with the wrong sort?" Elizabeth crossed to the front door, then turned back. "The problem with you, Rebecca, is that you like to play at being just like everyone else, then you get angry when you're treated that way. There's nothing wrong with the world of privilege. There never has been. You could have had everything. Instead, you tossed it all away. Play whatever game you want. I don't care."

She left. Rebecca stared after her, refusing to feel the sharp pain in her heart.

"You never have," she whispered to the empty room.

Jayne pulled the cookie sheet of mini taquitos out of the oven, glanced at the clock on the stove, and swore. She was running late. She set the taquitos on the cooling rack, then glanced around her kitchen to see what else had to be prepped.

David walked in and saw the cookie sheet. "Those look good."

"Don't even think about it. You can wait until everyone else gets here."

"Bossy. I like it." He winked at her.

"Then you'll enjoy carrying in that bowl of tortilla chips and the salsa. Does everything fit on the coffee table? Will we have room for drinks?"

Instead of grabbing the food, he moved close and put his hands on her hips. After lightly kissing her, he said, "Relax. Everything will be fine."

She let herself get lost in his eyes because the alternative was to panic, and shrill was not her best look. "You don't know that. What was I thinking? These are my friends. And you're . . . not who they're going to be expecting. There will be awkward questions and knowing looks."

He kissed her again, lingering this time until she was close to whimpering. "I live for awkward. We're going to talk jewelry. They'll love it."

"*You're* going to talk jewelry. There's a difference."

"They'll adore me."

"Are you sure you can manage the chip bowl? Because that ego looks kind of heavy."

He chuckled and reached for the two bowls. While he went to put them on the coffee table, she transferred the taquitos to a plate, then pulled the guacamole from the refrigerator.

"They're all nurses, too?" he asked when he returned and swiped a taquito. "At the breast center?"

"Katie and Charlotte are. Gigi works up front, in the office."

He leaned against the counter. "Why do you work there and not a hospital?"

"My mother died of breast cancer."

"I'm sorry." He frowned. "You were still in high school, right? That's when you moved in?"

She nodded. "My mom wasn't diagnosed until she was stage four. She never went to the doctor, probably because of money. By the time we knew what was going on, it was too late. She only had a few weeks to live. The radiology nurses were my favorite. They would answer all my questions. They didn't pretend everything was going to be okay. It was scary, but knowing the truth was better than wondering."

He moved toward her, then stopped. "You didn't have any other family?"

"None. Rebecca helped, but she was in high school, too. One of the nurses, Sylvia, took me out to dinner a couple of times and told me what was going to happen with my mom. What the last couple of weeks would be like. She prepared me. She also told me that the type of cancer she had was random rather than genetic. Which also helped. I wanted to be like Sylvia—making a difference."

She pulled a bottle of white wine from the refrigerator and handed it to him, along with the opener. She collected glasses.

"The night my mother died, Elizabeth invited me to come stay. When I got close to high school graduation, she and Blaine offered to pay for college. Blaine already knew I wanted to be a nurse, and he was very supportive."

"More so than my mother," David said, pulling out the cork. "She would be more interested in how it looks than for paying it."

Jayne agreed, but didn't want to say that. "They were both there for me."

"And you'll always be grateful." He reached for the bottle of red on the counter.

"Life is nothing if not complicated." She drew in a breath. "But I can't keep doing it," she said slowly. "Acting as Elizabeth's assistant. Paying back the never-ending debt."

David set down the wine. "Elizabeth does feel she has a claim on you."

Jayne swallowed and stared into his amazing blue eyes. "It's not just her. I'm as much to blame. I've let this situation go on too long. And it's time to fix things."

He drew his eyebrows together. "Why do I get the feeling I'm not going to like what you're saying?"

"I don't know. It's not going to make any difference to you, that I can see." She drew in a deep breath. "I'm moving to Dallas."

David studied her. "Okay."

She told him about the job she'd accepted. "I'm putting my condo up for sale and leaving in two months."

"To get away from my family." He wasn't asking a question.

"To do a lot of things. It's a great opportunity."

"Sounds like it."

She wanted to ask if he was mad, but that would be stupid. David might enjoy her company, but she was never going to be important to him.

"Does my mom know?" he asked.

She nodded.

His expression turned sympathetic. "I'm guessing it didn't go well."

"No. Rebecca wasn't happy, either."

He stunned her by moving forward and pulling her into his arms. As he hugged her close and kissed her, he murmured, "I apologize on behalf of Wordens everywhere." He straightened. "I'll miss you. I've enjoyed getting to know you."

"I'll miss you, too." *Desperately and with every breath.*

"Can I come see you in Dallas?"

He was being polite, she told herself. He really didn't mean it. But the words made her feel all gooey inside.

"You can," she said.

"Naked?" he whispered in her ear. "Can I see you naked?"

Her mind went blank. Was he serious or kidding? How on earth was she supposed to respond?

Her doorbell rang. "Perfect timing," she said, and escaped into the living room.

Her friends had arrived together. Charlotte and Gigi were both tall. Charlotte had dark hair and was model thin, while Gigi was more curvy and had a lot of gray in her blond hair. Jayne introduced all of them to David.

"I remember you from the hospital," he said as he shook Katie's hand. "Good to see you again."

Katie grinned, looking him up and down. "Good to see you, too." She looked at Charlotte and Gigi. "See?"

Jayne held in a groan.

"See what?" David asked.

"You don't want to know," Jayne said, glaring at her friends. "Behave."

"I am behaving," he said.

"Not you."

"Katie said you were pretty," Gigi offered. "Although my eight-year-old granddaughter says boys can't be pretty. She'll figure it out as she gets older."

Charlotte sat on the sofa and reached for a handful of chips. "So you're the new boyfriend."

Jayne willed herself not to blush. "We had this conversation carlicr. David is a friend, nothing more. He wants our help with his business. You're all going to cooperate and not say anything that will embarrass me."

Katie laughed. "Nice try." She sat in the kitchen chair

Jayne had pulled into the room. "Why aren't you and Jayne dating? We love her. Why don't you?"

Jayne tried to speak, but the words got caught in her throat. She gestured wildly at Gigi and Charlotte, both of whom ignored her and waited for David to answer.

"I'm getting to know her," he said.

"And?" Katie prompted.

He grinned. "Impressive."

"You are all totally out of control," Jayne announced. "Now behave, or there's no wine for any of you."

"She looks like she means it," Katie grumbled.

"I do. Now sit, all of you."

She didn't wait until they were settled, but instead escaped to the kitchen where she collected more glasses. But her hands were shaking and she had a bad feeling that her cheeks were bright red.

"They're teasing you because you're important to them," David said, coming up behind her. "You okay?"

She nodded without turning. "I'm sorry."

"Why? Because you have people who care about you? Isn't that the whole point of life? They're comfortable here, with you. And I like them."

Somehow she was turning and facing him and he was standing really, really close. "They are good friends. I'm lucky to have them."

"Yes, you are. Ready to go back?"

She would rather stand here, next to him, his hands braced on either side of her. She liked the heat of his body easing in hers and the way she felt safe. As if she could count on him. As if this were real. As if he really wanted to see her naked.

"I'm ready," she whispered.

He stepped back and picked up the glasses. She took the two bottles of wine and they returned to the living room.

David had already laid out a couple of dozen pieces of jewelry. Several were from his trip to the mall, while others came from the Worden store. A couple were Jayne's QVC purchases, and there were three pieces Rebecca had given her. He asked her friends to look over the jewelry and then tell him what they liked and didn't like.

"These are yours, right?" Gigi asked Jayne, holding up a pair of faux-diamond hoops. "I love these. Sparkly and I don't have to mortgage my house to afford them."

Katie picked up a pendant from the Rivalsa collection. "I love this," she said. "Look at the lines. It's so beautiful." She rubbed the curves. "It's real gold, right? A couple of thousand dollars?"

Jayne shrugged. "It was a gift, but yes, it's expensive." She happened to know that pendant sold in the high five figures, but there was no point in mentioning that.

"What do you like about it?" David asked.

Katie handed it to Charlotte. "How it looks. The weight of it. I don't know. I just like it."

"Me, too," Charlotte said. "Are there earrings like this?"

Jayne nodded.

"Would you like it in sterling?" David asked. "If you could buy it for, say, a couple hundred dollars?"

"I would," Katie said.

"I'd want the earrings."

David took them through the rest of the pieces. Of the mall jewelry, only two pairs of earrings were a hit. Everyone loved the Worden pieces, but it was like wanting a house on the beach—lovely in theory, but not in this lifetime.

"Unless the lottery comes through," Gigi added.

He listened carefully, taking notes and asking specific questions, obviously interested in their opinions. Jayne watched her friends watch him, noting the looks they exchanged. There would be plenty of phone calls tomorrow, she thought. Mostly to ask if he had a brother.

David cleared off the table and asked the women to show him their favorite pieces from their own jewelry boxes. Katie held out a pretty sapphire-and-diamond ring.

"My mom adored Princess Diana," she said. "Bought all the books when she got married. She even had a collector's edition doll. The Christmas after Mom had me, my dad got her this. It's like Diana's engagement ring. A sapphire surrounded by diamonds. A couple of years ago, she gave it to me."

"What do you like about it?" he asked.

"The stone is beautiful. It changes color in the sunlight. The ring is lovely, but what I like most is that it makes me think of my mom when I wear it." She shrugged. "That's probably not helpful."

He made more notes. "Sure it is. The setting is classic. Do the rest of you like it?"

Gigi shrugged. "Maybe with an emerald."

"I want diamonds," Charlotte said. "In any form. If you have some loose ones you can't get rid of, I'll take them."

An hour later, they'd gone through the rest of the jewelry. Jayne's friends left.

"I am *so* calling you tomorrow," Katie whispered on her way out.

"I already knew that," Jayne told her and shut the door.

She turned back to face David, who stood by the table, still making notes.

"A lot of information," he said when he'd finished. "Good stuff."

"I'm glad it helped."

"It did." He put down his notepad and grabbed his glass of wine. "They were fun."

"They thought you were nice."

He grimaced. "Thanks."

She held in a smile. "You don't want them thinking that?"

"No guy appreciates that title. It's usually followed by 'Let's just be friends.'"

She laughed. "Sure. Because that happens to you *all* the time. Poor David. Too rich and handsome to get the girl."

As soon as the words were out, she knew she'd made a hideous mistake.

He put down the wine and walked toward her. His eyes had a dark gleam, and his expression was satisfied. "Handsome, huh?"

She took a step back. "Well, you know what I mean."

"Not really."

"You come from a great gene pool." She took another step back.

He moved forward.

"It's all a matter of luck," she said, aware she should just shut up or at least change the subject. "And appearance is subjective. Culturally, what we find attractive here in this country is very different from what—"

He pulled her against him and kissed her. She melted into his embrace because it was better than babbling and because she wanted to. Kissing David was always the best part of her day.

But there was something different this time, she thought as he quickly deepened the kiss, stroking with his tongue. An insistence. A need. He moved his hands up and down her back, then slipped them to her hips. She found herself hanging on, as her legs began to tremble.

If she didn't know any better, she would swear he had no plans to stop with just a kiss.

As if reading her mind, he straightened and looked into her eyes.

"I want to stay."

Four little words that meant nothing apart but could be the whole world when strung together.

She had a moment of indecision. Even as various parts of her body sent up a cheer, her brain pointed out this could be a really bad idea. One that would leave her desperately in love with a man who was just passing time. It was a recipe for disaster.

Unless she was careful and kept her heart out of the process. Could she? Did she dare allow David into her bed? Or was the real question, Would she ever forgive herself for passing up an incredible opportunity?

She stared into his blue eyes and knew she had to find out the truth. Was David Worden as good as he looked?

Eleven

JAYNE TOOK HIS HAND and led him into her bedroom. Light spilled in from the hall, leaving most of the room in shadow. While she didn't usually insist on having sex in the dark, some lack of illumination seemed like a good idea. After all, David had been with some of the most beautiful women in the world. She, on the other hand, couldn't remember the last time she'd done a sit-up.

He reached for her, then paused. "Tell me you have condoms."

"You don't travel prepared?"

"Not as a rule."

"I have condoms."

An unopened box of three in her nightstand.

He reached for her again, then they were kissing and his hands were moving over her body. He touched her back, her side, then slid his fingers up to her breasts. He cupped her curves, then teased her tight nipples.

Pleasure flooded her. He kissed his way down her neck, then pulled off her sweater and took advantage of the exposed skin. He was attentive, determined, and patient, easing her out of her clothes with an expertise that left her breathless. Then he was naked, too, and they were on the bed.

He kissed his way down her body, lingering at her breasts, before dipping between her legs to lick her into surrender. She was still gasping when he entered her, all hard and thick. Rather than get lost in what he was doing, she found herself watching his face as he thrust into her. His features tightened as he got closer. She felt and saw the exact moment he came and knew she would never get tired of the view. Even if this ended badly, she would always have the memories of tonight.

She pulled up the sheet as he retreated to clean up in the bathroom. When he returned, she started to sit up. No way she was going to miss the show of his getting dressed. But instead of reaching for his clothes, he slid into bed next to her and propped his head up on his hand.

"That wasn't dinner, was it?" he asked. "I'm thinking Chinese. Is there a place that delivers close by? Or we could go out if you want."

"You're hungry?"

He grinned. "Aren't you?"

"Yes, but . . ." Nothing about this made sense. "Aren't you leaving?"

"Do you want me to?"

"No, but . . ."

"Yes, but. No, but. Jayne, you're going to have to pick a direction."

She would have put money on his being the type to do the deed and then run.

"Hey." He touched her cheek. "I can go if you want. I'd prefer to stay. We can have dinner, watch a movie, then use up the rest of the box of condoms. I know how you hate anything to go to waste."

"I'm big on recycling," she said, confused and happy at the same time. David wanted to spend the night. With her. Here.

Sure, it was emotionally dangerous—but she'd already gone this far. She leaned in and kissed him.

"I know a great Chinese place, and they deliver. You don't even have to get dressed."

He kissed her back, then pulled her close. "I like that in a restaurant."

Two days later Jayne raced to her car and drove directly to Rebecca's place. As it was barely nine in the morning, she had to knock for a full three minutes before her friend opened the door.

Rebecca looked sleepy and rumpled and still incredibly beautiful. Jayne pushed past her and headed for the kitchen.

"I'll make coffee. I need you awake."

"Morning to you, too," Rebecca said, trailing after her. "Did I forget we had something planned?"

"No. This is an emergency."

"Can it wait until I brush my teeth and pee?"

Jayne found the filters and the coffee. "Sure. Hurry."

"Will do." Rebecca paused. "Are you okay?"

"Do I look okay?"

Her friend frowned. "You're a little wild-eyed."

"Good. I'm feeling panic. It ought to show."

"Then be happy. I'll be right back."

Jayne finished making the coffee, then tapped her foot impatiently as the brew slowly dripped into the carafe. By the time Rebecca returned, two cups were ready. Jayne handed her one.

"Drink," she said.

"Don't I get cream and sugar?"

"No. You take your coffee black."

Rebecca grinned. "Just checking to make sure you haven't been replaced by a pod person." She sipped her coffee and sighed. "Okay. I'm braced. What's going on?"

"David wants me to be his date for the dinner party Elizabeth is giving."

There was more, of course. The fact that she and David had had sex. But that wasn't anything she needed help with—at least not yet. The invitation, on the other hand, screamed crisis.

Rebecca stared at her. "The one for the purpose of finding him the right wife?"

"That would be it."

Rebecca's mouth twitched. "Doesn't he know why Mom's giving him the party?"

"I think he's ignoring that little fact."

Rebecca took another sip. "He asked you, like a date?"

"Apparently." Jayne paced the length of the kitchen.

"We were talking, and he mentioned the party. I said I didn't know if I would be there helping his mother. He said that wasn't going to work for him. I wanted to know why, and he said he wanted me to go with him. That Elizabeth would have to get by on her own."

She still couldn't believe it. There she'd been, eating a bagel out on her patio. She'd thought the most incredible part of the morning had been waking up next to David. Then she'd decided it was showering with him, an experience she longed to repeat. Then she decided it was their eating breakfast together and talking . . . like a real couple.

But she'd been wrong. The invitation was the most startling event.

"I can't go with him," she said, turning and pacing the other way. "Do you know what your mother would say? Your mother who, by the way, has already called me and asked for my help."

Rebecca stared at her. "Really? The all-powerful Elizabeth Worden actually picked up the phone and asked?"

Jayne hesitated. "It was more of an assumption than a question. She called with a timetable and a list."

"Then all is right with the universe."

"It was until David asked me to be his date! This isn't information that would brighten her day. She wouldn't be happy. We're not dating."

"You and Elizabeth?"

Jayne glared at her. "Don't be funny."

"Why not? Come on, this is fabulous. My mother is

combing through the richest families of Beverly Hills to find her perfect son the perfect wife. And he wants to take you."

There was an ouch buried in there, Jayne thought, trying to accept the comment as it was meant. "The hired help."

"She doesn't even pay you. You have to see the deliciousness of it."

"No, I don't. David wasn't happy when I told him no."

"Don't you want to go with him?"

"Of course not. How could I? He's not serious about me. Elizabeth has gone to a lot of work to put this party together. I might not be completely thrilled with her at the moment, but I'm not willing to ruin everything. I'm leaving in less than two months. I want to go quietly."

"That may not be an option." Rebecca set down her cup and tightened her silk robe. "So you like him?"

Jayne felt the yawning coldness of the trap that opened beneath her feet. She loved Rebecca, but she wasn't willing to trust her with the secret of her crush. Or the fact that she and David had slept together. Not just yet.

"He's a great guy, and yes, I like him. There's a lot to like. I see a bit of Blaine in him, which is pretty cool."

"But you're not falling in love with him?"

Jayne relaxed. "Do I look stupid?"

"David would be lucky to have you."

That was the friend part of Rebecca talking, Jayne thought. "Yes, he would, but that's not the issue."

"Maybe he's trying to screw with Elizabeth," Rebecca said. "Or, at the very least, tweak her plans."

"Maybe." Now that she was a little calmer, she wished she hadn't come over and told Rebecca about the invitation. "You're right. That has to be it. I should have realized it."

Rebecca grinned. "Are you sure you don't want to date him? Just for me?"

"You mean to mess with Elizabeth."

"That would be the point of it, yes. Come on. One date? I'll pay."

"Your warm and loving support overwhelms me."

"I do what I can."

Elizabeth circled the set tables, studying everything from the china to the flatware to the centerpiece. Jayne stood off to the side, imagining which she would pick. Not that she would ever throw a party like this. Ignoring the cost, it was too formal, too fussy. Although she liked the idea of a buffet.

"The flowers," Elizabeth said slowly. "Jayne, what do you think?"

Jayne knew she was to be more of a sounding board than actually offer an opinion. "The tall arrangements are pretty, but difficult to talk over."

"I agree." Elizabeth circled another table. "I want more intimate seating this time. More tables of two. Would we even want a centerpiece on those?"

The catering manager made frantic notes.

"Set up tables for two," Elizabeth said, then glanced at her watch. "Jayne will check back in fifteen minutes."

"Certainly, Mrs. Worden."

Jayne followed Elizabeth out of the living room, where the sample tables had been set. Most people went to the catering office for setups, but not Elizabeth. People came to her.

Instead of going toward her office, Elizabeth stepped outside and breathed deeply. "I've had honeysuckle planted. Can you smell it? Not my favorite, but it's very romantic. There's night-blooming jasmine as well. All in pots. As soon as David's made his choice, I'll have it taken away." She glanced at Jayne. "Have you and David looked at any more houses?"

"No. Not since the last one. I, ah, think he's been busy with work."

"I hope not," Elizabeth snapped. "I swear, if Blaine is making him work long hours, I'll be furious. David needs to focus on what's important. Right now that's finding a house and getting engaged. Although I suppose the good news is if he doesn't find a house before that, whoever she is can help. God knows, someone will need to take him in hand. He hasn't mentioned anyone?"

A question Jayne could answer honestly. "He hasn't said a word."

"There's someone. I called him close to ten the other night, and he wasn't there."

If she'd phoned in the past two nights, Jayne knew exactly where he'd been. "Maybe he was out with friends."

"That's possible." She glanced around at the patio. "I would like to have the party out here. The ambiance is better than the house, don't you think?"

Jayne didn't answer.

Elizabeth sighed. "I'm having comedians at the party."

"What did you say?"

"I know. The antithesis of elegant, but I need some kind of entertainment, and this will give the women something to talk about. Also, I can watch to see if they laugh inappropriately."

Jayne didn't know if that meant discovering if they laughed at the wrong thing or if their laugh was wrong. *Note to self: As amazing as David is, no guy is worth this.* She would remind herself of that should she inadvertently get more involved than she wanted.

Elizabeth crossed to a pot of white roses and inspected the petals. "I saw Rebecca."

"Oh."

"She hasn't changed at all. She's still difficult. You kept in touch with her while she was gone."

It wasn't a question, but Jayne answered it anyway. "E-mail, phone calls. I saw her when I went on vacation."

Elizabeth turned slowly and raised her eyebrows. "You never mentioned any of that."

"I didn't think you wanted to talk about her. After she left, you never said anything. It was like she'd never been here."

"And you think that's wrong." Elizabeth's calm expression never changed. "Perhaps I should have cried or ripped out my hair?"

"I remember how much I missed my mom when she died. It was like a part of *me* went missing. When Rebecca left, I wanted to say something, but I didn't know how to start the conversation. It was a little like losing my mom all over again. At least for me. I wondered what it was like for you."

Elizabeth looked away. "Of course it was difficult. I'm her mother."

"You never said anything. I wanted to talk to you about her. I missed her." Jayne remembered feeling torn. She knew in her head Rebecca had been looking for an excuse to run away, and the stolen necklace had given her that. But it had been Jayne who had taken it in the first place. She'd been the one to give Rebecca the means to run.

"You're a very loyal friend," Elizabeth said. "I hope she appreciates that."

"She does." Jayne drew in a breath. "I know she's difficult and loves to make trouble, but you're her family. Her mother. She can't ever forget that."

"But that's not the question, is it? What is important is if she wants to—and I think we both know the answer to that."

Jayne wanted to say that wasn't true, that Rebecca didn't want to disconnect herself from Elizabeth. Unfortunately, her friend did, and a case could be argued that she had earned the right.

Elizabeth's cool, calm expression never flickered. "I appreciate that you want to help, Jayne, but as you said, Rebecca is family. This matter is best left between us."

A kiss on the cheek, followed by a neatly placed slap. Jayne told herself that in less than two months she would be gone. The Wordens would be part of her past, and she would never have to deal with them again. Well, Rebecca would still be her friend, but the rest of the family could go to hell, and she wouldn't care in the least.

"I'll go check on the tables," she said, and walked inside the house.

"Wow, could you look less happy?" Rebecca said with a snort. "Sullen was cute when you were eight, but now it just makes people wonder if you're constipated."

David ignored his sister as he stood by the window and glowered at the room. There were about sixty people milling around, with more arriving every few minutes. And while there were plenty of "friends of the family," there were several women he didn't know. Twentysomething women who wore elegant clothes and expensive jewelry. Who were well spoken, attractive, and constantly glancing at him.

"I've already been welcomed back," he grumbled. "Why is she throwing another party?"

"You already know the answer to that, my young prince." Rebecca waved her hand toward the guests. "Welcome to your own private marriage mart. Twenty-four-hour convenience. Yours for the choosing."

He glanced at his sister. "You're enjoying yourself, aren't you?"

She laughed. "What's not to love? The food will be excellent; our mother hates that I'm here. Have you noticed the stabbing glances? If looks could kill, she would so be booked for murder. My date is less than stellar, but I'm doing my best to ignore him. And there are endless possibilities on the entertainment front."

"Trouble with Jonathan?"

"More boredom than trouble. While I keep reminding him this is a meaningless fling, he acts as if we're long lost lovers. I'll be ending things, just as soon as I figure out the best way."

He had a feeling "the best way" would be the most expedient plan for her, Jonathan's feelings be damned.

"But this isn't about me," she continued, leaning her head on his shoulder. "However much it pains me to say that. This is your night, David. And what a special night it is."

"Go to hell."

"I would, but my mother lives there."

He saw Jayne walk toward the patio. She didn't look toward him or acknowledge him in any way. It was as if he wasn't there.

"You didn't expect her to come with you, did you?" Rebecca asked, following his gaze. "As your date?"

"Why not?"

"Because this is your own private version of *The Bachelor.*"

"The what?"

"It's a reality show on TV. I watched it on the Internet when I was in Italy. One guy, twenty-five women vying for his attention."

"No, thanks." That many women could only be trouble.

"Why are you pissed? Her relationship with Elizabeth

is complicated. It's why she's leaving L.A. This whole party is about finding you Ms. Right. Do you really want Mom coming down on Jayne? Does she deserve that? It's not as if you're serious about her. Speaking of which, don't make her think it's more than it is. Jayne's my friend."

His annoyance grew. "Because I can only be the bad guy?"

"David, I love you like a brother."

"Thanks."

She smiled, then turned serious. "I mean it. Jayne is wonderful, but she's not like the other women you get involved with. Or rather, don't get involved with. You haven't had a serious relationship in years. You enjoy the company of women, and then you move on. I'm not sure Jayne plays by your rules. I don't want her hurt, and if you were the least bit nice, you wouldn't want her hurt, either."

"I don't," he admitted, still pissed but slightly less so.

"So do the right thing. Keep it friendly, but don't lead her on."

"Because there's no way I could get involved with Jayne?"

Rebecca laughed. "Oh, please. She's way too good for you. Wait and see. You'll choose one of the women here. Or a bride just like them. Rich, groomed in the ways of our world. Your own personal young princess."

He agreed that Jayne was too good for him, but not with Rebecca's assumption about the woman he would marry. He didn't want a clone of his mother, God forbid.

Or someone just like him. He wanted to marry a woman he could be friends with, laugh with.

He had no idea if that was Jayne, but that wasn't the point. He should be able to find out without creating a crisis with his mother. Or his sister. But everyone had bought into the idea of what his future wife should be—including Jayne.

He told himself he didn't give a damn about her. If she wasn't willing to stand up to his mother and come as his date, then he was through. Sure, the sex had been great, but so what?

"I need a drink," he said. "Want one?"

Before she could answer, Jonathan joined them. "I've been looking for you," he told Rebecca. "Hello, David."

"Jonathan."

Rebecca looked at him and rolled her eyes. David made his escape and headed for the bar in the corner. As he did, he looked out toward the patio and saw Jayne looking in. Their eyes met. For a second, maybe less, he saw such longing and sadness there, his chest ached. Then she blinked, and it was gone. Elizabeth walked up to her and said something he couldn't hear. His mother pointed at one of the tables. Jayne nodded and disappeared toward the kitchen.

As he watched her go, he remembered what she'd said about her mother dying. How she'd been all alone, and the Wordens, mostly Elizabeth, had taken her in. He'd never known that kind of tragedy or fear. To be still in high school and completely alone in the world. She'd done the best she could with what she had, and when it became impossible to separate herself from Elizabeth's unreasonable demands, and possibly Rebecca's, she'd done the only thing she could. She'd decided to leave.

Who was he to get in the middle of that? To make trouble now, when she was so close to escaping? He should do what he could to make the situation better, not worse. Except he didn't want to let her go. He wanted . . . something else.

Ordering a scotch from the bartender, he'd barely gone two steps when Elizabeth and one of the potential brides joined him.

"David, you remember Wendy."

"Of course," he said, smiling at the beautiful redhead. "Nice to see you again."

"Thanks. Great party."

"My mother's doing."

Elizabeth brushed off the compliment. "Wendy's a lawyer. High-powered corporate law, but she also volunteers as legal counsel at a women's shelter."

Wendy, tall and slender, dressed in a fitted suit he would guess cost more than Jayne and all three of her friends made in a month, smiled modestly. "I think it's important to give back."

"Of course it is, dear. Wendy's father is our banker. Her mother and I serve on several boards together. Isn't your sister pregnant?"

"Six months and counting," Wendy said. "I can't wait until the baby gets here. I love children." She turned to David. "Don't you?"

David nodded. "If you'll excuse me for a second, I

need to talk to my mother." He took Elizabeth's arm. "This way, Mother."

"Whatever it is can wait. I'm sure Wendy is hungry."

"I'll be right back," David promised, and propelled his mother through the living room and into the first room off the hall. It happened to be Blaine's office, which was empty at the moment. David shut the door and faced Elizabeth.

"You have got to stop," he said.

"Stop what? Introducing you to women like Wendy? She's perfect, by the way. I've been asking around. No drugs, moderate alcohol. There was a touch of bulimia when she was in college, but that seems to be under control."

"Enough," he said, his voice a low growl. "I appreciate that you want me to find the right woman, but the key part of that statement is *me* finding her. Not you."

"I'm facilitating the process."

"You're holding a contest, and I'm the prize."

"This is an important decision."

"Which I will make on my own."

She shook her head. "You've been gone a long time. The dating pool is very different. I'm offering you good choices."

"I'll find my own girl. This has *got* to stop."

"You knew the reason for the party weeks ago. Don't pretend you didn't."

"I expected something more casual. I appreciate the opportunity to get to know your guests, but stop presenting them to me. I don't need to know their credentials up front." He ran his hand through his hair.

"You're acting like your sister," Elizabeth snapped. "So there are too many pretty girls. Isn't your life hard and full of pain? Grow up, David. This is how it's done. You're not just getting married, you're making an investment in your future. This woman will be the mother of your children. Her credentials are important, as is her family and her past. Play all you like, but when it comes to a wife, you can't afford to screw around."

"Like Blaine did with you?"

Elizabeth froze in place. Her eyes widened, as color exploded on her cheeks. David immediately felt like a jerk.

"I shouldn't have said that," he told her.

"No. And you shouldn't have thought it, either."

She walked out of the room, her head high, her shoulders stiff. David thought longingly of escaping somewhere less complicated, like the Australian Outback. Right now blinding winds and burning temperatures seemed like a reprieve.

As that wasn't an option, he returned to the party, determined to get another drink. But as he walked into the living room, he realized that dealing with his mother might be the lesser of two evils. Rebecca stood by the patio, Jonathan reaching for her.

"Stop," she said, stepping back. "Just stop. Stop following me, stop talking to me, and stop touching me." She grabbed his hand and pushed it away.

"Rebecca," Jonathan pleaded. "Don't do this. You're important to me."

"Too bad, because you're not important to me. I told you this was nothing but a fling. Why can't you listen?"

Jonathan glanced around at the interested guests. "Please. Not here."

"This is as good a place as any." Rebecca tossed her head. "It's over, Jonathan. I don't want to see you again. Ever. Don't call. Don't stop by. This was a mistake from the beginning. You're too old and too boring for someone like me. Now do us all a favor and go away."

Twelve

THE SILENCE THAT FOLLOWED seemed to fill the large living room and press down, as if everything had suddenly gotten too heavy.

Jonathan turned white. "You'll regret that," he said with an anger Rebecca had never heard before. His eyes flashed with a fury that made her take another step back.

She became aware of the people around them. Watching. Listening. For the first time in a very long time, an uncomfortable sensation poured through her, making her feel small and foolish. She read judgment in the gazes of the guests and finally identified the emotion as shame.

Dumping Jonathan was one thing, she admitted. Doing it in public might have been a mistake. Not that she would let anyone know she had regrets. Instead of cowering or disappearing, she tossed her hair over her shoulder, smiled, and took a glass of wine from a passing server. She toasted those still watching her, then took a sip.

Conversation slowly resumed. Rebecca glanced around, looking for someone to approach, a safe conversation to be had. Then the skin on the back of her neck prickled in a way that had her instantly on edge. There was only one man on the planet who could get her attention simply by walking into a room.

It wasn't possible. He couldn't be here.

She turned slowly, bracing herself for the inevitable. Then she saw him. Tall, tanned, and ruggedly handsome. Like an actor out of a commercial featuring cowboys and cigarettes. Nigel moved toward her, his walk more swagger than stride.

His dark hair was too long, his eyes burned with desire and appreciation, his mouth turned up with the hint of a smile.

"Becca Blue," he said as he got closer, as always his Australian accent making her weak at the knees. "You do have style."

She told herself that he was married and that she had to be strong. That whatever brought him here and whatever he wanted, it couldn't be good. Not for her. But when he pulled her into his arms and kissed her, she felt like she'd found her way back home . . . for the first time in months.

For Elizabeth, rage was hot and white and burned in her chest and her stomach. If she had a gun, she would have cheerfully shot Rebecca—consequences be damned.

It wasn't just that her daughter had once again ruined David's party, it was *how* she'd done it. Publicly, and to Jonathan.

Good manners demanded that she go to him and apologize for Rebecca's behavior and somehow try to smooth things over. But her own affair made her hesitate. Twelve years ago, she'd been the one to end things. Was he thinking, Like mother, like daughter? She didn't want to anger him more and risk his telling Blaine out of revenge. She'd always trusted Jonathan to act like a gentleman, but Rebecca was capable of pushing anyone past the breaking point.

Not knowing what to do was nearly as horrifying as the scene itself. Someone needed to teach that little bitch a lesson. To think Rebecca was her child. If only she had been adopted—Elizabeth could blame someone else. As it was, she could only assume there was some mental weakness, some flaw inside of Rebecca. If she were younger, she could be locked away. Something Elizabeth should have thought of years ago.

But it was too late, and she had a party to salvage.

She forced herself to smile, as if Rebecca's outburst had been in her plan all along, and mingled with her guests. As she spoke and waved over servers to refill drinks, she searched for Blaine. Finally she spotted him talking to that drab Marjorie Danes. Why someone with that much money dressed so plainly, she would never know.

She crossed to him. "Hello, Marjorie. Blaine, I need you to circulate among our guests. Provide a distraction."

"All right," he said absently. "A distraction from what?"

Marjorie patted his arm. "He was in the restroom and missed Rebecca's . . . conversation. I wasn't going to say anything."

Blaine frowned. "What happened with Rebecca?"

"She broke up with Jonathan in front of everyone," Elizabeth said, annoyed that Marjorie hadn't told him and that he hadn't stopped it in the first place. Rebecca took after him—this was his fault for indulging her while she was growing up. "He was humiliated, and now everyone is talking."

"He was too old for her," Blaine said. "What was she thinking?"

"God only knows with that girl. Blaine, the party? Can you talk to a few people and act as if everything is all right?"

"I'll go with him," Marjorie said, slipping her arm through his. "My oldest daughter just told me she was pregnant. I didn't want to take away from David by telling anyone, but under the circumstances . . ."

Idiot, Elizabeth thought grimly. "Yes, please. Tell everyone you're about to have another grandchild. How delightful."

She walked away thinking that of course Marjorie was the type to happily announce she was a grandmother. She probably called it "aging with grace" instead of "letting oneself go," too.

She left her husband with Marjorie and started looking for Jayne. At least *she* would understand the disaster and give her an honest assessment of the situation. People tended not to notice Jayne and speak as if she wasn't in the room.

Elizabeth spotted her heading into the kitchen and went to catch up with her. As she moved across the room she saw Rebecca with a tall, good-looking man. He was casually dressed, but his clothes were expensive. Not American, she thought. English, perhaps? She walked faster.

Jayne stood by the large kitchen island with a list in her hands. Probably confirming the entrées were ready to go out to the buffet table, Elizabeth thought, relieved to know she could always count on Jayne.

"Leave them to deal with the food," she said, motioning for Jayne to follow her into the pantry, where they would have some privacy. The small room was maybe twelve feet square, with rows of shelves, two freezers, and a long counter and sink for prep work. "How bad is it?"

Jayne didn't pretend to misunderstand. Sympathy flared in her brown eyes. "From what I can tell, about ten or fifteen people heard the whole thing. They're spreading the word."

"Of course. I'm sure they're exaggerating the story."

"I'm not sure they have to. She was fairly brutal. Jonathan stalked out into the garden. I don't know if he's left."

"He's probably sulking," Elizabeth said absently, wondering if there was any way to save the party. "Jonathan has always been sulky." She pressed her lips together before she said too much. "Would you go check on him? If he's still lingering, pretend concern and get him to leave."

"Sure." She moved toward the door.

Elizabeth grabbed her arm. "Wait. There's a man with Rebecca. Tall, dark, very nice looking. Mid-thirties. Scar on his chin. Probably not American. Do you know who he is?"

Jayne stepped back and clasped her hands together in front of her waist. "Um, yes. Probably. His name is Nigel. He's Australian. I didn't know he was coming here."

"So Rebecca knows him?"

"They were involved for a while. It didn't work out."

"No doubt my daughter is responsible for that," Elizabeth snapped. God forbid Rebecca make a relationship work. "What does he do? Is there money in the family? Is it possible she's found someone wealthy and appropriate? Dare I hope?"

Jayne's eyes narrowed. "I'm sure the question you meant to ask is, Who is he as a person? Is he good for her? Does he make her happy? Isn't that more important than any money he might have?"

Elizabeth couldn't have been more surprised if the can of beans on the shelf next to her had spoken. "How dare you?" she breathed. "You are *never* to speak to me like that again. You forget yourself; you forget who I am and what you owe me."

"I'm clear on who you are," Jayne told her, sounding more angry than contrite. "It's my role that gets confusing. Not the hired help, exactly. I don't get paid for what I do. As for Nigel, he's part owner of a diamond mine. So yes, he has some money. From your perspective, I'm guessing that's good enough. Wealth makes up for a lot. At least for you. Little else matters, right?"

Fury burned hot and bright, making Elizabeth want to slap her. "Get out," she breathed. "Get out of my house. After all this time and all I've done for you, I finally see the person you are. Ungrateful. Disrespectful. When I think of how foolishly I took care of you. This is my reward? You disgust me."

"Then we're even. And Elizabeth, in case you were wondering, you're the reason I'm moving a thousand miles away."

Jayne walked out of the pantry. She felt oddly disconnected from her body, as if she were floating alongside of it.

She couldn't explain what had happened. Something inside of her had snapped. One second she'd been feeling bad about how Rebecca had humiliated her family, and the next she'd wanted to shove a pie in Elizabeth's unnaturally tight face. It was the other woman's comments about Rebecca. And, okay, the fight with David.

Every one of the Wordens was insane, with the possible exception of Blaine. He was too clueless about what was going on to qualify as crazy. David wanted to bring her to the "let's find a wife" party as his date and then had gotten pissed when she'd refused. Rebecca chose to embarrass a perfectly nice man whose only flaw was in adoring her a little too much and not being the married man she was still in love with. Elizabeth was a psycho bitch determined to maintain appearances, despite whatever reality threw at her. For her, there was only the perfect son and the mistake of a daughter.

Jayne didn't have whatever was necessary to live in this world anymore. She'd done her best to thank Elizabeth for taking her in. She'd been an unpaid servant for years. It had to be enough. She was done. Totally and completely done.

Texas would be better, she promised herself. Quiet and normal. She would find a nice guy to fall in love with. Someone whose idea of a good time was dinner with family or taking his dog for a walk. She couldn't even care if he liked to spend all Sunday afternoon watching football.

She wanted normal. Boring. Right now, boring looked really, really good.

She opened the closet and pulled out her small handbag.

"You're leaving?"

She shut the door and found David next to her, in the quiet hallway.

"I want to talk to you," he told her.

"This isn't a good time."

She tried to move past him, but the hallway wouldn't allow that, not without their touching. And despite everything that had happened, she couldn't brush against him without wanting to lean in and beg.

"This time works for me," he told her.

"Then that's what matters, isn't it?" she snapped, feeling her temper flare. "Because it's all about you. What I want isn't important. You have spoken. Let David's will be done."

He folded his arms across his chest. "The sarcasm is a nice touch."

"You like it? You earned it. What do you want? Obviously not to respect my request that we not do this here and now."

"I respected your wishes. I wanted you to come as my date, and you refused. I didn't push."

"No. You were sullen and obviously pissed. Not the least bit gracious. You didn't try to see my side of things. But you didn't push. Yay, you."

"Jayne," he began, dropping his arms to his side. "I didn't mean it like that."

"How did you mean it? We're talking because this is a good time for you. I'm supposed to quiver with gratitude because you didn't push. Let's be clear. Your asking me out to something doesn't obligate me to go with you."

"I know."

"Do you also know what this party is about? It's your chance to find the right kind of girl to marry. Your mother has some very clear ideas on that, and obviously you don't disagree, because you were fine with the party. Then you invite me as your date. What the hell is up with that? Are you too frightened to stand up to your mother? Is some twisted passive-aggressive response better? You won't tell her no, but you'll bring someone like me just to piss her off? That's mature. And doesn't it do great things for my relationship with her?"

Not that Elizabeth was going to be speaking to her anytime soon, but that wasn't the point.

She slung her purse over her shoulder, then planted her hands on her hips. "Where do you get off using me like that?"

"I'm not using you," he growled. "I wanted you to be my date because I wanted to spend time with you."

"At *this* party? Does anything about that strike you as smart? Or even reasonable? You told your mother you'd come home to L.A. to get married. Were you lying?"

"No."

"Then go find a wife. I'm busy."

She started to push past him, but he wouldn't let her. He shifted in front of her, blocking her exit.

"That's it?" he asked. "You don't care that I'm supposed to find my future bride here?"

"It has nothing to do with me." She might be wild about him, but she wasn't an idiot. Unlike some others she could name.

"We slept together, Jayne. Doesn't that mean anything to you?"

It meant more than he could ever know. The night had been magical, but not as perfect as the man. It wasn't just the things he'd done to her body—it was the way he'd made her laugh. How they'd talked until two, then made love again. It was him in her shower, yelling that her shampoo was going to make him smell like a girl.

She stared into his impossibly blue eyes. "It was meaningless."

A muscle in his cheek twitched. "To you."

"No, David. It was meaningless to you."

He swore. "Because I'd have sex with anyone who was convenient?"

"I'm sure there are standards."

"Are you?"

She flinched. "I know we had a good time together.

But I'm not going to pretend I believe the sex is significant to you."

"I'm not sure who that speaks worse of," he said. "Me or you."

She watched him walk away. Part of her wanted to call him back, to say that she hadn't really meant it. That if he thought there was even the slightest chance they could make it work, she would sell her soul for the opportunity. Then she reminded herself that she'd already given the Wordens plenty over the years. They could manage very well without her soul.

The garden smelled sweet. The air was cool, but not unbearably so, although Rebecca had a feeling she wouldn't notice the temperature even if she was standing in the center of the sun. She was with Nigel, and little else mattered.

He sat next to her, on a low stone wall, his arm around her. She could feel the steady beat of his heart and breathe in the familiar scent of him. It had been so long, she thought, both thrilled and apprehensive about his presence. Too long.

"The whole sky is different," he said, staring up at the clear night. "The stars. It's freaky."

"It's a different hemisphere. Besides, you should be happy to see any stars at all. This is L.A. We don't get to see the sky very often."

"Then I'll enjoy the view down here." He leaned in and kissed her. "Hey, Becca Blue."

She could so easily get lost in him. She'd done it a thousand times, giving up everything about herself in the effort to please him. Then it got to be too much, and she had to leave. The first time, she'd run clear to Italy. He'd found her, and she'd succumbed again.

And so it had been, through nearly a decade of loving and wanting, pulling back and then missing him. Until finally she'd been ready to let him win her once and for all. She'd been willing to say the words he told her he needed to hear. That she loved him. That she would marry him. That had been six months ago. Three days later he'd arrived in Italy and told her he was marrying Ariel.

Now he angled toward her and cupped her face in his hands. "God, I miss you," he said, his voice low and tempting. "I can't go an hour without thinking about you. I made a mistake marrying Ariel. I know that now. You're the one for me; you always have been."

The words eased pain in places she hadn't realized hurt. They made her want to fly and dance and sing. Everything about her life had been off—black-and-white in a world of color. Everyone had been happy but her. Without Nigel, she couldn't breathe, couldn't create. But with him, she could do anything.

He leaned in and kissed her. Just a light touch at first, then deeply. His tongue plunged into her mouth.

After months of feeling nothing, of being dead inside, she came to life with a burst of passion. Hunger burned as blood raced through her. For the first time in weeks, she was alive and aching for a man. No. Not a man. For Nigel. Always Nigel.

She clamped her lips around his tongue and sucked. He responded by groaning, and the sound ripped through to her heart. They reached for each other.

She wore a short, sleeveless dress. He found the zipper and jerked it down. She pushed the fabric to her waist, he unfastened her bra. Then his mouth was on her breasts. He licked and teased, before biting on the very tips of her nipples, just the way she liked. Between her legs she swelled in anticipation. The need was so desperate, she parted her thighs, then dropped her hand to begin rubbing herself. The thin layer of her thong got in the way, and she pulled it off.

Nigel straightened. "Pull up your dress," he demanded.

A shiver of excitement rippled through her. She did as he asked, then opened her legs wide and once again found her swollen center. Her gaze locked with his, she circled the spot, moving faster and harder, her breath coming in pants.

It took only a few seconds, then she was coming for the first time in months. She forced herself to keep her eyes open, to let him watch her experience her release. He fumbled with the belt on his trousers, unfastened the zipper, pulled out his hard dick, and shoved it into her.

She welcomed him with a moan. After wrapping her legs around his hips, she hung on for the ride as he pumped in and out of her.

The fast and steady pace was familiar, as was the man. She was close again in seconds, crying out her need, begging him not to stop.

"Never," he promised.

On the verge of her second climax, she heard a sound and opened her eyes. Jonathan stood in the shadows, staring at her. His face was a mask of intense loathing. Then Nigel thrust in again, and she screamed out her release. Her eyes sank closed as pure liquid pleasure poured through her. She came and came, as if making up for all the times she hadn't while they'd been apart. She barely noticed when Nigel finished. When she opened her eyes again, Jonathan was gone.

Good. Let him think about all the times he'd been unable to please her. It was what he deserved.

Nigel stepped back. She pulled up the top of her dress. Her bra was somewhere, but she wasn't worried about it. He finished dressing and bent down to pick up her thong.

She shook her head. "Let the gardener toss it."

Nigel grinned. "I'll keep it then. As a memento." He shoved it into his pocket, then took her hand and drew her to her feet. "Come back to me."

The last bit of her world righted itself. "What about Ariel?"

"I'll leave her. You're the one for me. You always have been. You're the one I want. Say yes."

He pulled her close and kissed her. She went willingly, surrendering to the inevitable. She and Nigel belonged together. They always had.

As he kissed his way along her jaw, he murmured, "I'll move in with you tonight. We'll stay in L.A. for a while, then take off for anywhere you want. Just the two of us. And the blue diamond."

Agreement hovered on her lips, then died as his words sank in. Reality was a bitch, she thought bitterly, pushing him away. She might love Nigel, but she also knew him.

"That's what this is all about, isn't it?" She reached behind her and zipped up her dress. "You're not interested in getting back with me. This is all about the blue diamond."

He shifted slightly. "I need it back. Things aren't going well, and I have a buyer. I need the money, Becca Blue. Something you've never had to deal with."

Few things hurt more than the death of a dream. It was like someone stabbed her in the gut and was now turning the knife. The pain made her nauseous.

"Would you really leave her?" she asked, already knowing the answer. "Can I buy you with a blue diamond?"

He frowned. "There's no reason to be nasty."

"Isn't there? Does your wife know you're for sale? Or is it a cool game of bait and switch? You promise me everything, get the diamond, then go back to her? How stupid do you think I am?" She held up her hand. "I already know the answer. Good-bye, Nigel."

She lifted her head, squared her shoulders, and started toward the house. Every part of her hurt, but he didn't have to know that.

"You know you want me," he yelled after her. "No one can do what I do, Becca Blue. You can't walk away from me."

She glanced over her shoulder. "Apparently I can."

Thirteen

"ANOTHER MARGARITA?" REBECCA ASKED, holding up the pitcher.

Jayne squinted toward the horizon. They were facing west and the sun wasn't in view yet, which meant going for another drink this early in the day was a bad sign.

"I think I'll hydrate," she murmured, reaching for her bottle of water.

"I'll do the same," Rebecca said, "but with tequila." She filled her glass, then took a sip. "Much better. I almost don't care. How's that for progress?"

"Impressive."

"He's a shitty little bastard," Rebecca muttered. "I hate him."

"He's disgusting," Jayne agreed. While her evening hadn't been especially stellar, it had been a whole lot better than Rebecca's. "At least the sex was good."

Rebecca adjusted her sunglasses. "With Jonathan watching. Talk about a total perv." She raised her glass. "To me. I have absolutely no taste in men."

They were stretched out on lounge chairs on Rebecca's

large balcony overlooking the Santa Monica beach. It was about eleven Sunday morning on a perfect kind of day. Blue sky, warm breeze, lots of good-looking guys parading by on the sand below. Jayne kept telling herself there was no bad here, but she was having a little trouble believing.

"What happened last night has nothing to do with your ability to pick men," she told her friend. "You never picked Jonathan. He was a convenient way to screw with your mother." She winced and rubbed her temples, then pulled her straw hat a little lower over her eyes.

Rebecca sighed. "I used him, and it came back to bite me in the butt. I guess there's a lesson there." She took another sip. "I can almost feel bad for him. I guess I should have told him in private. But he was really pissing me off."

"Men do that. It's easy for them."

"Tell me about it."

Jayne turned toward her. "I'm sorry about Nigel."

"Me, too."

Rebecca wore a hat even bigger than Jayne's. It was one thing to lie in the sun; it was another to allow actual skin to get tanned. At least nothing above the waist. They were both covered in sunscreen. Jayne wore shorts and a T-shirt, while Rebecca had on a tiny bikini that probably cost as much as a living room set.

Rebecca had called a couple of hours earlier, asking Jayne to come by. Over coffee and bagels—only Jayne had eaten the bagels—Rebecca had told her about her garden encounter with Nigel and how he was willing to sell his wife for a blue diamond. Or buy Rebecca. That part wasn't clear.

And unlikely to get clear if she kept drinking margaritas. She gulped more water, then let the warmth of the sun soak away her pain.

"I shouldn't be surprised," Rebecca said slowly. "He's always been a jerk. I know that, so why can't I get over him? Why was I so happy to see him? It took me all of fifteen seconds to start having sex with him."

"You missed him, and then he lied to you. He took advantage of you."

"I'm the strong one," Rebecca said. "No one takes advantage of me. I should have sensed something was wrong. It was too easy. Nigel's a lot of things, but easy isn't one of them."

"Do you think he'll go back to Australia?"

"I don't know how badly he wants the diamond."

Yet another problem the average person didn't have to wrestle with. "Do you think he'll try to steal it?"

"Maybe, but first he has to get into my safe, and then he has to find it. I feel fairly confident that technology will win over greed." She smiled. "He can't even accuse me of taking it, because that would mean admitting he had it in the first place. I don't think Ariel's father would appreciate knowing his baby's new husband had found and kept a prize like that for himself."

"Not to mention his giving it to you."

"Exactly."

Jayne glanced at her watch.

"What?" Rebecca asked. "You keep doing that. Do you have to be somewhere?"

"I have a meeting with my real estate agent at one. I'd like to be vaguely on time and sober for it."

"As if she'd notice." Rebecca reached for her margarita, then turned her attention back to Jayne. "Wait a minute. Why are you meeting with her?"

Jayne hesitated. Her second call of the morning had been to set up the appointment. "Apparently I have an offer on the condo. She says it's close to full price. The buyers are a young couple. They're prequalified, and their parents have given them the down payment."

Which meant there was no reason to refuse it. "I'm in shock. The condo has barely been on the market a week. But it's in a great location, and I priced it to sell." She was still trying to absorb the news. "The timing is slightly off. I'll close before I'm ready to move, but that's better than being ready to move and not being able to sell my place."

Rebecca swung her feet to the floor of the balcony, then shifted so she was facing Jayne.

"Oh, God. You're really leaving. I mean, I knew it, but I was trying not to think about it. I don't want you to go."

Jayne told herself to accept the statement in the spirit it was meant and not to get pissy because Rebecca was thinking only about herself.

"I appreciate that, but you can visit me in Dallas. There's great shopping there. And cute cowboys."

Rebecca pressed her lips together. "There's nothing I can say to change your mind?"

"Not even for money."

"Why do you say it like that?"

"Your mother and I had a moment last night at the party," Jayne admitted, not sure she wanted to talk about it. Of course the alternative was whining about David, and that didn't seem thrilling, either.

Rebecca leaned toward her. "Please tell me you called her a bitch and slapped her."

"Close."

Rebecca drew in a breath and grinned. "Tell me everything. Start at the beginning and talk slow."

Jayne picked up her water. "She was upset about you."

"A side benefit."

"She wanted to know about Nigel."

Rebecca wrinkled her nose. "What did you tell her?"

"His first name, where he was from. Her only question was whether or not he had money. I shouldn't have been surprised. That's very her. But I didn't want to hear it. I just . . . snapped."

"How? Did you throw anything?"

"I told her that you were her daughter and the right question was whether Nigel was good for you."

"That must have pissed her off."

"Pretty much. She told me I was ungrateful and didn't know my role."

"She didn't!"

"Either role or place. I can't remember. I told her I agreed, then said something about being an unpaid servant. Then I walked out."

Rebecca grabbed her free hand and squeezed her fingers. "You're my hero, and I love you. Thank you for supporting me."

"A lot of cheap talk."

"I'm so proud."

"You're happy I upset Elizabeth."

"Yes, but what matters is you stood up for yourself." She released Jayne's hand and grabbed her margarita. "Are you okay? You and Elizabeth have one of those twisted, confusing relationships."

"One of the reasons I'm leaving town. Maybe the main one." She paused to consider the question. "I'm not happy. I didn't want to have a fight with her. But I'm not sorry I told her the truth." She thought about David. "The Worden clan is big on assumptions."

"Meaning?"

"Because that wasn't sucky enough, I followed it up with a fight with David. He's still pissed that I wouldn't be his date at his special find-a-bride party. How passive aggressive is that? He tells his mother he's fine with the party, then wants to bring a date? Why not just tell her no, if that's what he wants? And why me? Is this more about being the hired help?"

"Because you're helping him find a house?"

"It's complicated. He's . . ." Charming? Handsome? Perfect in nearly every way? She sighed. The unfortunate answer was yes.

"I warned you about not getting involved," Rebecca said.

"I know, and I'm listening. He's the one making it difficult. We don't have a relationship. We never will. I'm clear on that. Why isn't he?"

Rebecca leaned forward. "Have you and David gone out?"

"You mean like to dinner and stuff? We have, but that's not the point."

"Then why would he . . ." She put down her drink and removed her sunglasses. Her blue eyes, very much like her brother's, were wide with shock. "You've slept with him."

"I hate it when you're insightful," Jayne muttered, and tried not to squirm. "Yes, we had sex. It didn't mean anything to him. I'm clear on that. It just kind of happened."

"Please, please say you told my mother."

"No, and this isn't about you."

Rebecca slumped back on the lounge chair. "Where's the fun in that? So you and David did the wild thing. By the way, thank you for not giving me details."

"He's your brother. You don't want to know."

Rebecca put on her sunglasses. "Only if he's shaming the family name."

"He's not."

"Good. So after sex, he asks you out, and you refuse. That's playing hard to get."

"I'm not playing," Jayne grumbled. "He didn't ask me out to dinner or the movies. No, he asked me to his mother's bride-hunting party."

"That *was* stupid. Typical guy." Rebecca glanced at her. "You know to be careful, right?"

"You've already warned me. Don't risk my heart. He's not going to fall for anyone." Jayne was clear on that. "I tried to explain that all to him, but it didn't go well. I almost think I hurt his feelings."

"I'm not sure that's possible."

That's what Jayne was telling herself, and yet there was something about the way he'd acted. Something almost . . . defensive.

"I don't know what to think," she admitted. "I feel guilty."

"You feel guilty about too much," Rebecca told her, leaning back in her chair. "Let it go."

Probably good advice, but somehow it didn't sound right. "Maybe I was too harsh."

"Not possible. You're the nicest person I know."

"It's not exactly a tough competition."

"Still. Let it go. He's fine."

Jayne wanted to believe that, but she wasn't sure. Maybe her concerns about David were a twisted response to her fight with Elizabeth. Or maybe they were because she'd been a bitch. Either way, she was going to have to do something or let it go. Living in the middle was impossible. And denial, while Rebecca's specialty, wasn't a skill she'd ever learned.

But apologizing to David would mean offering an explanation, and she didn't know how to do that without confessing her lingering feelings. Talk about a disaster waiting to happen.

* * *

David spread the samples across the table in the smaller of the two conference rooms. Some pieces he'd commissioned from local artists. Some came from inventory, three had been ordered from QVC, and the rest were from his trip to the mall.

He'd already put the two binders on the table. They contained his proposed business plan. He'd done his research, had a list of suppliers he wanted to talk to, and had several designs he'd commissioned from the same artists who'd made the samples.

He'd spent the past week working on his proposal. There had been plenty of time—he still hadn't been given a whole lot to do around the office. His father had told him to study the books and learn about the business side of things. He could spend only so long staring at computer printouts. His evenings were quiet. Despite his mother's not-very-subtle requests that he take out each of the women who attended his party, he wasn't in the mood. The only woman he wanted to spend time with was Jayne, and that pissed him off.

A week after the party he was maybe, just maybe, willing to admit that he might not have thought through the consequences of taking a date to a party designed to help him find a wife. When he'd invited Jayne, he hadn't been thinking about that. He'd been thinking that he wanted to spend more time with her. Which was the point she'd blithely ignored.

But it was her assumption that he didn't care about their having sex that had prevented him from calling her. He knew that wanting to be right rather than working things out wasn't something he could be proud of. But there were principles at stake here. And pride, he admitted grudgingly.

He didn't sleep with just anyone. He'd given that up years ago. For him, the thrill was no longer about volume and much more about connecting with someone he liked. And he liked Jayne.

The mistake had been in telling his mother he was back to find the right woman and settle down. She'd taken the idea and run with it—not exactly a surprise. But finding the right person on paper was different than finding her in person. There was something about Jayne . . . something intriguing. He wanted to spend more time with her, but because of the great marriage hunt, there were complications.

The conference room door opened, and his father walked in. Blaine had a mug of coffee in each hand.

"If this meeting is as boring as the rest of my meetings, we're both going to need the caffeine," Blaine teased.

David took the mug. "I'll have you on the edge of your seat."

Blaine sat across from him, in front of the display of jewelry. "An eclectic collection," he said, picking up one of Rebecca's pieces. "This has been selling well."

"Classic, with a fresh twist."

"That was the marketing campaign." Blaine leaned back in his chair. "All right, David. This is your meeting. Why am I here?"

"As you suggested, I've been studying the business side of our empire."

Blaine smiled. "What did you find?"

"We do well. We have a reputation for excellence and innovation. Our clients are loyal and nearly forty percent of them make multiple purchases a year. Mothers bring daughters. Brides want to be able to tell their friends their ring is from Worden's."

Blaine picked up his coffee. "But?"

David pointed to one of the necklaces Élan had made. "As someone asked me recently, Does the world really need another one-hundred-and-fifty-thousand-dollar necklace?"

"It's our market."

"Agreed, and it's a good one. But what about everyone else? Do you know who is the largest jewelry retailer in the country?"

"Walmart."

David grinned. "Go, Dad. You're right. Walmart. Sears, JCPenney, and QVC are also in the top ten."

"Our market share is small, but we make considerably more on each piece." Blaine picked up a dented snake chain. "Do you want to sell something like this?"

"No, but there is a fifty-billion-dollar-a-year market out there, and we're not part of it. There's a big difference between this"—he pointed at Élan's piece—"and cheap crap. What about the middle ground? What about a more entry-level collection? Tiffany does sterling. That's an option. There have also been technological innovations with cladding. And stainless steel is an emerging market. It's harder to work with, but the material is cheap, and if the pieces are well made, they'll last forever."

He leaned forward and touched Rebecca's pieces. "We find two or three designers willing to start a line exclusively for us in silver, clad, or stainless. Maybe one of each. We approach QVC and offer them one of the lines for a start. We take the other two retail." He passed his father one of the folders.

Blaine took it and read through the first couple of pages. "Interesting," he said. "You have numbers?"

"I have estimates of costs, a list of potential retailers, the steps necessary to get a product on QVC, and some rough profit percentages."

"I've seen QVC a few times," Blaine said. "They want a personality to go with the product."

David couldn't get past the first part of the statement. "You watch shopping on television?"

His father grinned. "Not regularly, but every now and then. It's interesting and impressive. They move massive amounts of merchandise. From what I've seen, a new line requires a person selling it. Have you talked to Rebecca? Would she be willing to be our front person?"

David didn't know what to say. Rebecca, as in his father knew she was Rivalsa? "I, ah . . ."

"She'd do well on television. She's beautiful and flashy. As long as she didn't put her foot in her mouth. We could get her some media training." Blaine eyed him. "Or you. They have men selling jewelry. The Tacori spokesperson is a member of the Tacori family."

"You know they sell Tacori on QVC?"

"I know a lot of things."

David figured there was no point in pretending. "How

long have you known about Rebecca's designing jewelry?"

"Since you showed me her first piece. That talent's in the blood. I had an aunt who did some design work. There was a similarity. Your mother doesn't know."

"I'm not going to tell her," David said quickly.

"She'll figure it out on her own."

"You think?" David asked. "That would mean assuming Rebecca has ability."

"Not Elizabeth's strong suit," Blaine admitted. "Now that Rebecca's back, it will come out, one way or another. Secrets have a way of doing that. In the meantime, I'll talk to her. Let her know I'm proud of what she's done and see if she's interested in coming on board with your project."

David felt a flush of excitement. "We're moving forward?"

"I think you've come up with an excellent plan. Let's get a couple of designers lined up and get samples made. That will give us products to take out. From there, we'll work margins and put it in progress." Blaine closed the report. "I'll finish this later and give you any thoughts I have. I'm glad you came up with this idea, David. It's why I wanted you here, helping me run things. We have a long history of making beautiful jewelry."

"That's not going to change."

"I agree." Blaine reached for his coffee again. "Are you settling in all right? Getting bored being in one place?"

"No. I was ready to stop living out of a suitcase. I've seen the world. Being home is a great alternative."

"What if you marry an adventurous bride? Your mother mentioned that's why you've come back. To settle down."

Blaine said the words as if they were a statement, but David heard the question in them.

"I'm ready," he said slowly. "It's time."

"Meet anyone interesting at the party last week?"

"There were some nice girls."

Blaine looked at him. "I've left you to find your own way. My father micromanaged my life, which caused me to rebel in some ways I've regretted. I've done some things . . ." His voice trailed off.

For a second, David wondered if his father was talking about his affair with his secretary. Which led to a pregnancy and a quick marriage. Was it possible Blaine and Elizabeth's union hadn't been a love match?

Knowing his mother, it was easy to say yes. But marriages were private, and it was difficult for anyone on the outside to understand which dynamics made one relationship work and another fall apart.

"I didn't want that for you," Blaine continued. "I wanted you to be free to make your own decisions and live with the consequences. I don't want you to think I don't love you."

David felt slightly uncomfortable but told himself to go with it. "I know that, Dad. I love you, too. I've always felt your support, and I've appreciated being left to follow my dreams in my own way."

"Marriage is a tricky business. Don't tell your mother I said this, but worry less about the right family or connections. Other things are more important. Does she make you laugh? Is she kind? How do you feel about seeing her personality in your children? Does that make you excited or afraid? Pay attention to your gut."

"I will," he said, wondering if any of this described his mother. He wasn't sure Elizabeth made Blaine laugh very often and doubted anyone would describe her as kind.

He had the thought that Blaine was speaking from the wrong end of a bad marriage. Not that he would ask. There were topics simply never discussed in his family.

"How's the house hunting coming?" Blaine asked.

"Slowly. So far all I've seen are huge places with too many bathrooms. I'm seeing another place tomorrow. I told my real estate agent I want something more reasonable than a mansion."

Blaine chuckled. "Don't let your mother hear you say that, either."

There were disadvantages to being in the loop, Jayne thought as she drove north on Pacific Coast Highway toward Malibu. David's real estate agent didn't know about their fight, so she had called Jayne to let her know about the showing this afternoon. Knowing meant making a decision. And making a decision meant it was time to apologize.

In theory, she could have gone to David's hotel just about any evening. She could have set up an appointment with his assistant at the Worden offices and seen him there. But neither of those locations had felt right.

Not that David had made any move to come see her. Still, she wasn't happy with how she'd acted, and she wanted to make it right.

She found the quiet, narrow street and turned onto it, then promptly drove past the address. Houses for sale in the rich parts of town didn't have big signs out front. Most of them didn't have signs at all. She managed to turn around in someone's driveway, a security camera following her every move, then went back to the correct house. As luck would have it, David was pulling in at the same time. He, of course, had gone to the right house in the first place.

She sat in her Jetta, staring through the passenger's-side window, while he stared back. Damn, he looked good. Tanned and handsome, with his hair a little too long. Her insides did some kind of twisty dance that made her wonder if she was going to throw up.

He didn't look angry, but he didn't smile at her, either. Knowing there wasn't any way to escape at this point, she got out and locked her car. He did the same.

"Your real estate agent called me," she said by way of an explanation. "About the appointment. I thought maybe I'd come and . . ." She cleared her throat. "I wanted to talk to you, and this seemed like more neutral territory."

"Switzerland west."

"Right." She tried to smile. It didn't go well. "I, ah. I wanted to say I'm sorry. I was upset at the party. I appreciate that you wanted to spend time with me. I don't think you were setting me up with your mother." Not much of an issue now, she thought. Elizabeth hadn't been in touch with her since that night, and Jayne had no plans to make the first call.

"It was a dumb invitation," he said, surprising her. "You were right. I was there to meet my mother's selections. It would have been like bringing a date to a singles bar."

She inched around the front of her car, moving closer to him. "It was weird, but instead of getting mad, I should have said that. And maybe offered an alternative date."

"It's not your fault," he said, his voice kind. "You weren't yourself."

"Who was I?"

"We'd just made love," he said, closing the last few feet between them, then taking her hand in his. "You were still dazzled by my incredible skill and passion. There probably wasn't enough oxygen getting to your brain."

She pulled her hand free and slapped his arm. "You're lucky I'm not hitting you with my cast," she told him. "I was not overwhelmed by your amazingness."

"You're embarrassed about it. Don't be. I'm used to the problem. I should have warned you so you were prepared." His humor faded. "That night meant something to me."

"I know. I'm sorry about that, too. Saying what I did, I was wrong."

They looked into each other's eyes. It was one of the most intimate things she'd ever done—almost like staring into his soul. She felt heat between them, but it wasn't all sexual. Her chest felt funny, too. Kind of tight and achy.

"Is this as bad as it gets?" he asked.

"What?"

"You. How you acted. The fight. Was that you at your worst?"

"I don't know. I can get mad, just like everyone else. I try to fight fair. I would say stealing the necklace was the worst thing I've ever done. I'm not that person. I don't take what doesn't belong to me."

"It was a long time ago."

"That doesn't mean it wasn't something that changed me. I always try to figure out why things go wrong, then learn from the experience." She smiled. "Why are you asking? Are you filing a report with the character police?"

"I tried, but their Web site is down." He reached for her hand again, this time linking their fingers together. "Come on. Let's go spend twelve million dollars."

She nearly stumbled as she went with him to the gate and waited while he pressed the button. "T-twelve million? Are you sure?"

"Something like that. But the house is right on a private beach."

"For twelve million you should get an island and be worshipped as a deity."

"That's what I say," David told her.

They walked into a private courtyard, then up the stairs to the front door. Before he knocked, he leaned in and lightly kissed her.

"I don't want to fight anymore," he said.

As always, his kiss was magic. "Me, either."

The house was smaller than the others. Only about thirty-two hundred square feet, with four bedrooms and a couple of baths. But none of that mattered when compared to the view.

As David had promised, they were right on the beach. Both levels had floor-to-ceiling windows that looked out directly on the ocean. Stairs led down to the sand. The agent pointed out the remodeled kitchen, the slate flooring, the electronic blinds, but all Jayne could do was stare out at the tumbling sea.

"This one," she breathed. "It's perfect."

"You like it?" he asked. "I'm surprised."

The agent disappeared upstairs.

"Why?" Jayne asked, crossing to the windows and staring out. "It's amazing. People will come to your parties just to say they'd been invited. Any woman would be thrilled to come home to this. Even the housekeeper will love the bragging rights."

"So it's what you'd like?"

She laughed. "After I win the lottery? Make that two lotteries. Thanks, but no. Not my style. But you look good here. You might have a problem with Rebecca. Once she sees it, she'll never want to leave."

"But if you had the money, you wouldn't buy it?"

He came up behind her and wrapped his arms around her. She leaned against him. Maybe it was just short term, but it was a great way to spend an afternoon, she thought, resting her hands on top of his.

"It's the best location by far," she said. "You'll have celebrities all over and nice restaurants close by."

"Stop trying to sell me on it. Why doesn't it work for you?"

She hesitated. "It's not homey enough. I want a regular house, not some fantasy palace. I want to know my neighbors, not be recorded on security cameras. I want a safe yard for kids and a place for a dog to run. I want grass and trees and maybe a fountain."

"The ocean doesn't count?"

She laughed. "Fair enough. I want a slightly smaller fountain."

He turned her in his arms. "Then that's what we'll find."

If only, she thought longingly. "You can't buy *my* dream house. You have to buy your own."

"You're influencing me. I had a meeting with Blaine yesterday. I talked to him about developing a line of high-quality, affordable jewelry. He's excited by the idea, and we're moving forward with the research-and-development stage."

Her mouth fell open. "You're kidding? You're doing that?"

"Your point about the hundred-and-fifty-thousand-dollar necklace was a good one. I know how to listen."

"But I don't understand. You're taking my advice?"

He nodded. "You're more than a pretty face, and I respect that."

It was too much for a single brain to take in. Without thinking, she raised herself on tiptoe and pressed her mouth to his. As his arms came around her, he deepened the kiss. She hung on to him, being careful not to knock him in the back of the head with her cast.

It wasn't just that he'd taken her advice or accepted part of the blame for the fight or asked her opinion on the house. It was all of it. The real David Worden had turned out to be so much more than any man she might have imagined. And that was the danger. Falling for him seemed as inevitable as breathing.

Somehow she was going to have to stop herself before it was too late. Loving him would make leaving harder, and she wasn't about to fool herself into thinking it could work. She would have to back off.

His mouth moved against hers.

Later, she thought hazily. She would come up with a plan later.

Fourteen

REBECCA'S WORKSHOP HAD BECOME a haven. It was loud and busy. There were bursts of fire and steam as freshly poured molds were plunged into pails of tepid water. Buffers and sanders screamed, and every kind of music imaginable blasted well into the night. It wasn't the kind of space that allowed introspection, and even if she started to miss that shithead Nigel, all she had to do was stroll past one of the welders. The whistles and the suggestions they yelled immediately made her feel better about herself.

She adjusted her magnifying glasses and studied the carving in her hand. It was the first step in a long process that would end with a beautiful gold ring embedded with diamonds. It was her second attempt, and so far she didn't love any of it. The proportions were off, she thought as she pulled off her goggles and tossed them on the scarred worktable.

"I need to start over," she muttered.

"Am I interrupting?"

She looked up and saw her father standing in the entrance to her alcove. Well dressed and elegant, Blaine should have looked out of place against the paint-splashed walls and dented floors. Instead, he looked perfectly at ease.

"Hey, Dad," she said, standing and walking toward him. "What are you do—"

Reality sank in. The Rebecca her parents knew had no business being somewhere like this. But with the carving in her hand and her tools all around, it was difficult to think of a good explanation.

"What are you . . ." she began. "How did you . . . What's going on?"

"May I?" Blaine sat on the bench across from her stool. "I wanted to talk to you about your work."

Damn. She sank onto her stool. "Who told you?"

"I figured it out for myself, years ago. It was the first bracelet David brought me. My aunt Rose designed jewelry as well. Your pieces are a lot like hers." He chuckled. "Maybe more sensual. Aunt Rose was a fairly prim spinster."

"That doesn't mean she didn't have a good time with the gardener."

He winced. "Let's not go there. She was old when I knew her."

"Want to keep her all for yourself?"

Blaine grinned. "Thank you, no. But back to you. When I saw the bracelet, I suspected. Over the next year, I was sure. The name was a big clue. Rivalsa. Revenge is never a good idea."

"You sure about that?" she asked.

"Yes, but regardless of your motivation, you do beautiful work. I'm very impressed."

"Thank you," she murmured, hoping she wasn't blushing. She was too old to need her father's approval, but the words were nice to hear. "I studied in Italy. Milan. David kept telling me he would buy my pieces, but I was afraid he was being too much the big brother." She'd also been afraid to believe in herself. "Eventually, I gave him a few things, and they sold."

"Extremely well," her father told her. "The mystery helps, of course. Very romantic. Have you thought of announcing yourself to the world?"

"Not really. I like being anonymous." She fingered the carving. "Does Mom know?"

"No. She's never said anything, and it's not the sort of information Elizabeth would keep to herself." He leaned toward her and smiled. "It makes her crazy, you know. She's constantly pestering David to tell her. She wears several of your pieces and loves them."

Rebecca felt both vindicated and bitter. "Until she knows they're mine." The years seemed to fall away. She was nine again and feeling hurt and snubbed by her mother. "All those times I told you she didn't want me. You'd never talk about it. Never admitted I was right. You told me she was my mother and of course she loved me. You were wrong."

Blaine's mouth straightened. The lines on his face seemed to deepen. "I shouldn't have dismissed your feelings. I'm sorry, Rebecca. I was trying to make things better."

"Don't you mean easier on yourself?"

"That, too. I'm not proud of how I acted. You're my

daughter, and I can't imagine not loving you. Elizabeth is her own person, with her own rules."

"You should leave her." It was advice Rebecca had given him countless times over the years. "Why do you stay?"

"I won't discuss this with you."

"I hope you're discussing it with someone. You deserve better. She tricked you into marriage, and she's made your life a living hell ever since."

"That's not for you to say."

"Fine. Play the martyr. But don't you ever wish you could be with someone you actually liked? I'm not talking about a great love, but a friend. A woman who bakes cookies and makes you laugh. Someone willing to fly commercial."

Blaine was quiet for a minute or so, then he said, "I came here to talk about your work."

"Not a very subtle transition."

"But one we'll make all the same. As you know, David has come home to learn about the business side of what we do."

"No more roaming the world for precious gems?"

"Exactly. He's come up with an intriguing idea. Part of the appeal of our brand is the exclusivity, which is usually defined by our unique selections and price. He suggests we start a second division selling inexpensive pieces through traditional and nontraditional markets."

Rebecca wanted to cover her ears and hum. "You're getting a little technical, Dad. What does it mean?"

"Have you ever considered working in sterling or stainless steel?"

"Sterling wouldn't be that different, but I don't know anything about stainless. I've heard it's difficult to work with."

"But once created, a piece is much stronger."

"Sure. Stainless is a serious metal."

"We're looking to feature two or three designers in our new line. One of the places we'd like to sell is QVC. They're very successful, and they can move merchandise. One thing that seems to help is putting a face to the brand. I suggested you as that face."

"I wouldn't know what to say. Or how to act."

"There's media training for that. I think you'd be a natural. You're young, beautiful, and talented, and you have passion for your work. But first you'd have to decide if you want to take on the challenge."

Be a spokesperson for Worden's Jewelry? "It would mean coming clean about being Rivalsa."

"You'll have to do that eventually," Blaine told her. "We can keep it quiet through the negotiations. In the meantime, I'd need you to work up some sketches, maybe a few samples."

The thought of being on TV was exciting, but she was more intrigued by the idea of learning to work with a new metal. "I'd lean toward stainless rather than silver," she said, considering her options. "It's less traditional."

"Like you?"

She laughed. "Exactly. Stainless and precious gems. I wonder if there's a problem with settings. Movado does beautiful watches in stainless. They're elegant and classy." She rubbed the carving. The gold wasn't working for her right now. Moving in a new direction could really help her creativity.

"I'll do it," she said. "Give me a couple of weeks to get some ideas on paper."

"I can't wait to see what you come up with."

"Just don't tell Mom."

Blaine hesitated. "Elizabeth will have to know at some point."

"But not right now. I don't want her messing with me, and you know she will. I need time, Dad."

"All right. I won't tell her you're working with us on this. But the longer it takes until she finds out, the less pleasant it's going to be for everyone."

"Something I'm used to."

After dinner, Elizabeth finished responding to her many invitations. That dreadful Marjorie Danes had actually sent an invitation through e-mail. So tacky. Elizabeth had refused without bothering to read the particulars. What was next? Wedding announcements via text message? Would it kill people to keep a good supply of embossed card stock and lined envelopes? Her work finished for now, she tapped her pen against her desk as she considered how to deal with the David problem.

Through subtle probing, she'd discovered that he hadn't been in touch with any of the women she'd invited to the party. It made no sense. He'd been the one to return to Los Angeles. He'd specifically said he was looking to settle down and get married. She'd offered to help, and he'd agreed. There had been nearly a dozen perfectly eligible women there that night. He had to have been interested in at least one or two. So why wasn't he asking them out?

She rose and walked down the hall to Blaine's study. Blaine had been extremely cheerful at dinner, something she found annoying. He was so chatty when he was happy, and she couldn't figure out how to shut him up. Well, if he wanted to talk to someone, he could call his son and find out what was going on.

Blaine sat on one of his leather sofas, reading some kind of report. He looked up as she entered.

"I need to talk to you," she said, moving to the sofa opposite his and sitting down. "About David."

Blaine removed his reading glasses and set down the report.

"David hasn't contacted any of the women who were at the party," she began. "I've checked with them all. The point was to give him a chance to meet suitable young women in a controlled setting. He knew the plan, so it's not that he wasn't interested. It's been over a week. If he doesn't call soon, they're going to think he's never going to call."

Blaine looked at her. "I don't see the problem."

"We're talking about your son's future. I know you care what happens to him. He needs to get going on this. He's in his thirties. If he wants to still be alive when his children graduate from high school, time is ticking."

"The men in my family live well into their eighties," Blaine said, reaching for the report. "He'll go out with the

girls he wants to. He's never lacked for female compan-
ionship."

"I'm not interested in his having a good time for the
weekend. This is about the rest of his life."

"David knows what he's doing."

She held in her frustration, when what she really
wanted to do was scream and throw whatever was in that
stupid folder across the room.

"Obviously he doesn't," she said between clenched
teeth. "I want you to talk to him."

Blaine sighed and lowered the report. "What should
I say?"

"That he needs to start asking out these women. What
if they meet someone else before he can decide if one of
them is right for him?"

"Then he'll learn an important lesson."

"Don't you want grandchildren?"

"Yes, but I'm surprised you do."

She bristled. "What a terrible thing to say. Of course I
want David to have children."

"But not Rebecca?"

She narrowed her gaze. "What has gotten into you
today? At dinner you were so happy, you were practically
singing. Now you're . . ." Talking back, but she didn't want
to say that. "Now you're being difficult for no reason."

"I'm sorry, Elizabeth. I'm not trying to be difficult."

"Then imagine what you could accomplish with a
little effort," she snapped. "Why would you think I don't
want grandchildren?"

"Because they imply a certain age. Something you have never been comfortable with. You're constantly pointing out that you think Marjorie is an idiot for bragging about her grandchildren and not trying to pass for thirty."

"I'm not suggesting she should pass for thirty, but Blaine. Please. The way that woman dresses. So frumpy. And she hasn't had any surgery. Not even Botox. You can tell just by looking at her. If she doesn't want to go under the knife, fine, but get a peel or something."

"I think she's lovely."

"You're a man, and you don't notice that sort of thing. She's a tedious little woman and not the point of our conversation. What are we going to do about David?"

"Nothing."

She wasn't even surprised. "I don't accept that. He obviously needs our help."

"He's busy with work. He has a new project." There was pride in Blaine's voice.

"What is it?" she asked cautiously. "Another store?"

"No. A different direction. David came to me with the idea of expanding our customer base. We'll still keep the exclusive line, but also branch out. Offer less-expensive jewelry at different retailers. Maybe on one of the television shopping channels."

Elizabeth's heart stopped. She felt it lurch in her chest, then there was nothing. If she'd been standing, she would have collapsed. As it was, she could only keep telling herself to breathe.

"You're not serious," she said with a gasp.

"Do you know the largest jewelry retailer in this country is Walmart?"

"No, and I don't care."

"I do. David's idea is to offer quality pieces at low prices. We'll get two or three collections together. One of our designers is interested in working with stainless steel. We'll do another line in sterling."

Metal and silver jewelry? Worden classic pieces sold at the mall? "You can't," she said, breathing deeply. "This is impossible. The Worden name means something. You can't cheapen it by making horrible mass-market items and selling them who knows where."

"It's an excellent way to expand," Blaine said, motioning to the report. "The numbers are impressive. David's report—"

"David came up with this? I don't believe it. He would never consider this without someone else pointing him in that direction." She glared at Blaine. "Who was it? You?"

"No. He gets all the credit."

"I doubt that. Was it Rebecca? This has her written all over it? Only she has no interest in the company at all."

Who could have talked to David about this? Who could have planted the idea? Someone who knew about cheap jewelry and didn't mind destroying the family's good name. Someone with something to prove.

For a second, no one came to mind. Elizabeth might not have a lot of close friends, but she didn't have any enemies. At least none who would risk everything to go up against her. Besides, David wouldn't listen to someone like that. He would have to be tricked by someone who appeared trustworthy. Someone who—

"Jayne," she breathed. "This started with Jayne."

"Why would you say that?" Blaine asked, which wasn't the same as denying.

"I didn't tell you what happened at the party," Elizabeth said, still furious at the memory. "She was rude and disrespectful. She implied—well, what she said isn't important. What matters is that she's bitter and resentful. She probably has been for years. We've helped her beyond what anyone could have expected. We've practically been her family. And her way of showing thanks is to try to ruin us."

Blaine rubbed his forehead. "You're being dramatic, Elizabeth. While Jayne may have mentioned the idea to David, it wasn't done to, as you put it, ruin us. This could be very lucrative. You've never objected to increasing our income before."

"But not like this," she said, ignoring the dig about her spending. "She's probably been planning this for years. I wonder what she'll do next. Tell all our secrets to some tabloid or sue us for something."

"Stop it," Blaine told her. "Jayne has always been a sweet girl. You've gotten your pound of flesh from her, many times over."

Elizabeth stared at her husband, bile and loathing boiling in her throat. "What does that mean?"

"Yes, we helped Jayne. It was the right thing to do, but our reasons were more about trying to get Rebecca raised than taking care of Jayne. She's been nothing but loyal to you. Don't go assigning her evil motives after the fact."

"You don't know what you're talking about. She's changed. Or maybe she's always been lurking around, waiting for her chance."

"You're right," Blaine said, sounding weary. "When her mother died, leaving her completely alone in the world, she came up with the idea that in ten or twelve years she would have the chance to influence David into selling inexpensive jewelry. She's too smart for us, Elizabeth. What are we going to do to protect ourselves?"

Embarrassment joined anger. Elizabeth stood and smoothed down the front of her silk blouse. "Mock me, Blaine. I know how you love to make me feel bad. A new business venture *and* humiliating your wife. This has been a good evening for you."

He rose. "I'm sorry. That isn't what I meant. I was trying to point out that you're making Jayne the enemy, and she hasn't earned that." He reached out to touch her.

She moved away. If they had still been sleeping in the same room, she would have thrown him out.

"Do you love me?" he asked.

"What a ridiculous question. With everything we have going on, right now, I don't have time for this, Blaine."

"I take it that's a no."

He spoke lightly, as if they were playing. Elizabeth didn't know what he wanted from her, and she didn't care. Her head hurt, she was still angry, and the David problem hadn't been solved. Just as frustrating, now she had to deal with Jayne, and nothing about that would be pleasant.

"I'm your wife," she said. "Isn't that enough?"

"You'd think it would be."

Tiresome man, she thought as she left his study.

One problem at a time, she told herself. She would deal with Jayne, and then she would talk to David. She would get him to see reason, both on the jewelry and on going out with one of the women she'd chosen for him. He'd always needed a firm hand to guide him. Someone to show him the way. If Blaine wouldn't help, she would work around him. She'd been doing it for years.

Jayne parked in her space at her condo, then turned off her car and climbed out. Her new cast, a cheerful yellow, was the last one she would need, according to the doctor she'd seen that morning. It would come off in ten days, allowing her to return to light duty at work for the last four weeks before she left for Dallas. She'd been given some simple exercises to do at home and would start physical therapy as soon as the cast came off.

Healing was good, she thought as she let herself into her condo. The swelling had gone down, so this cast was more comfortable than the one before. Once it was off, she wouldn't have to worry about accidentally hitting herself with it or keeping it dry in the shower—a daily challenge.

She'd barely put down her purse when there was a knock at the door. Hoping for David, but willing to accept a kid selling cookie dough or wrapping paper, she pulled it open. Then wished she hadn't.

Elizabeth stood there, looking furious enough to breathe fire. Jayne involuntarily took a step back.

"You seem surprised," Elizabeth said, stepping past her and entering the condo. "No doubt you hoped to slip away unnoticed. But I've learned what you've been up to, and if you think you're going to get away with it, you don't know me at all."

Discussing her sexual relationship with Elizabeth's son was not her idea of a good time, Jayne thought, closing the door. What was she supposed to say? That she knew it was meaningless, but she was willing to accept a short-term fling with David because he was just so much fun? That she loved the way he laughed and teased, but she was more impressed by his kindness and compassion. That he was smart but not scary smart? She knew she wouldn't be mentioning that he was practically a god in bed.

"Elizabeth—"

"How dare you?" the other woman demanded, speaking quickly, her voice laced with fury and resentment. "When I think of all the years you've been working against us, all the things you've done that I don't know about. How you've hurt all of us."

Jayne held up her hands in the shape of a T. "What are you talking about?" Sleeping with David hardly hurt anyone else. It sure didn't hurt him.

"Your plan to destroy us all. Even your precious Rebecca won't appreciate what you've done."

Rebecca already knew, Jayne thought, more confused.

"We have a proud family tradition. Worden's Jewelry is an American icon. Women dream of being able to buy just one piece and then pass it on to their daughters. We are an institution, and we will *not* become some cheap wholesale business."

"Oh," Jayne said, relieved they weren't going to be talking about her sex life. "David told you about the new designs and the plans to expand."

"I heard all about it. Disgusting. This is *your* fault. I know better than to ask you to fix it. You may think you've influenced my son, but you're wrong. He's going to need approval to get this started, and that isn't going to happen."

"But I thought Blaine was already on board with this. They had a meeting."

"It's a family decision," Elizabeth snapped. "One that has nothing to do with you." She clutched her handbag more firmly in her hands. "You have gone too far, Jayne. You have been nothing but a disappointment to me from the beginning. I helped you because it was the right thing to do, and all you've given in return is grief. You are nothing without me. Just another average young woman. You're not pretty or especially smart. This"—she waved at the condo—"is the best you'll ever do. You're pathetic."

The reprieve was over, Jayne thought. She folded her arms across her chest.

"Okay," she said. "I've put up with crap from you for years. Mostly because I was grateful you took me in. I knew you wanted me to be an example for Rebecca, which was fine. Doing the right thing was easy. I liked being the good girl. I admired you so much. You were beautiful and gracious, in a cold, snakelike way. But you were the closest thing I had to a family, and I was willing to put up with a lot."

"I won't listen to this," Elizabeth said, glaring at her.

"There's the door." Jayne pointed. "Feel free to go. In the meantime, let me say I've more than paid my debt to you. I've been your personal minion for ten years. I've helped you plan parties, written thank-you notes, done shopping, wrapped presents, looked after the house while you've been on vacation. I've been your sounding board, kept your secrets, and tried desperately to convince myself you actually gave a damn about me. But you didn't. Not ever. I was a way to demonstrate how wonderful you are. Nothing more. As long as I acted like a well-behaved pet, you were happy to keep me around."

"If you were a pet, we could have you put to sleep," Elizabeth said, and crossed to the door. "Go to hell, Jayne. And stay there. You are dead to all of us."

The door slammed, and Jayne was alone. She stood in the center of her tiny foyer. She drew in a breath, then another, cautiously probing her feelings, half expecting an emotional crash and burn. She and Elizabeth had passed the point of no return. Their relationship was damaged beyond repair.

There wasn't any grief, she thought cautiously. No real pain. If anything, she had a sense of lightness. Something big and heavy had slipped off her shoulders, leaving her with the sense that she could almost fly.

She was free. No more answering to the angry queen, no more trying to please a woman who prided herself on being difficult. No more errands to run, no more canceling plans because Elizabeth needed her.

She was also alone, but that was nothing new. She'd been alone since her mother died. Living on the fringes of Elizabeth's life had allowed her to pretend otherwise, but that's all it had been. An illusion.

She turned to look at her small condo and smiled. It seemed like the perfect day to start packing. Out with the old.

Her cell phone rang. She picked it up and recognized the number.

"Hi, Rebecca," she said.

"Hey, you. It's beautiful outside. Want to have lunch on the beach? We can watch the pretty people go strolling by and know they're wishing they were us."

Jayne laughed. "That sounds like the perfect plan. You have a restaurant in mind?"

Rebecca gave her the name and address.

"I'll be there in twenty minutes," Jayne told her.

"I'll save you a seat."

The day was warm, the restaurant right on the beach, the waiter deliciously attentive. Rebecca ordered a lemondrop martini and eyed the bread basket with interest. She'd been eating a lot of carbs lately. She was going to have to up the length of her morning walks on the beach or risk not getting into her jeans. But that was to think about tomorrow, she thought as she reached for a roll.

"Rebecca?"

She looked up and saw Jonathan standing next to the table. Well, there went her appetite.

She set down the roll and sighed. "Why are you here?"

"To give you a copy of this." He handed her a thin folder. "It will be in the paper tomorrow. It's a good picture. That will make you happy."

She opened the folder and stared at the copy of an article. "Heiress Aids Terrorists," the headline screamed.

> Five years ago the rich and famous scrambled to purchase expensive and exclusive jewelry by mysterious and talented designer Rivalsa. While dozens speculated as to the designer's identity, no one knew the truth. Except the Worden family. Rivalsa is none other than only daughter Rebecca Worden. She's been designing her pieces from her palatial mansion in Italy. But why so secretive, Rivalsa? Is it because the beautiful diamonds everyone admired were purchased on the black market? Illegal conflict diamonds are bought and sold every day, the profits going to fund worldwide terrorism.

"What?" Rebecca screeched as she sprang to her feet and tossed the folder at Jonathan. "You bastard! None of this is true. I can't believe you'd be this much of a shit. My diamonds come from Australia and Canada. I would never use conflict diamonds."

"You screwed me in public," he said with a thin smile. "Now it's my turn."

"If you'd done a better job of screwing me in private, none of this would have happened."

His nasty little smile never wavered. "Face it, Rebecca. You're ruined. And you'll take your family down with you."

Then he turned and walked away, leaving her frothing with rage and clueless as to how to fix any of it.

Fifteen

REBECCA SAT IN THE book-lined conference room and tried not to let anyone know she was nervous. The article had appeared that morning, and she'd already received nearly a dozen calls.

David walked into the conference room. She resisted the need to run to him so he could make her feel better.

"I don't need a lawyer," she said instead. "I haven't done anything wrong."

"Not just a lawyer," he said with a grin. "A team. We have a spin consultant and a media specialist coming, too."

"Goody."

"Along with Mom and Dad."

She stood. "No way. I'm not staying if she's going to be here. I don't want to listen to whatever it is she's going to say."

But Blaine and Elizabeth appeared at the doorway before she could make her escape. Rebecca sat back down, wishing she hadn't had that extra shot in her latte. It wasn't sitting well in her stomach.

She'd called David after Jonathan had stalked out of the restaurant. He'd promised they would fix whatever problem Jonathan had created. While she believed him, she was seriously pissed that there was something that had to be fixed. Maybe she could have been slightly more sensitive when she'd broken up with Jonathan, but that was no excuse for what he was doing.

"Don't worry," Blaine said, moving toward her. "We'll make this right."

She stood and hugged him. "Thanks, Dad. Jonathan is being ridiculous. Conflict diamonds. I would never do that." She stepped back. "I shouldn't have told him about the jewelry at all."

"But so interesting that he knows," Elizabeth said coldly. "About your being Rivalsa. Apparently you all know, and no one thought to tell me. Now I'll have to pretend to be excited and have a coming-out party."

Rebecca watched Blaine and David try not to squirm. She felt a flicker of sympathy. None of this was their fault.

"Why would anyone tell you?" she asked Elizabeth. "You never showed any interest in me before. Your own daughter took off when she was eighteen, and you did nothing."

Elizabeth pulled out one of the chairs and sat down. "Here we go again. I didn't look hard enough. Poor, poor you."

"You didn't look at all," Rebecca said coldly. "Admit it. You were relived not to have to worry about me."

"Because every move everyone makes is about you. God forbid anyone go five minutes without considering what you might be doing or thinking. The world would cease turning."

"Elizabeth," Blaine said, putting his hand on her shoulder. "This isn't helping."

"Oh, and if we're not helping Rebecca, we're not doing the right thing," Elizabeth said, her voice thick with anger and contempt. "How foolish of me to forget."

"Admit it," Rebecca said, refusing to let her mother's words hurt her. "You're pissed because you love the pieces and you had no idea they were mine. Now it's all going to come out, and you're going to have to pretend you're proud of me, that you knew all along. You're going to have to convince your friends that it was a happy secret, when you'll be left feeling like a fool."

Elizabeth's blue eyes turned cold. "How little you know me, Rebecca. My friends will be nothing but jealous to find out my daughter has been delighting them all with her jewelry. There's no convincing. You've made me a celebrity. How that must annoy you."

"Not as much as your not knowing it was me in the first place," Rebecca said. "David's known from the beginning. He helped me. Did you know that, Mom? Gave me a place to stay, looked out for me."

David sighed heavily. Rebecca knew she was selling him down the river, but making her point with Elizabeth was more important.

"Dad came out to Australia to make sure I was all right," she continued. "The rest of the family gave a damn, but not you. You couldn't be bothered to check up on the mistake you'll always regret."

Elizabeth stood and faced her. "Look at this mess. Look at what you've become. Why wouldn't I have regrets where you're concerned?"

"Elizabeth." Blaine's voice was sharper now. "She's your daughter."

"I'm well aware of that, Blaine. But while you left for work every day, running the family business and enjoying yourself, I was left with an uncontrollable child whose only goal was to make my life a living hell. She was rude, defiant, and insulting to my friends. She skipped school, drank, slept with her friends' boyfriends. She worked hard at destroying her life and taking me down with her."

She turned to Rebecca. "You brought this on yourself. I'm not going to help you fix it."

With that, she left. Rebecca didn't watch her go. Instead, she turned to her father. "Dad, you really need to think about finding someone else."

Blaine bent over and kissed the top of her head. "I'll get right on that."

David took the chair next to her and grabbed her hand. "What's with the two of you?"

"She's a bitch and can't stand my perfection."

He squeezed her fingers. "That must be it."

She pulled back her hand. "I'm okay. She's always been like this. It's not new."

"No, it's not," Blaine said, sitting on her other side. "I'm sorry."

Andrew Tannin, the aging family attorney, walked into the conference room.

He greeted them all, then took a seat opposite and put down several sheets of paper.

"Well, young lady," he said, smiling at Rebecca, "you're in a bit of a pickle."

Despite everything, she laughed. "That's one way to describe it."

"Conflict diamonds are a serious business. Very serious. The government is likely to get involved. So why don't you tell me what happened?"

Andrew Tannin was about a hundred and eight, Rebecca thought. Would talking about sex kill him?

"My daughter ended a relationship," Blaine said, surprising her by speaking first. "The man in question was angry. He knew about her work as a jewelry designer, knew she worked in diamonds, and planted the story."

"Hardly gentlemanly behavior," Andrew said, then tutted. "Do you have documentation on the diamonds?"

She pulled the folders out of her large tote and set them on the table. "No one wants to be accused of selling conflict diamonds," she said. "Customers don't want to think they're supporting terrorism. I get my white diamonds from Canada and my colored diamonds from Australia. They're more expensive, but we know exactly where each stone came from. The Canadian diamonds have a microscopic etching of a polar bear or a maple leaf on them. The Australian diamonds are numbered."

She pushed the folders toward Andrew. He pulled a pair of glasses out of his suit jacket pocket and put them on.

"Like a dog pedigree," he said, flipping through the papers.

"Sort of." She tried not to smile. "I would never use conflict diamonds. I haven't done anything wrong."

Andrew looked up. "Don't you worry, young lady. This is all fixable." He glanced at Blaine. "Do you want to sue for damages?"

"David and I will handle that."

"I won't ask any questions." Andrew put his glasses back in his pocket and rose. "I'll get started on this right away. Rebecca, make sure my staff knows how to get in touch with you. You're not planning on leaving the country anytime soon, are you?"

"No. But I'll want to eventually."

"We should have this cleared up in a matter of weeks. I know people." He winked, then left.

"He's a weird little man," she said when the door closed behind him. "But I like him."

"He's the best." Blaine stood. "I think that's everything."

Rebecca thought about her safe at home and the hidden blue diamond Nigel would do just about anything to get back.

"Not exactly," she said, and told Blaine and David about the stone. "It was my consolation prize," she said. "Now Nigel's in L.A., and he's made it clear he wants the diamond back."

She didn't mention the sex in the garden. It wasn't something either her father or her brother would want to know.

"You don't have any paperwork on it?" David asked.

"No. I suppose he could claim I stole it, but then he would have to admit that he had it in the first place. And I did smuggle it into the country."

"You won't like prison," her brother said cheerfully.

"Gee, thanks for your support."

Blaine shook his head. "I'm not worried about that. Is it possible Nigel and Jonathan are working together?"

"No." She paused and considered the question. "Maybe. Nigel's not a happy guy."

The men exchanged a look she couldn't read, then David patted her on the shoulder and stood.

"We'll take care of it," he said. "Don't worry. But next time, could you pick somebody who won't want to crucify you in the press?"

She stuck out her tongue. David laughed. Blaine followed his son to the door.

"Your brother is right," he told her. "This is manageable. I want you to spend your time learning about stainless steel jewelry."

"I promise," she said, collecting her bag.

She walked out after them. Despite the article and the two angry men after her, she felt good. Loved and protected by those who mattered. As to Elizabeth, she could go to hell.

Rebecca celebrated her legal soon-to-be victory with a mocha Frappuccino, no whip, then drove to the studio. She felt inspired and ready to get to work on her stainless steel designs. She'd already done about a dozen sketches, and a couple of the ideas were keepers. She was playing with a signature look. A leaf design that would—

She rounded the corner, heading for the parking garage next to the design center, only to have to stop behind a half dozen police cars parked in front of the building. It took her ten minutes to work her way around them and into the garage. As she parked, she fought against a bad feeling in her stomach. A sense that she wasn't going to like what she found inside.

Sure enough, she'd barely made it to the first floor of the building when two of the other jewelers came running toward her.

"Somebody broke in and stole all your stuff," one of the women yelled. "They trashed your space and even broke the bench."

Rebecca's stomach flipped, making her regret the Frappuccino, whip or no, and followed the women inside. After she'd shown the police her ID, she was allowed to climb the stairs to her workspace and survey the damage.

Someone had destroyed everything. Her sketches were in ruins, her small safe broken open and everything missing. The only thing still in one piece was her stool, with a note attached. Block letters suggested that she TRY FUCKING ON THIS NEXT TIME.

"Do you know what it means?" one of the LAPD officers asked.

She had a good idea it was connected to Jonathan's watching her make love with Nigel in her mother's garden.

She wasn't afraid. Jonathan's actions were childish and spiteful. But inside, she felt an emotion she didn't usually allow herself. Guilt.

Jayne was right—Jonathan had done nothing worse than not be Nigel. She'd cruelly and publicly humiliated him in front of his peers. She'd destroyed what mattered most to him, his reputation, and now he was trying to destroy what mattered most to her. At the lawyer's office, she'd been annoyed, but now she was simply ashamed.

"Do you know who did this?" the police officer asked.

She nodded slowly. "I doubt he did it himself, but I know who's behind it." She gave them Jonathan's name, his work and home address. "He's a banker," she added. "A very rich banker."

The officer grinned. "My favorite kind."

Blaine poured more coffee. "We need a plan."

"What about beating the crap out of both of them?" David asked. "Or at least threatening it. That would work on Jonathan."

"An interesting idea. But from what I remember about Nigel, he would be happy to take you on."

David chuckled. "I thought you'd be doing the fighting."

Blaine grinned, then settled back in his chair.

They were in Blaine's office in the Worden building. Andrew would handle the legal end of the mess, but David and Blaine had to come up with a way to silence Jonathan and keep Nigel away from Rebecca.

"Nigel and Rebecca have a history," David said, reaching for his mug. "I warned her about him years ago, but you know Rebecca."

"Not one to listen."

"Not on purpose. From what I can tell, their relationship has been volatile. She moved to Italy to get away from him. He followed a few months later. When he wanted to get married, she didn't, and so on."

"We can't let him mess with our baby girl."

David thought about Nigel. While going after him with a bat and breaking a few bones would be satisfying in the moment, they needed a better plan.

"He's married to Ariel Cunningham. The wedding was a few months ago."

Blaine's expression turned satisfied. "I know Ariel's father. Eric isn't a man who likes to be messed with. He's killed men who have stolen his diamonds. Not that anything's been proven."

David wasn't surprised. The rules were different in a diamond mine. Accidents happened.

"Have you seen the blue diamond?" Blaine asked.

"No." He would like to, though. Blue diamonds were a once-in-a-lifetime sight.

Blaine pulled a quarter out of his pocket. "Want to flip for who gets to threaten whom? Or should we take care of the bastards together?"

David raised his mug. "I say we work together."

"I agree." His father chuckled. "It's been a long time since I put the fear of God into anyone."

"Seriously?"

"It was a long time ago. I was young and foolish." He put the quarter back in his pocket. "Where do you think you got your wanderlust from? Your mother?"

"Good point, Dad. Now who was the last guy you threatened? I want to hear everything."

But before Blaine could start the story, David's cell phone rang. He picked it up.

"Hey, sis," he said. "We were just talking about the men in your life. We—" He paused, listening to her, then hung up. He stared at his father. "The problem just got bigger."

David knew Nigel well enough to guess he wouldn't leave town until he'd found what he'd come for. A few calls to local hotels landed him the information that Nigel was registered at Shutters in Santa Monica—less than a mile from Rebecca's rented condo.

"Got him," he said, hanging up. "I asked to be put through to his room, and he picked up. So he's there now."

"Let's go."

They took Blaine's Bentley, a dark blue monstrosity that had been cared for with the love and attention usually reserved for spoiled lapdogs.

"You've got to get a new car," David said, running his hands along the smooth, butterlike leather. "This car is older than I am."

"It's a classic, and there's nothing wrong with it."

"You have to keep a mechanic on call."

"I keep Raoul on salary so he's always available if something goes wrong."

"Which it does. Can you even get tires for this thing?"

"Of course. Your mother wants me to get a Mercedes. She hates this car." Blaine grinned at him. "It's a chick magnet at the beach."

David laughed. "Tell me you're not cruising PCH looking for hot girls."

"I'm not, but with this car, I could."

The valet at the hotel practically whimpered when he saw the shiny car. "S-sir," he breathed, nearly trembling as he took the keys. "I'll guard it with my life."

"Keep it up front," Blaine told him. "We won't be long."

They went into the hotel and walked to a house phone.

"You want to make the call, or should I?" Blaine asked.

"He'll probably come down for me before he comes down for you," David said. "I'll pretend I don't know there's any trouble."

Twenty seconds later, he'd been connected to Nigel's room.

"Hey, there," David said, sounding happy to talk to his old friend. "It's David Worden. I heard you were in town. I'm here at your hotel. Want to grab a drink?"

Nigel hesitated just long enough for David to know he was nervous. "I'm kind of busy right now, David."

"You can spare half an hour. I'm flying out tonight to"—he paused—"London. I won't be back for weeks. Come on. I haven't seen you since I was last at the mine."

"Okay. Sure. One drink. I'll be right down."

David and Blaine split up. David went out onto the rear terrace to make sure Nigel didn't try to slip out the back way. A minute later, he walked into the open lobby and glanced around. David moved back inside while Blaine joined Nigel.

The tall Australian man looked surprised, and not in a happy way. "You didn't tell me your father was with you," he said, then forced a smile. "Blaine. Always good to see you."

"Likewise."

They shook hands, then made their way through the lobby and outside, onto the beach.

"I thought we were getting a drink," Nigel said, pushing his hair off his forehead. "Don't you want a drink?"

"Too many people," Blaine said. "Let's talk privately."

Nigel swallowed. "I don't know what Rebecca told you but—"

"She said you were a nasty little weasel," David told him. "I'd love to beat the shit out of you right here, but that wouldn't teach you anything, would it?"

Nigel turned back toward the hotel. "I'm not going to listen to this."

"You can talk to us, or I can talk to Eric," Blaine said conversationally. "You choose."

Nigel stopped in midstep.

"Eric and I have known each other for years." Blaine adjusted the sleeves on his linen jacket. "I remember when all he had was a deed to land no one else wanted and the belief that he would find diamonds. He came to me for a loan. Did you know that?"

Nigel shook his head.

David hadn't known that either. No wonder Worden's got first right of refusal on every diamond.

"Everyone told me I was throwing my money away, but I believed in Eric. I gave him the money he needed to start production. You know what happened next. It was one of the largest finds of the last fifty years. Nearly as big as the Argyle mines. Eric and I go way back."

"Look, Blaine—"

"I'm sorry Elizabeth and I couldn't make it to the wedding. I understand it was beautiful. But you got our gift?"

"Ah, sure. Yeah. It was great."

"You're happily married now, aren't you?"

Nigel shoved his hands into his front pockets and hung his head. "Dancing with joy."

"Good. Because I wouldn't want to have to tell Eric his only daughter has a lying cheat for a husband. I'm sure you wouldn't want that, either."

"What *do* you want?" Nigel asked, sounding resigned.

"Never see Rebecca again," David said.

"What if she wants to see me?"

"I suggest you run in the other direction."

"Fair enough."

"Good," Blaine said. "You still in the mood for that drink?"

Nigel blinked. "No, thanks. I'll go to my room and pack."

"An excellent idea. Oh, and Nigel? Anything you gave Rebecca is hers. Don't try to get it back. If you do, I'll start to wonder where you got it in the first place. That will mean asking a lot of questions."

Nigel nodded once, then headed back to the hotel. David watched him go. "What did she see in him?"

"You're asking me?"

"What was I thinking?" David's pleasure at the moment faded. "On to Jonathan?"

Blaine nodded. "Did I tell you I know a man who used to be in Special Forces? He's now a bodyguard. He also does extra work on the side. Based on what Jonathan just did, I think we should pay him a little visit first."

"Apparently Jonathan folded just as quickly as Nigel," Rebecca said as she passed Jayne a carton of tuna salad. They were having their delayed lunch on Rebecca's balcony. There was takeout from Whole Foods, a chilled chardonnay, and male eye candy from here to Venice Beach.

"He and Blaine have worked together for years," Jayne said. "It must have been tough for both of them."

"David was very impressed. He said Dad totally missed his calling. But it's weird. When the police went to arrest Jonathan, they couldn't find him at first. It turns out he was in the hospital. He fell down the stairs at his office and broke his leg. Apparently he was really banged up." She shrugged. "Oh, but that's not the best part." She leaned forward and lowered her voice. "Dad knew about the affair Mom had with Jonathan. He actually mentioned it, saying he knew Elizabeth needed that at the time, but Jonathan's sleeping with me was going too far. David thought Jonathan was going to have a heart attack right there in his hospital room. And he has police guards. He's been arrested and everything."

"Your reputation is restored," Jayne said.

"It's pretty damned amazing." Rebecca grinned. "Who would have thought my brother and father could moonlight as enforcers?"

Jayne tried to picture Blaine with a gun and couldn't. "You should feel good. They're taking care of you." One of the pluses of family, she thought wistfully.

"I feel like a character out of Jane Austen," Rebecca said, pressing the back of her hand to her forehead. "I'm only a woman. I need a big strong man to take care of me."

"Yeah, that's you."

They laughed.

Rebecca pointed at Jayne's arm. "Is your cast a different color or am I imagining things?"

"Yes, and it's smaller. My last one. I get it off in a few days, and then I start physical therapy. I'll also be going back to work doing light duty."

"And then you're leaving. I'm still not happy about that."

"And the decision is still not about you," Jayne told her.

"You should be touched that I'll miss you desperately."

"The knowledge of your discomfort keeps me up nights."

Rebecca rolled her eyes, then tossed half a roll across the table. "Sometimes you're a total brat."

"Part of my charm."

A faint bell sounded.

Rebecca stood. "Doorbell. I hope that's the dessert

sampler I ordered. Six flavors of crème brûlée. Could you just die, or what?"

"Are you insane? Six desserts?"

"I need a sugar fix."

Which meant Rebecca would take a single bite of each and try to hand the rest off to Jayne. Just what she needed. Fourteen thousand calories taunting her from her refrigerator.

There was the sound of conversation behind her, but Jayne didn't bother turning until she recognized a voice she didn't want to hear.

Elizabeth.

Jayne's first thought was to go over the balcony, but it was a three-story drop to the sand. Not exactly smart. Besides, she hadn't done anything wrong. She could face Elizabeth with her head held high—and then run really, really fast to her car.

She rose and walked into the house. Elizabeth stood with her back to the balcony. Rebecca shrugged as if to apologize.

"Who are you speaking with?" Elizabeth asked, then turned. "Oh, it's you."

Her tone implied that a cockroach would be more welcome.

"Hello, Elizabeth." Jayne grabbed her purse. "I'll leave you two to talk."

"Don't go," Rebecca said. "Please, don't go."

"Jayne should leave," Elizabeth said. "I want to discuss a family matter. There's no need for her to be a part of that."

"But we're not speaking," Rebecca whined. "We had a big fight. Remember?"

"This is more important than any small disagreement you and I might have had."

Jayne made her escape into the hallway, but before she could reach the stairs and the path to freedom, Elizabeth followed her and called her name.

She hesitated. Common sense said to run, but her mother had always pressed her to be polite. She could be civil to Elizabeth for ten or fifteen seconds. Just long enough for the other woman to get off an insult or two.

She turned back. "Yes?"

"I'm here to speak with Rebecca about her brother, but it occurs to me you might have the information I need. I've had reports that he's been seen dining with a young woman twice this week. No one knows who she is, which is troubling. Now, I realize you have your own issues and misunderstandings about how you were treated in the warm embrace of my family. However, I will still ask you, as someone I once considered a friend. Do you know who she is?"

There were a dozen things she could say, Jayne thought. But she was tired of hiding, tired of trying to make things right when they never would be.

She slipped her purse over her shoulder. "It's me, Elizabeth. David was having dinner with me."

Elizabeth's eyes widened. "But that's not possible. David was on a date. He was seen kissing . . ." Her hand covered her mouth.

Jayne nodded. "All me. I'm the mystery girl. Rebecca will confirm it."

"No," Elizabeth breathed. "Anyone but you."

Jayne hesitated, but what was there to say? She walked down the three flights of stairs without once looking back.

Sixteen

DAVID RETURNED FROM A very fruitful meeting with marketing only to find his mother pacing in his office. She saw him before he could make his escape. Talk about bad timing.

"I need to speak with you," she said. "It's important."

The need to bolt increased, but running wasn't an option. He shut the door, then motioned to the corner, where two sofas had been set up.

"Would you like something to drink? Coffee? Tea?"

Elizabeth shook her head. She moved to the sofas but didn't sit down. David noticed her normally sleek blond hair seemed mussed somehow. Her lipstick had faded, and there was a smudge of mascara under her left eye.

"Are you all right?" he asked.

"No, I'm not. Something terrible has happened."

As he'd just seen his father in the meeting, he knew it wasn't him. "Rebecca?" he asked, knowing it couldn't be. Elizabeth would hardly be so . . . distraught over her daughter.

Elizabeth set her small handbag on the coffee table

and laced her fingers together in front of her waist. She stared at him intently.

"Is it true?" she asked. "Are you seeing Jayne? Dating Jayne? Are you together?"

Hot damn. Jayne had finally told the old lady. Good for her, he thought, knowing this meant she was taking them seriously.

"I am."

"You seem very happy about it."

"Why wouldn't I be?" he asked. "Jayne's amazing. Smart and funny. She cares about people, and she's incredibly self-aware. There aren't any games with her. I know where I stand."

"Which all sounds very laudable, but isn't the point. How is this possible? When did you start going out with her? How could she have betrayed me this way?"

He knew what his mother meant, but it seemed smarter to put her on the defensive. "Gee, thanks, Mom. Betrayed you? Are you saying, Jayne doesn't have high enough standards?"

Elizabeth's expression turned cool. "That's not what I'm saying, and you know it. Jayne seeing you? A totally unacceptable situation. You're a Worden. You have a family tradition to uphold. I can't imagine how either of you let this happen." She relaxed her arms to her sides. "How long has this been going on? Are you sleeping together?"

He would give her full points for recovering quickly, he thought grimly. So much for leading the conversation.

"My sex life isn't your business."

"It is when it concerns your future." She pressed her

lips together. "Dammit, David. You should know better. I've given you the opportunity to meet appropriate women. Accomplished and beautiful single women who would like nothing better than to fall in love with you. But could you see one of them? Ask one of them out? Of course not. And Jayne, of all people."

"Why do you say it like that? What's wrong with her?"

"Nothing, if you were a junior accountant from the Valley. You're a man, so I don't expect you to understand, but Jayne will do anything to get ahead. I should have realized it before."

"Now you're scaring me," he muttered, thinking his mother was going over to the dark side.

"She's doing this on purpose. Throwing herself at you. Telling you her sad little story and getting you to feel sorry for her."

"I feel a lot of things for Jayne, but I don't feel sorry for her. Mom, have you ever had a conversation with Jayne? Not just handing out a to-do list or instructions, but a real conversation? Do you know what she does with her life?"

"What? Of course I do. She's some kind of nurse. A job she got after college, which we paid for, I might add. Jayne has been fortunate to have me in her life, and here she is repaying me with this." Elizabeth moved toward him.

"You have to listen to me, David. You're not thinking, or if you are, it's not with your brain. Jayne Scott will do anything to trap you. She'll lie, deceive, and very possibly trap you by getting pregnant."

"She's nothing like you."

Elizabeth narrowed her gaze. "I see you're still trying to hurt me. Fine. Go ahead. Be disrespectful. Dig in the knife. But while you're doing it, know that no one will ever love you as much as I do. No one will ever care about you like I do. Do you think Jayne worries about you and your future? Do you honestly think she wouldn't love to give up her crappy little apartment for life with you?"

Frustration built inside of him. It shouldn't have to be like this, he thought grimly. "You're wrong about her. She's so determined to get away from this damned family that she's moving halfway across the country. If she was so enamored with all things Worden, why would she do that?"

"It's all part of her plan to get your attention and sympathy."

Weariness tugged at him. He didn't like drawing a line in the sand—it often made things worse rather than better. But he wasn't going to let Elizabeth run his life.

"Mother, you don't know what the hell you're talking about. I respect that you're genuinely concerned about me, but there is no way in hell you're coming between Jayne and me. I'll keep seeing her, and you will stay out of our way."

"We'll see about that."

"No, we won't. If you do anything or say anything to turn Jayne away from me, if you make trouble of any kind, I will turn my back on you forever."

She sucked in a breath as the color faded from her

face. "You're not choosing that opportunistic little whore over me. I forbid it."

"You don't get a vote. Don't push me. I'll push back, and you'll be the one with regrets."

She stared at him for a long time before reaching for her purse, then sweeping out of his office. David watched her go.

This was going to end badly. He could feel it. One way or the other, someone was going to get hurt. His job was to make sure it wasn't Jayne.

Jayne knocked on the hotel room door, telling herself not to be nervous. So what if David was waiting for her? They were going to have dinner, then sex. No big deal. Except there was something vaguely illicit about going to a man's hotel room.

The door opened.

"What?" David asked. "You look funny."

"A compliment to make me all fluttery inside."

He smiled, then pulled her close and kissed her. "You look like you're worried about something."

She kissed him back, enjoying the immediate heat that flared between them and the liquid desire that took up residence in the most interesting places.

"I was thinking I don't go to many men's hotel rooms."

"No moonlighting as a call girl?"

"I tried it for a while, but I hated the hours."

He led her into the room, which turned out to be a

suite. The living room held a sofa, a TV in a cabinet, a desk, and a couple of chairs. The bedroom beyond was big, with a king-size mattress. Both rooms faced west and had French doors that opened onto balconies. This being spring in Los Angeles, the late afternoon was plenty warm enough for the doors to be open. The sounds of traffic drifted up to them.

"Very nice," she said, glancing around. "Understated elegance. Are we ordering in or eating in the dining room?"

He moved close and took her in his arms. "Whichever you'd like. I have champagne."

Of course he did. "Because no good seduction should be without champagne."

He walked into the bedroom. She followed and saw the freestanding ice bucket tucked beside the bed.

"Very subtle," she teased.

He opened the bottle while she collected glasses from inside the armoire. After he poured, they toasted each other. She took a sip.

Even though you could buy it at Costco, there was something decadent about drinking Dom Pérignon while it was still light out.

"Nice," she said, staring into his blue eyes and meaning more than the champagne. "Very nice. You're spoiling me. I could get used to that."

"Good."

No. Not good. It was bad. Very bad. Getting used to his spoiling her meant getting used to him. And then she was on a slick highway to Broken Heart Town. Not a place she needed to be right now. Her life was supposed to be about new beginnings, not getting caught up in a relationship that had been a risk from the beginning.

She wanted to say it wasn't her fault. That her fantasies about David had predisposed her to falling for him, but the actual fall itself was because of who he'd turned out to be. Nice. Funny. Charming. Caring. How was she supposed to protect herself against that?

"Let's go enjoy our champagne," he said, putting his hand on the small of her back and guiding her to the other room.

"You don't want to have sex with me?" she asked before she could stop herself.

He laughed. "How come I didn't find you years ago?"

"You met me when I was still in high school. You weren't interested."

They sat next to each other on the sofa. She angled toward him.

"I was a fool," he told her.

She touched his glass with hers. "I'll drink to that." She studied his face, the perfect curve of his mouth and the light reflected in his blue eyes. "You want to talk about something."

"How do you know?"

"You have talk-face."

She forced herself to smile when she really wanted to run. If she left before he could say anything, she wouldn't be hurt. And right now not being hurt seemed like a damned good plan.

"My mother came to see me," he began.

"Oh, God. Because of me." She put her glass on the coffee table. "I should have said something. I was so angry, and I should have warned you. I'm sorry."

"I'm not."

"Excuse me? How can you not be sorry? I'm sure she's furious. She's going to come screaming for an explanation." She held in a groan. "Which she already has, because that's how you know."

"She came to the office this afternoon, wanting to know if it was true we were dating."

Jayne wanted to sink into the floor. "I totally screwed this up, huh? I'd offer to talk to her, but I don't think that would help. Maybe if Rebecca got in touch with her or—"

He pressed his fingers against her mouth. "Shh. It's all good. I wanted her to know we're going out."

"Why?"

"So she'll get off me about going out with someone else. You're the one I'm seeing. You're the one I want to keep seeing, Jayne. Why do you think I asked you to be my date to the party?"

"But I . . ." She picked up her glass and took a big swallow.

She told herself not to get too excited by the information. It didn't mean that he was falling for her or that she was more than someone he was casually dating. If she read too much into his words, she would only get hurt more.

"Okay," she said cautiously. "But your mother is upset."

"So?" He leaned in and kissed her.

"There's going to be trouble."

"We can handle it."

Her heart fluttered. "I'm not sure you're worth it," she joked.

"I am." He touched her cheek. "I don't expect you to do anything about my mother. I just wanted you to know that she's not happy. Forewarned and all that. I can handle it, can you?"

"I've been dealing with Elizabeth for years. I'm an expert."

"Good." He set down his glass, then moved a stack of magazines on the table, revealing a large, flat, dark purple box with "Worden's Jewelry" embossed in gold. "I have something for you."

If it had been a ring box, she probably would have had a heart attack and died right there on the sofa. As it was, she found it difficult to breathe, what with her entire body frozen. Frozen *and* trembling. Talk about a trick and a half.

"You're not like anyone I've ever met," he said, holding out the box. "I want you to know that you're important to me, and in my family, we say that with diamonds."

He waited. She stared at the box but made no move to reach for it.

"You're not going to open it?" he asked with a smile.

"I'm not sure I can."

"Then allow me."

He turned the box so it was facing her, then raised the

hinged lid. Inside on a bed of white satin sat a graduated diamond necklace. The diamonds went all the way
around to the back, with the larger stones in front. The
center stone had to be at least two carats. The perfect diamonds winked and sparkled in the afternoon light.

She knew she was breathing. She could feel air moving
in and out of her lungs. Even so, her chest felt tight, and
her mind was amazingly blank.

The necklace was possibly the most beautiful thing
she'd ever seen. "It's much nicer than the one I stole," she
whispered.

He laughed, then pulled it out of the box. "Let's see
how it looks on."

She put down her glass and scrambled to her feet. "I
can't. It's too expensive. I don't have a lifestyle to support
that kind of thing, and even if I did . . . It's lovely, David.
I appreciate the gesture, but it's too much."

He rose and moved toward her. "If I owned a tire
place, I'd bring you tires. This is what I do. Come on. At
least see how it looks."

She held up both hands to protect herself. "No way. If
I let you put that on me, I'll be lost. I have to be strong
and resist."

"Why?" The humor faded from his eyes. "Jayne, I'm
falling for you. You're my girl, and I want you to have this."

He couldn't have persuaded her any other way. Four
simple words. "I'm falling for you." She didn't know if he
meant it or not, and she wasn't sure what his definition
of "falling" was, but she was unable to resist him.

He came up and slipped the necklace around her neck.

She held up her hair so he could fasten it, then together they moved into the large marble bathroom. He flipped on the light.

She wore a sundress she'd bought at Kohl's for thirty dollars and minimal makeup, and she really needed to consider highlights. But none of that mattered. While the necklace was a once-in-a-lifetime dream she would probably never take off, what captured her heart and wouldn't let go was David staring at her as if . . . as if . . .

As if she really were his girl.

She turned in his arms and kissed him.

"Thank you," she whispered.

"It looks good on you."

"Being with you looks good on me."

"Jayne."

Then his mouth was on hers and nothing else mattered. As long as they could be together, touching, yearning, taking, and giving. Love swelled up inside of her. The words threatened to burst out, but she held them back. Saying she loved him was admitting too much. Not because he would ever use that against her, but because then she would have admitted the truth to herself. There was no going back from that.

She might have David's attention now, but for how long? Eventually he would realize she wasn't a long-term relationship. That everyone knew he was going to marry the "right" sort of woman. Then he would break her heart. Better for both of them if she didn't admit that what had once been a crush had grown into a life-changing love that she would carry with her forever.

*   *   *

Rebecca turned off the CD player. She'd just finished the second CD of Tony Robbins's *Get the Edge* program and could already see how she was totally screwing up her life. She took plenty of time for herself, but not in a way that mattered. She wasn't focused, didn't have goals. She floated through life, thinking she was entitled, which left her with plenty of fawning but no fulfillment. Except for Jayne, she didn't have friends. On the surface, she had it all, but underneath, she was totally empty and devoid of happiness.

She poured herself a glass of wine, then walked to her laptop and turned it on. Maybe she could find some seminars to go to and be healed. Or try a meditation retreat.

She felt on the brink of an important discovery. Having her father and David take care of Jonathan and Nigel had somehow freed her. The need for revenge had faded. She almost didn't care that her mother was upset with her.

While her laptop booted, she crossed to the kitchen table, where she'd started working on her ideas for the stainless steel jewelry. She'd been reading about the process, and while it was challenging, she knew her creations would be beautiful. To think she could bring happiness to millions of women just by making pretty jewelry. It was almost too much to take in.

Her doorbell rang, followed by someone pounding on her front door. The rhythm was frantic, as if something was really wrong. She set down her wine and hurried to unfasten the lock.

Big mistake. Elizabeth burst in.

"You're home," her mother said. "I was afraid you'd be out, and I didn't want to call first because you'd just leave. We have to talk."

Rebecca's good mood bled away. "Hello, Mother." There was a lot more she wanted to say—like ordering her out of her house. But now she was conscious of a greater good, of the universe moving all around her. She could afford to be gracious.

Elizabeth picked up Rebecca's glass of wine and drained it in a single gulp. "Your brother is sleeping with Jayne."

Rebecca breathed deeply and let a feeling of calm flow through her. "It's all right. I know, and I think this is good for David. Jayne's lovely. He's back, having a little fling. She's leaving town in a few weeks. It's all right. I know it delays his finding the bride you're so eager for, but you have to trust this will work out the way it's supposed to."

Elizabeth glared at her. "Are you on drugs?"

"No, I'm calm and focused. I've been practicing breathing. You should try it."

"I should have you committed. This isn't a situation I can ignore, and neither can you. David isn't just seeing Jayne. I think he's in love with her."

Rebecca drew in another breath. David in love with Jayne? "You're overreacting. He's having fun, nothing more."

"I tried to talk to him."

Rebecca walked into the open kitchen and found another wineglass. "Big mistake. You'll make him feel trapped. He'll push back."

"He already did. He said that if I tried to come between them, he would turn his back on me. His own mother. He's choosing Jayne over me. He's in love with her. I don't know if he's realized it or not, but he is."

Hearing the words was like being plunged into an icy pool. At first Rebecca felt nothing. Then there were sharp, cold knives slicing her everywhere. She wanted to throw up, to scream, to protest to the universe that this couldn't be happening!

David in love with Jayne? Sweet, sensible, funny Jayne? Jayne was *her* friend. David couldn't have her. Couldn't. She wouldn't allow it. It was impossible. Jayne already had Katie. If she had David, too, if they were together, what would happen to Rebecca? Who would love her best? Who would take care of her?

"No," she breathed, hanging on to the counter, half afraid she would pass out. "They can't."

David had been there for her whenever she needed him. The same with Jayne. But if they had each other, they would be too busy. They would talk about her together, take each other's side. She would be left alone, with nothing. No one.

"You have to do something," Elizabeth told her. "You have to stop this. Do you know what a disaster it would be if they got married?"

Married? Together always? Forever shutting her out?

"I won't let them."

"Can you stop this?" Elizabeth asked.

"I have to." Rebecca had never been more certain of

anything in her life. She straightened. The pain receded, but the panic remained. "I'll go see him. Talk to him."

"He's not going to listen."

"He's my brother. He'll listen." She walked into the bedroom and picked up her purse.

"You have to be delicate," Elizabeth said, following her. "You have to say it the right way, or you'll push them together."

"I know that."

"I should come with you."

"Because your last conversation with him went so well?" Rebecca asked, moving toward the door. "I'll do it. I'll make him understand this isn't possible."

Then she was running down the stairs because the elevator would take too long.

She got in her car and started the engine. Thoughts swirled in her head as she drove east on I-10, then exited and drove north to the Four Seasons. Traffic was a bitch, as usual, but she didn't mind the delay. It gave her time to think.

The knot in her stomach didn't go away. No matter how she considered the problem, there was no good solution. David and Jayne together meant she was abandoned. They were the two people she loved most in the word—how could they do this to her?

"I trusted you," Rebecca whispered, wiping away tears. "I trusted you to be my friend."

She pulled into the hotel and gave the keys to the valet. "I won't be very long," she told him.

He flashed her a smile. "I'll have your car right here."

She nodded and walked into the cool, elegant lobby.

The elevators were to her left. She pushed the up button, then rode to the fifth floor and turned left again. When she was outside of David's door, she knocked loudly.

It opened seconds later. David, wearing jeans and nothing else, was already talking. "That didn't take long. Are you sure those steaks are . . . Rebecca?"

His hair was mussed, and he didn't have shoes on. Those should have been clues. Later she would remind herself she hadn't been thinking. Or maybe she had known exactly what she was doing.

"What the hell is wrong with you?" she snapped. "Dammit, you know better. Dating Jayne and sleeping with her is one thing, but falling for her? You fuck the help, David. You don't marry them."

There was a sound. Not quite a gasp, but a sharp intake of breath. Rebecca looked past her brother and saw Jayne standing in the doorway to the bedroom. She wore David's shirt, a diamond necklace, and nothing else. Her cheeks were red, as if she'd been slapped, her brown eyes wide.

For the second time in a week, Rebecca felt shame.

Jayne closed the bedroom door. David grabbed Rebecca's arm and shook her.

"What's wrong with you?" he demanded. "How could you do that? She's your best friend."

"Not anymore," Rebecca whispered. "Not anymore."

Seventeen

JAYNE SCRAMBLED TO GET into her clothes. There was something wrong—she couldn't see very well. When she wiped her face, she felt dampness. From what? Tears? She couldn't be crying. Not over anything to do with the Wordens.

She pulled on her panties, then ripped off David's shirt and grabbed her bra. There were voices coming from the living room, but she didn't bother listening. Neither of them could say anything she wanted to hear.

She knew this wasn't David's fault. His only sin was being a Worden. He had a biological connection to the insanity. But there was no way to separate him from them. No way to have one without the other. And as she'd teased earlier, he simply wasn't worth it. Later, when breathing didn't hurt so much, she would tell him.

She stepped into her shoes, then tugged at the necklace around her throat. She couldn't get the clasp to open at first. There was a sharp pain as she scratched herself, but finally it came free, then tumbled into her waiting hand.

The diamonds winked up at her, all sparkly and perfect. She would never own anything like it, probably never even see one like it again up close. Which was fine. Like with David, the price of the necklace was too high.

She pulled open the door to the living room. Rebecca and David stood close together, obviously having a heated conversation. Jayne looked at the beautiful blonde standing next to him. Tall and lovely, the kind of woman who stopped traffic.

Jayne knew everything about her. She knew her moods, what she found funny, what annoyed her. She'd seen Rebecca happy and sad and sick and exhausted. They'd traveled together, had endured the flu together. They'd shared hopes and dreams and clothes. They'd grown up together. Jayne had thought they would always be friends.

She'd been wrong.

She and Rebecca weren't friends—they'd *never* been friends. Theirs was a relationship born of proximity and loneliness. Under ordinary circumstances, they never would have met. And if they met now, they would have nothing in common. They weren't friends, and it had been Jayne's mistake to assume they ever could be.

They'd used each other. That wasn't friendship. That wasn't anything.

"Jayne, wait," David said coming up to her. "Please, don't go. I don't know what shit my sister has going on, but it has nothing to do with me. Don't go."

He was so beautiful, she thought sadly. Everything a man should be. Not perfect, but perfect for her. She could have loved him forever. Maybe she would, but he would never know.

She held out the necklace.

"No." He backed up, tucking his hands behind him. "I won't take that back. I want you to have it. Dammit, Jayne, don't do this. Don't listen to her."

"She knows I'm telling the truth. Jayne, I care about you, but this is impossible."

David turned on his sister. "Shut the fuck up," he yelled. "What are you doing here anyway? Why are you doing this?"

Jayne didn't know why Rebecca had turned on her. Jayne's relationship with David had been amusing before. Something that could be used to annoy Elizabeth. Except Jayne had told the woman she was dating her son, and Elizabeth had panicked. Did she know about the diamond necklace? Had she talked to her son and realized that maybe this was more than a game?

Jayne wanted that to be true, wanted a moment to hold the thought inside. But there was no point. Whatever David felt for her didn't change the fact that he was indelibly connected to the rest of the Wordens.

She couldn't do it anymore. Not the drama, the hysterics, the assumptions. She just wanted normal. She dropped the necklace onto the coffee table.

"Good-bye," she said to both of them. She picked up her purse, then walked out.

David came after her. He grabbed her arm and spun her to face him. "Don't," he pleaded. "Rebecca's leaving. I want you to stay. Jayne, please."

"This isn't about you," she told him. "I'm sorry. I can't do this anymore. I thought I could. I thought we had a chance. We don't."

"I love you."

It was a perfect moment. If this were a Lifetime movie, Rebecca would burst out of the room, eyes filled with tears. She would apologize and admit she'd been wrong. She would tell them both that she wanted them to be happy. David would sweep Jayne up in his arms, and they would kiss.

But this wasn't a movie. It was her life, and she'd been avoiding reality long enough.

She thought about telling him she loved him, too. That he was everything she wanted, but there was no point. So she simply turned her back and walked away. David was a proud man—he wouldn't come after her a second time.

And he didn't. She made it to the elevator without hearing another word.

Elizabeth hovered in the hallway, listening for the sound of Blaine's arrival. Normally, she waited in her office or in the family room. Not that she was ever excited that he was home, but it did mean the rest of the evening could begin. Usually he ran late, meaning she had to usher him through getting changed for whatever event they had on the calendar.

Tonight was a quiet evening. Just the two of them. For the best, she thought as she glanced at her watch again.

They needed to talk, and interruptions wouldn't make the conversation go any faster.

Finally she heard the door to the garage open, then close. She moved into the kitchen and waited until Blaine had entered.

"We have to talk," she announced.

"Hello to you, too," he said.

She flicked her wrist. "Yes, yes. Hello, I'm fine. I'm sure your day was excellent. Is that enough?"

He put down his slim briefcase. "As always, your romantic declarations make me love you all the more."

She did her best not to glare. "Are you being funny? Is this humor?"

"Apparently not." He walked into the butler's panty and opened the liquor cabinet. "Scotch?"

"Yes, please. Then we can talk."

"About?"

"David and Jayne. They're together."

Blaine stepped back into the kitchen. "They're going out?"

"Yes." She finally had his attention. Talk about a miracle. "Apparently it's serious. They're sleeping together, which today doesn't mean anything. But they're also involved. David seems quite taken with her. I can't imagine why."

"Why not? She's a bright young woman. Hardworking."

"Which is an excellent characteristic for a housekeeper, but not how I want my future daughter-in-law described."

"You'd rather she was lazy?"

Elizabeth forced herself to breathe slowly. "Blaine, I swear, you look for ways to annoy me."

He retreated to the butler's panty, then reappeared with two drinks. He handed her one. "I don't plan. Sometimes the opportunity presents itself, and I succumb to temptation."

"Resist," she snapped. "We have to talk about what to do. Jayne is nobody. There's no family, no money, no connections."

Blaine sipped his drink. "David has enough for both of them."

"You can't seriously expect me to believe you approve. If your son walked in right now and said he wanted to marry Jayne Scott, you'd be fine with it?"

"He could do a lot worse."

"Yes, perhaps someone from the local prison population."

"You're a snob."

"And you're naïve. This is important. We don't want him marrying a nobody. If we're not careful, she'll trap him, and we'll all be stuck."

Blaine's blue eyes darkened. "We wouldn't want our son being tricked into marriage, would we?"

Elizabeth stiffened. "If you're going to take that tone with me, we're not having this conversation."

Blaine picked up his briefcase and started out of the kitchen. "Then this might be an excellent evening after all."

*   *   *

The reception was held at Worden's Jewelry in Beverly Hills. Rebecca hadn't really listened when Elizabeth had said something about a reception "launching" her as Rivalsa, but as she entered the normally quiet and elegant space, she was greeted by a tall, handsome man in a tux. He offered her a martini, "shaken, not stirred," then guided her into a transformed store.

There were white lights everywhere, competing in brilliance with a room filled with diamonds. The display cases held the usual beautiful pieces, along with hundreds of loose stones Rebecca assumed were fake. No one's inventory was that impressive. Armed guards in tuxedos stood against the walls, watching everyone. Music from various James Bond movies played in the background, and several faux roulette wheels had been set up for the guests.

On top of the display cases reclined scantily dressed young women wearing Rebecca's designs. Beside each model was another armed guard. These looked beefy and quite capable of taking out anyone willing to risk stealing something shiny.

Rebecca took it all in, then sipped her martini. She'd been reluctant to attend Elizabeth's reception, but she had to admit, her mother had done a great job pulling it all together.

She scanned the crowd. There were the usual collection of the very rich, a few Hollywood types, and the serious jewelry collectors. Now that word was out as to who Rivalsa really was, she'd been getting calls from people asking about custom pieces. Business had always been good—now it was excellent.

She should have been thrilled, and she was. Sort of. The only minor annoyance was that David still wasn't speaking to her. She'd left several messages, which he hadn't returned, and she had even stopped by his office two days ago. He'd walked out on her.

She also hadn't seen Jayne, which was more upsetting than she would have thought. When she'd lived in Italy, she could go several days without talking to her friend, although they always kept in touch through e-mail. Now there wasn't anything.

Rebecca hadn't made any calls there. She knew Jayne needed time to get over being angry. The truth was Jayne knew she wasn't right for David. She would be the first one to admit it. However, it was possible that Rebecca's crude assessment of the situation had been a little over the line. Accurate, but more hurtful than she would have liked.

Still, Jayne knew she was in the wrong, so she could take the first step.

"Ms. Worden."

Rebecca watched a heavyset Russian man approach. "I see you are as beautiful as your pieces."

"Thank you. Call me Rebecca."

"And I am Aleksei. I am buying that necklace." He pointed to a woven chain with three large pink diamonds.

"For your wife?"

Aleksei smiled. "For my mistress. My wife doesn't appreciate fine jewelry."

"Perhaps if you gave her more of an opportunity," Rebecca murmured, then took a sip of her martini.

"Perhaps," he agreed, sounding amused. "I would like to commission matching earrings, also in pink diamonds. The larger stones, of course. As the necklace is eight hundred thousand U.S., the earrings will be close to that price, yes?"

She thought about her diamond inventory. "I have two pink diamonds that are similar. They're a perfect pair, three carats each. The earrings will be one-point-two million."

"I see you are as strong as you are beautiful."

"I could easily sell the stones to someone else."

"Very well, one-point-two million. How long will it take you to make them?"

"About two weeks. If you'll give your card to my brother, he'll write up the order."

Aleksei nodded, then reached for her free hand. He kissed her knuckles, then excused himself.

A man from China and his translator were next, followed by a representative from the Sultan of Brunei, asking about her inventory of yellow diamonds. The fawning attention made her feel better about pretty much everything. She replaced her empty glass with a full one and went searching for David.

She found him finishing an order. When he'd shaken hands with both the businessman from China and his interpreter, she moved next to him.

"Still not speaking to me?" she asked in a teasing voice. "You can't stay mad at me forever."

"I'm not mad," he said, barely looking at her. "I'm disappointed. There's a difference."

Her good mood deflated like a punctured balloon. "Wait a minute. What did I do except tell the truth?"

He slipped the order forms into a concealed drawer and locked it. "Because none of this could be your fault? Hide behind the truth, if it makes you feel better. We both know you were a complete bitch. Not a real surprise, you've always had the tendency, but your target was unexpected. I thought Jayne was your friend."

"She is. We've been friends for years. You know that."

"With friends like you, I can see why she's moving away."

Rebecca stared at him. "Jayne isn't moving because of me. She's moving because of Mom."

"Keep telling yourself that. Maybe it will be true."

"No, I'm not the reason. Jayne is probably a little pissed right now, but her being sensitive doesn't change facts. She's not someone you can be with, David, and you know it. The truth is, you're the one playing with her heart, not me. Leading her on, making her think she can win you."

"I'm not a prize to be won or lost," he said, glaring at her. "Neither is she. We had a relationship, one you've done your best to ruin. I care about her, Rebecca. I'm in love with her."

She swallowed. "You've never said that about anyone before." Her chest tightened. Love? He couldn't love Jayne. He had to see that.

"I've never been in love before."

"She's totally wrong for you."

"Why? Because she's not rich?"

"Partially." Partially, because if they had each other, they wouldn't need her.

"I'm rich enough for both of us."

"Fine," she grumbled. "There's more. She doesn't have any connections. She wouldn't fit in with your friends."

"She'd fit in fine with mine. You're saying she wouldn't fit in Elizabeth's world of charity events and parties. She doesn't know the right people. You think I give a damn about that? I don't need her to introduce me to anyone. I have plenty of connections on my own. What I want is a woman I can respect. Someone who challenges me and sees me for who and what I am. I want someone to call me on my bullshit. Someone who makes me laugh. I want to be excited about growing old with her. Jayne is special. I would expect you to be telling me I don't deserve her, but you're not really her friend, are you? You're just like Mom. Using Jayne because it's convenient and makes you look good."

His words were a punch in the gut, but not as devastating as the contempt she saw in his eyes. "It's not like that," she began.

"I expected it from Mom," he said. "But not from you."

He walked away from her. There was something about the way he moved, as if he couldn't wait to put some distance between them. As if she was someone he didn't like anymore.

Her eyes burned, but she refused to give in to tears. Not in public. She hurried to the restroom, wanting to check her reflection. She felt small and ugly and needed to know that none of that showed on the outside.

After reassuring herself, she returned to the party, but she found she couldn't stay. A few more people stopped her, wanting to talk about her work or to place orders, but their words seemed flat and false. The lights overhead were too bright, and the burning in her stomach seemed as if it would never go away.

How could Jayne have let things get this far? She had to have known it would never work out, but she continued to see David, taking him from Rebecca, probably turning him against his own sister.

The music was too loud, the crowd too large. The need for escape, for air, pressed in on her. She set her drink on the glass display counter, bumping it against the hip of one of the Rivalsa girls, as people had taken to calling them. The busty blonde rolled in Rebecca's direction, stretching out on the glass.

"Hey, you're the designer," she said, fingering the diamond bracelet around her wrist. "Great stuff."

"Thanks," Rebecca mumbled as she headed for the door. She had to get out.

She'd barely managed to push through the door when she bumped into a woman trying to enter. A woman Rebecca had never met but knew on sight.

They stopped inches from each other. Staring. Rebecca's sense of unease grew until she was afraid she was going to throw up.

"Ariel," she said, stepping away from the door, wishing she had her car parked in front so she could jump inside and drive away. She had to run, had to be anywhere but here.

"Rebecca."

Nigel's wife looked tall and elegant in a beaded designer gown. Ariel, a former model, had long auburn hair that tumbled to her waist, green eyes, and a mouth that had once been named the sexiest on three continents.

Now those green eyes filled with tears, and that famous mouth trembled. "I came here to see you."

The last thing she wanted to hear, Rebecca thought, pressing a hand to her midsection. "I'm really busy now. I have to go."

"This will take just a second. It's about Nigel."

Rebecca had already guessed that. There were only a handful of reasons a bride followed her new husband to a different country, and very few of them were good.

Ariel straightened and squared her shoulders. "Is he still in love with you?"

Pain joined the tears. Rebecca watched the other woman brace herself for the inevitable. It would take only a second to pay back Nigel for the crap he'd tried to pull. A matter of a word or two to shatter both their lives. Saying yes was the easiest thing in the world. God knows Nigel had earned it.

She could tell Ariel about the blue diamond that Nigel had not only stolen but given to her. She could ruin them all and walk away without looking back.

"You can say it," Ariel told her. "I know something's wrong, and you're not the kind of woman men forget."

"True," Rebecca said slowly.

The need to hurt someone else was powerful. All that stopped her was the realization that if Nigel was free, he would come after her again. She would probably fall for his lines and then be stuck with him. He wasn't anyone she could trust. He could never make her happy. Better to leave him where he was—safely out of reach.

"He's not in love with me. I don't think he ever was. We had fun, but our relationship was never serious. He likes the connection with the family. Rubbing elbows with the rich and famous."

Ariel looked as if she desperately wanted to believe.

Rebecca took pity on her. "You're the one he married. Not me."

"Because you wouldn't say yes."

"Does it matter? You have him now. Are you going to fight for him, or are you going to become some whiny, clingy doormat who begs for attention? Nigel always wants what he can't have. Be *that* woman. You already know how—you wouldn't be married to him if you didn't."

Ariel wiped the tears from her cheeks. "You're right. He picked me, not you. I have to remember that. Thanks."

"You're welcome."

Ariel sniffed. "Any cute guys I can flirt with inside?"

"Cute? Not so much. But there are plenty of rich ones."

Ariel smiled briefly, then went into the party. Rebecca leaned against the building and wondered what she was supposed to do next. Fate answered that question in the form of her mother, who stepped out onto the sidewalk.

"There you are. Everyone's asking about you. I went to all this trouble to invite these people. The least you can do is mingle."

"Fine. Sure. I'll mingle."

Elizabeth studied her. "Are you all right?"

"Never better."

"David is still angry," Elizabeth said, following her daughter inside. "This problem has to be fixed."

"Agreed."

"What are we going to do?"

There was no "we." At least that's what she wanted to say. Only there was. They were the only ones who saw the potential for disaster and were willing to head it off.

"I'll talk to Jayne," Rebecca said. "She'll understand why she has to break things off with David."

"And if she doesn't?"

"Then I'll get nasty."

Eighteen

JAYNE SAT IN THE waiting room, her hand tightly holding Lori's. The eighteen-year-old shook slightly, although she was trying not to show her nervousness.

Three years ago, Lori had been referred to the breast center by her pediatrician after she'd found a lump in her breast. Lori had been one of the very rare cases of teenagers with breast cancer. Surgery, radiation, and a lot of prayer later, she had been pronounced cancer-free. But twice yearly mammograms were required.

Normally Jayne performed the mammograms, then took her break right after so she could keep Lori and her mom company while they waited for the radiologist's report. Today, she was acting as a friend rather than a nurse. Lori's mom was away on a last-minute business trip.

"I know it's fine," Lori said, speaking quickly. "I'm healthy, I eat right, I rest. I'm playing softball with my sorority." She smiled. "We're not really great players, but we look good in the shorts and T-shirts. Last week we were playing Sigma Pi—that's one of the fraternities—and we were really behind. I hit a high fly ball. Mia was on second base, and when she saw the outfielder was about to catch it, she lifted her T-shirt and flashed her boobs. The guy dropped the ball."

Jayne laughed. "Whatever it takes to win."

"I don't want to be sick," Lori pleaded.

"I know."

Katie walked into the waiting room. They both looked at her. In her most professional voice Katie said, "If you'll come with me, please." Because all information was given privately, in an exam room. But right before she turned to lead the way, she gave Lori a big thumbs-up.

The teen exhaled sharply. "Did you see that?" she asked in a whisper.

"I did. Good news."

Better than good. With this "all clear," Lori could switch to annual mammograms. She would always have to be more careful than most young women her age, but the immediate threat had passed.

Later, when Lori had left and Jayne had said goodbye to her friends, she walked toward her car. Her cell phone rang. She looked at it, already guessing the caller was David. Sure enough, his name and number flashed on the screen.

As much as she wanted to pick up the call, she knew there wasn't any point. They didn't have anything to say to each other. Nothing that would change their circumstances. He was a Worden, with a history and a future that involved being rich and selling diamonds. She was a radiology nurse who wanted a level of normal he couldn't provide. She was leaving town in a few weeks, and his life was here. She pushed the Ignore button and kept walking.

Only to stumble to a stop when she saw Rebecca waiting by her car.

"When you weren't at home, I thought you might be here," Rebecca said.

Fierce gladness rushed through her. She'd missed her friend, had missed talking to her and laughing with her. Sure, Rebecca had been a total bitch, but it wasn't the first time. There was only one reason for her to be here, and that was to make things right. Rebecca wouldn't apologize—hardly her style. But she would get her point across.

Jayne knew that for the friendship to continue, she was going to have to have a serious talk with her. Put up some boundaries, that sort of thing. But later. Right now she just wanted to be happy to see her friend.

"I had to meet with a patient," Jayne said.

"You're working?"

"Part time."

Rebecca leaned against Jayne's Jetta. "I want to talk to you about what happened before."

"All right."

"You're taking it wrong. You know you can't be with David. Whatever is going on between the two of you is just a game to him. Practically a joke. It was never going to be serious."

If Jayne were smart, she would get a big, fat *L* tattooed on her forehead. *L* for loser, as a reminder. She would see it every morning and know that her relationship with any member of the Worden family, but especially with Elizabeth and Rebecca, was a party for one.

They weren't friends. How many times did she have to have that information thrown in her face before she would believe it? Why was she so damned slow? Rebecca Worden was not her friend and had never been her friend.

A friend was someone who loved you. A greeting card sentiment based in truth. Love meant giving more than receiving. Loving someone was about wanting the best for the other person—something Rebecca would never understand and had never practiced.

"You're great," Rebecca continued, "totally wonderful. Just not for him. You'd never fit in. You know that, right? The parties, the social thing. You hate that. You wouldn't know what to say or how to dress. Mom would make your life a living hell, and eventually she would wear David down. He's not strong enough to stand up to her. Am I making sense?"

"Every word is crystal clear."

Rebecca smiled. Actually smiled, as if they were connecting on an important level. "You're so important to me. I really care about you and your happiness. And David is not the guy to make you happy. This is better. You know that, right? Plus, hey, if you two fall for each other, where does that leave me?"

Jayne was pretty sure Rebecca meant that last comment as a joke, but it was the first honest thing she'd said.

"I'm doing this out of love," Rebecca added.

"Interesting," Jayne said slowly. "It's not how I define love, but I'm not like you, so what do I know?"

"Are you mad?"

"No, I wouldn't say mad defines how I feel. Disappointed works. I also feel very foolish. I still remember the first day we met, when I was wearing your hand-me-downs. I was terrified you were going to make fun of me and let everyone know I was the daughter of a house-keeper. But you didn't. You talked to me and were nice, and I was so grateful. Too grateful, because I didn't see you for who you really are."

Rebecca bristled. "I've been a damned good friend."

"Better than I deserve?" Jayne asked, raising her eyebrows. "Let me rephrase that. Better than someone like me deserves?"

Rebecca pressed her lips together.

"I'll take that as a yes," Jayne said. She supposed this was like ripping off a bandage. Better to do it fast and get all the pain over with at once.

"You liked hanging out with me because it made you feel better about yourself," she said. "I was dependable. I understood."

"You're not the martyr in this," Rebecca told her. "You got plenty out of our friendship. You lived in the big house like real rich people; you pretended my parents were yours, too. You like living on the fringes, Jayne. It makes you feel you belong without all that messy responsibility. You can come and go as you please, bad-mouthing us when we don't live up to your standards. It's easy to be critical when you're always on the outside."

"Do you think that's where I wanted to be?" Jayne demanded. "Do you think the vacations and used clothes were worth it? Does it occur to you I would have preferred a ratty one-bedroom apartment with my mother than living in that big house with you? I had no one. Yes, I pretended you were my family because the alternative was to be totally alone. I accept responsibility for that. Somehow I allowed myself to get sucked into a relationship with your family. My mistake was not ending things long ago."

A mistake she had paid for in blood, she thought grimly. "Somewhere along the way, I decided that being alone was the worst thing in the world. That I would do anything to be one of you. It was never about the money, although I don't expect you to believe that."

"Of course it was about the money," Rebecca told her contemptuously. "You loved being able to say you knew me, knew my family. It gave you power with your other friends. Something special that they didn't have."

Maybe she was right, Jayne thought sadly. Maybe she'd needed the Wordens to feel special.

"My goal was to belong," Jayne said quietly. "To be a part of something, in whatever form that took. At some point, I sold out who I was for that connection. I'll take responsibility for my actions. I gave too much of myself for too little. Which is why I'm leaving. Because I need a clean break."

"Oh, please." Rebecca rolled her eyes. "You're not interested in a clean break. You want to trap David into marrying you. Are you going to fake a pregnancy?"

There it was—the end point. With her words came pain, but no real surprise. Only sadness and regret. A list of "might have beens."

"You've known me since high school," Jayne said. "You've seen me at my worst and my best, and yet you ask that question? You're right—the rich are different. There's a lot less character development. You don't have to bother with it because you don't have anything to earn."

Jayne stepped around the other woman and opened her car door. She got in. Rebecca stared at her for a long time, then walked away. A few seconds later, a midnight blue Mercedes sped past and she was gone.

Jayne dropped her head to the steering wheel and gave in to the tears burning in her eyes. She cried for what was lost. For a friend who was no more. But mostly she cried for what she'd never had at all.

Still puffy and feeling more than a little broken inside, Jayne drove to Beverly Hills and found a parking space right in front of the Worden store. It was a miracle, or maybe just a sign. Either way, she was going to finish up things with the rest of the family and then be done. In three short weeks, she would be moving to Texas. Better to break things off cleanly now, she told herself.

Once inside, she told one of the sales associates that she was there to see David. Less than a minute later, he came through the showroom and walked toward her.

As always, her entire body sighed in appreciation

at the sight of him. Tall, blond, movie-star handsome. Completely crush-worthy. Of course she'd fallen for him years ago. He was the male ideal. Now she was in love with the man behind the pretty exterior, but that was a problem for another day. Once all this was over, she would figure out a way to heal and move on with her life. Teenage Lori had beaten breast cancer. Somehow Jayne could get over David Worden.

He smiled as he approached, making it tough to breathe. Then he took her hand in his and pulled her into one of the private rooms off to the side. Places where the very rich could sit and think about their two- or three-million-dollar purchase without being disturbed by the general public.

The space was small, with a sofa, a couple of chairs, and a table. The lighting was soft, and there were mirrors on the wall—all the better to see the glittery jewelry—and real china for coffee or a snack. Spend a couple million at Worden's and they gave you a cookie.

"I've been leaving you messages," he said, closing the door behind them and staring into her eyes. "I was starting to feel like a stalker."

She wished she could smile, or maybe had thought to touch up her makeup. No doubt she was blotchy and puffy.

David reached up and brushed his fingers along her cheek. "Have you been crying?"

"Yes, but that's not why I'm here," she said. "Or maybe it is. I don't know anymore."

He took her other hand in his. "Let me talk, Jayne. I'm

sorry about Rebecca. I'm sorry she can be such a bitch, and I'm sorry you had to hear that. But I'm not willing to let her come between us. I meant what I said. I love you."

The words should have been magic, and this should have been the happiest day of her life. There should be flowers and singing birds and music. Instead, she felt only dread and resignation.

She pulled her hands free, then cupped his face. She could feel the beginning of stubble on his jaw, see the small scar by his upper lip. His eyes were still that impossible color of blue, the lashes gold-tipped.

"You're better than the fantasy," she told him. "But I meant what I said, too. You're not worth it. We have to break the cycle here. Now. We're not going to see each other anymore. I'm leaving in a few weeks, and you'll find some perfectly nice girl to marry. I wish you all the best, David. I want you to be happy and live your life."

"You're going to let them win?"

"I'm not willing to let myself lose. I have to do what's best for me. I want that to be you, believe me. But it's not."

He grabbed her shoulders. "I don't accept that. I want you to date *me*, not Rebecca or my mother."

"I can't have one without the other, and I'm finished with them."

"I won't let you go."

"You don't have a choice."

"But I love you."

The Worden moment, she thought sadly. It was inescapable. "This isn't about you," she said, pulled free, then left.

* * *

Elizabeth sipped her cocktail. "Rebecca says that Jayne swears she and David aren't seeing each other anymore. I'm hopeful, but I can't be sure until I talk to David, and I want to give him space. I don't suppose he said anything at the office today?"

Blaine continued to read his magazine.

Elizabeth glared at him. "Blaine, I'm speaking to you."

"What?" He glanced up, looking over his reading glasses like an old man. "I wasn't listening."

"Obviously." She glanced at her watch. Dinner was late. She was going to have to have another talk with Carmine. The woman was getting tiresome. "I was saying that I think David and Jayne aren't seeing each other anymore, but I'm not sure. Did you and he discuss that today at work?"

"David broke up with Jayne? Why? I thought they were good together."

The man was an idiot. Despite the family name and money, he was a total fool. If she wasn't around to monitor him, he wouldn't be able to get dressed in the morning.

"They're not good together. They're a disaster. Which isn't the point. Has your son said anything?"

"No."

"Will you ask him?"

"Ask me yourself, Mother."

David walked into the living room and paused by the sofa.

Elizabeth felt his anger from several feet away, but she smiled so he wouldn't know. "David, darling. How nice to see you. Are you here for dinner? You didn't call, but I'm sure there's plenty. You know how Carmine loves to cook for twenty."

"I'm not interested in dinner. I want to talk to you."

Blaine stood. "Something to drink?" he asked.

"No." David's gaze slid back to Elizabeth. "You're going to back off, Mother. Starting now. You and Rebecca have no part of this."

She sipped her drink. "Sit down. You're hysterical."

"This is my life. Stop screwing with it."

She stiffened. "Excuse me?"

"You heard me."

"Blaine, are you listening to this? Your son is being disrespectful."

Blaine walked to the cabinet by the window and poured himself another drink. "What have you done this time, Elizabeth?"

"Me? Nothing but worry about those I love." She was doing her best to keep her only son from making a disastrous mistake, but did they appreciate that? Of course not.

"She and Rebecca have been doing their damnedest to break up Jayne and me, and they've succeeded."

Confirmation at last, Elizabeth thought with relief. Exccllent.

"Jayne won't see me. She says it's over."

"Then I don't see the problem," Elizabeth said. "I know it's always difficult to lose the girl, but there are so many others out there. Appropriate young women with good families. I have several names and numbers for you."

"I can get my own girl, Mother. I don't need your help. What I do need is for you to stay out of my life."

She rose and faced him. "So you can do what? Marry Jayne Scott? There's a disaster. I should have known this was going to happen. She's always been one to sneak around and slip into places she wasn't wanted. She's been using us for years, just waiting for an opportunity."

"Are you actually listening to what you're saying?" David asked. "Jayne isn't anything like that, and you know it. She's been a part of this family for twelve years. In all that time she's been kind and loyal. She's been your unquestioning lapdog, and you've never appreciated her."

"Jayne's a good girl," Blaine said. "I've always liked her."

"How lovely for you," Elizabeth said, wishing he would go back to his stupid magazine. "I know the truth. She's after money and power, and you're her way to get it. She's been planning this for years. She's been living her whole life in anticipation of trapping you."

"You're wrong," David said. "Were you always like this? A blind snob who assumes the worst about everyone?"

Elizabeth drew back. "Don't speak to me like that."

"Why not? It's true. Jayne is special. She's sweet and funny and unassuming. I like who I am when I'm around her, and I hope she feels the same way about me. I want to hear her opinions on everything. I want to show her the world and take care of her."

"You're not in love with her," she commanded, as if her words could make it so.

"I am. Not that it matters. She's giving up her life here because of this family. She's better than all of us, and we've been damned lucky to have her in our lives. And now she's leaving." He moved closer to Elizabeth. "Back off, Mother. Stay out of Jayne's life. Do you hear me? That's what I came to tell you. Stay the hell away from her."

Elizabeth had seen David in every mood imaginable, but she'd never felt such rage directed at her. She dropped to the sofa, suddenly afraid, although she couldn't say of what.

Then he was gone, and the room was still.

She felt sick inside. Hot and cold, with her stomach roiling.

Blaine set down his drink. "I don't know if this is a good time or a bad time," he began.

She drew in a breath. "I swear, I can't face another inane conversation with you right now."

"Then I'll make this quick. I'm leaving you, Elizabeth. My lawyers will be in touch with you in the morning."

He was speaking, but all she heard was a buzzing sound. Then she was gasping, as if all the air had left the room.

"W-what?"

"I'm done here," he said. "I want a divorce."

Nineteen

REBECCA TRIED TO UNDERSTAND the words, but it was impossible. All she knew for sure was that she'd never once seen Elizabeth cry, let alone hysterically. Her mother covered her face with her hands and rocked back and forth on the sofa, keening sharply between high-pitched cries of distress.

"What happened?" Rebecca asked again, hovering. "Where's Dad?"

Apparently the wrong question, she thought as her mother exploded into deeper sobs that seemed ready to rip her apart.

An hour earlier Rebecca had been eating takeout, ready to watch that adorable Anderson Cooper on CNN. Then her mother had called and asked her to come over. At least that's what she thought she'd said. It had been hard to understand the exact words. Now she knew why.

"Do you want a drink? Should I call a doctor?" She'd already brought in a box of tissues and didn't know what else to do.

Elizabeth sucked in a breath. Rebecca braced herself

for another round of tears, but her mother finally pulled herself together.

"It's Blaine," she managed, wiping at her dripping mascara. "He left."

"You mean to get you something?" Drugs seemed like a good idea. Something to calm Elizabeth down.

"No, you fool. He left *me.*" Elizabeth sprang to her feet and crossed to the open cabinet by the window. She poured scotch into a glass and gulped it down. "Your father left me. He wants a divorce."

Rebecca felt her mouth pop open as she let her handbag fall to the carpet. "What? Daddy's gone?"

"Apparently. I didn't see him actually leave, although I heard the door close. He said . . ." She pressed her lips together and poured more scotch. "I'm sure it's some type of crisis. Something hormonal."

A divorce? "But you've been married forever."

"Thirty-five years."

"I don't want to be from a broken home." It wasn't right. "Everything will change. I don't want that."

"This isn't about you!" Elizabeth yelled. "Can't you think of someone else for once? Your father left me. Do you know what that means? I'm ruined."

Rebecca shifted in her seat. "Maybe he'll change his mind."

"I doubt it."

"Is there . . ." She cleared her throat, not sure she wanted to know. "Is there someone else?"

Elizabeth just looked at her.

"Oh, God. Is she really young? Is she younger than me?"

"Oh, no. That would be understandable. That would allow people to take my side of things. But would Blaine do the reasonable, normal thing? Of course not. He has left me for Marjorie Danes."

It took Rebecca a moment to place the woman. She lived down the street, in an even larger house. "But she's old. She has grandchildren and doesn't color her hair."

Elizabeth gulped more scotch. After pouring a third drink, she returned to the sofa. "It's a disaster. That stupid cow of a woman. It's ridiculous. Have you seen her in a sleeveless dress? Her arms sag. I'm sure her breasts hang to her knees. She's done nothing to keep herself looking young, and yet she's the one he claims he wants."

"Did he say why?"

"Does it matter?"

Rebecca thought it might. There had to be a reason Blaine would leave his wife of thirty-five years to be with someone who was practically interchangeable.

"She's a tedious little woman who never has anything to say for herself," Elizabeth went on. "This couldn't have happened at a worse time."

She leaned back against the cushions and closed her eyes. "I'll lose everything. The house belongs to your father. I tried to get on the deed, but he wouldn't have it. Without this house, who am I? My friends will all abandon me. My social standing is linked to Blaine. Without him . . ."

Without him, Elizabeth was another abandoned middle-aged woman. A former secretary who had gotten pregnant with her boss's baby, Rebecca thought. There would be money. She knew her father would be more than generous. But actual cash only bought so much. There were rules in Beverly Hills, and one of the most unbreakable was the partner with the power kept the friends. In this case, that was Blaine. Elizabeth would only be a threat to her married friends. Worse, she would be a reminder that it could also happen to them.

"I'll have nothing," Elizabeth said, tears leaking out of her eyes.

While part of Rebecca felt badly for her, what she most noticed was that her mother never mentioned missing Blaine or being sorry she'd lost the man. She had a feeling that if he'd simply moved out and left Elizabeth without letting anyone know, her mother would have been perfectly happy.

"And with David acting the way he is . . ." Elizabeth murmured.

"What about David?"

Elizabeth opened her eyes and straightened. There were lines on her face Rebecca had never seen before. A droop to her mouth. Her hair had lost its shine, and her chin seemed to sag a little.

"He is in love with Jayne. He stood right in this room and told me."

That was nearly as shocking as hearing her father had moved out. "He can't be. He can't love Jayne."

If he did, she wouldn't have anyone. She would be completely alone.

"That's what I said. I don't know how it happened, I just know that bitch is to blame. For all of this. She's given him ideas." Elizabeth began to cry again. "I won't have anyone. I'll be all alone."

The exact echo of her own words made Rebecca want to jump out of her skin.

"He can't see what he's doing," her mother continued. "He'll ruin everything." She stretched out her hands to Rebecca. "You're all I have left. It's just the two of us." Her fingers shook with her sobs. "Promise me you'll never leave me."

Rebecca stalked into David's office the following morning. She was bleary-eyed with exhaustion and out for blood. Her mother hadn't let her sleep more than an hour at a time. Elizabeth kept coming into the guest room, where Rebecca hadn't wanted to stay at all, but her mother had insisted, going on about how everything was ruined.

Her brother barely looked up when she entered. "You're not my favorite person right now," he told her.

"You think I give a damn? Thanks to you, our family is disintegrating. Do you know Dad moved out?"

That got David's attention. He turned from his computer screen to look at her. "What?"

"Last night. After your performance, by the way. He announced he was leaving her. They're getting a divorce."

She collapsed into one of the chairs in front of his desk and removed her sunglasses. "I haven't slept, and I feel like crap. Mom's a total mess. Crying and drinking. I thought she was going to start pulling out her hair. I've never seen her like this. It's scaring me. You have to do something."

"What can I do? It's their decision."

"Do you want them to split up? Do you want to be from a broken home?"

"I'm nearly thirty-three. I can handle my parents getting a divorce."

"I can't. This is all your fault. You're making trouble, and it's spilling over into everything."

"I had nothing to do with it, and you know it."

Possibly, she thought, wishing she'd stopped for a latte. "David, this is serious. Dad says he's leaving Mom for Marjorie Danes."

David barely looked surprised. "I can see why he would."

"What? She's nobody. Okay, she has money, but he doesn't need that."

David's expression turned pitying. "You think this is about money?"

"What else matters?"

"I don't know. How about being with someone who makes you happy? Who acts as if she's happy to see you when you show up? Think about it. Would you have stayed with Elizabeth if you were Dad? Weren't you always going on about how he should leave her?"

Rebecca didn't like the question, so she ignored it. "You have to go talk some sense into him. Explain how bad this will look and how it hurts us."

"We've been out of the house for years," David told her. "I'm not going to ask one of my parents to put his happiness on hold because you're not uncomfortable."

She straightened. "What about Mom? What has she done to deserve this?"

"You're defending her? How about tricking him into marriage, having an affair, and belittling him every chance she got? I'm not sure she even likes him. He's a way into the lifestyle she enjoys, but is there anything else?"

"Not the point," she said. "I don't want my parents getting a divorce."

"Then you have a problem."

"David! You have to fix this."

"I can't, and even if I could, I won't. This isn't *about* you, Rebecca. It's something difficult for you to comprehend, but try. People have to be responsible for their own lives and decisions."

"This is all because of Jayne," she grumbled.

David stood and pointed to the door. "Get out," he told her, his eyes cold and his mouth pulled into a straight line. "I'm not discussing Jayne with you anymore."

She blinked at him. "What? I didn't say anything."

"Sure you did. What have you got against Jayne? What has she ever done to you?"

What was it with all the hard questions?

"She's been like a sister to you," he continued. "Loving, loyal."

"She's been well paid for her loyalty."

"Nice," David said sarcastically. "I always knew you were selfish, I just didn't know you were a bitch, too."

She stood and clutched her purse tightly to her stomach. "David, don't," she whined. "Why are you being mean? It's just Jayne. She's been around forever, and you never bothered to notice her before. Don't go all righteous on me just because you're screwing her now."

"I won't listen to this," he said, and started for the door.

She went after him and grabbed his arm. "Wait. I don't get it."

"Exactly," he said contemptuously. "You've never gotten it. You say Jayne doesn't fit in our world, but you're wrong. She fits in just fine. More impressive, she fits in anywhere. She has a level of class you can only aspire to."

"Oh, please. Have you seen what she wears to work? Those disgusting scrubs?"

"She's a nurse. Do you want her in Armani? But it's not about her clothes. It's about who she is." He paused, and his expression changed to almost . . . pitying.

"You'll never get it," he said. "You can't. Neither can Mom. But I see Jayne for who she is, and I'm not going to let either of you ruin the best thing that's ever happened to me."

He left then, walking out of his own office, leaving her feeling abandoned and oddly embarrassed, although she couldn't say why.

She stood there a second, not sure what to do next, then saw her father enter his office.

"Dad!" she yelled, racing after him. "Dad, wait. I have to talk to you."

While Elizabeth had looked old and haggard that morning, Blaine looked rested and happy. "Good morning, Rebecca."

"Not for me. I spent the night at the house."

"I'm glad your mother had someone there for her. I thought she might call one of her friends to be with her."

"As if. Do you know what they would be thinking? She's humiliated. How could you do this? How could you destroy our family?"

"The family you've ignored for ten years? This is between your mother and me. I've spent the better part of my marriage knowing I was a disappointment to my wife. I gave her everything I could think of to make her happy, but it was never enough. Eventually, I realized it would never be enough because I don't matter to her. She wants what I can provide, but she doesn't want me."

"This is too much information," Rebecca murmured. "Just go talk to her."

"We have talked. I'm not getting any younger, Rebecca. I don't think it's unreasonable to ask to spend the years I have left with someone who actually likes me. I hope your mother can find the same."

"But I—"

"No."

"Daddy! I don't want this."

"You would rather I was unhappy and living with your mother than happy somewhere else?"

"Yes."

"You've never cared about Elizabeth's feelings before."

"She says we only have cach other. There is no way I'm going to be responsible for her. That's your job."

His face took on the same expression David's had held. A combination of disappointment and pity. "Not anymore. Now you should leave. I have a lot to do today."

"But you have to go back."

"No, Rebecca. I don't."

Despite having grown up within spitting distance of Beverly Hills, Jayne had never been to Bel Air before. As she drove through the faux gates separating the exclusive neighborhood from the rest of the city, she told herself everybody got to be stupid now and then. It kept a person grounded and in touch with reality. This was her day for that.

David's real estate person had called the previous night to set up an appointment to see a house. Jayne had done her best to explain that she wouldn't be going on the house-hunting trips anymore, but the agent had insisted. This house was special. She felt it was "the one" and wanted Jayne to see it.

"In my next life, I'm going to have an actual backbone," Jayne murmured as she checked the address, then turned onto a side street.

The homes were nice. The deeper she went into the neighborhood, the more normal they seemed. There were big lots and tall trees. She turned another corner, then saw the FOR SALE sign in front. Imagine—a neighborhood where one actually put a sign in the front yard. Scandalous!

After she did a quick tour of the house, she would go by the movers and pick up more boxes. The guy who had given her the estimate had promised to tell her when they had used boxes in. Those were free to customers and, given the cost of new boxes, much more to her liking. She'd already packed up her spare room and would be starting on her kitchen that afternoon.

Jayne parked and walked toward the front door. It was only after she rang the bell that she realized the real estate agent's car wasn't in the driveway. Had she gotten the time wrong?

The door opened, but instead of a stranger or the agent, she saw David standing inside. She took a step back.

"What are you doing here?" she asked, trying not to be happy to see him.

"Waiting for you. Please, come inside."

She didn't want to. She should run in the opposite direction. Seeing him would only make a difficult situation worse. He looked too good in jeans and a leather jacket. She had to resist. Only she was weak where he was concerned, and five minutes in his company couldn't hurt anything, could it?

She walked inside.

The house was large but homey, with hardwood floors and pale walls. The entryway led into a big living room with French doors that opened onto a huge backyard. David put his hand on the small of her back and guided her toward the open French door.

"There's a dog run on the side, and the swing set stays," he said, pointing to the built-in play area. "There's a pool around the corner, and it's completely fenced."

He grabbed her hand, pulling her back inside. "The

kitchen has double ovens, just like you said you wanted, and a pantry. There are his and her closets, a media room. Built-ins in the dining room. The schools are great, or we can go private. There are plenty of those around."

He was talking too fast for her to follow what he was saying. "I don't understand. Why are you looking at this house? I thought you wanted to live in Malibu?"

Still holding on to her hand, he moved closer. "I want to be wherever makes you happy, Jayne. You said you wanted a family house. A place for kids and a dog. I remember everything you ever said you wanted, and it's here. In this house."

He looked happy and hopeful, while she felt sick to her stomach. "David, I—"

"Don't," he said, lightly kissing her, then releasing her hand. "Don't say anything."

They were in the kitchen of a strange house. It was a Tuesday. Things like this didn't happen on Tuesdays. Unbelievably, David Worden pulled a small box out of his jacket pocket. A ring box. Then he dropped to one knee.

"Jayne, I love you. I never thought I'd find anyone as wonderful as you. You're everything I ever wanted and more. I want to spend the rest of my life making you as happy as you've made me. I want us to grow old together, raise a family, live each day for all it's worth. Take a chance on me, please. Take this journey with me. Jayne, will you marry me?"

Still on one knee, he opened the box and showed her the beautiful diamond ring nestled in dark purple velvet.

It was a fairy-tale moment, she thought sadly, staring into his eyes. She loved him more than she had ever thought possible. If she said yes, she would have everything she'd ever wanted. And more.

And it was the more that made the situation impossible.

He'd gone to so much trouble to find the perfect house. He'd listened, which was a miracle, and remembered, which was even more amazing. He was caring, sweet, affectionate, and he'd waited long enough to be sure of what he wanted.

Her. He wanted her.

She reached for his hand and drew him to his feet. "I've had a crush on you since I was in high school," she whispered. "I couldn't seem to fall for anyone else because I kept comparing them to you, and they fell short of what I thought you would be. Then you came home and I broke my wrist and we actually got to know each other. You turned out to be even better than I'd imagined."

He smiled then, obviously happy with the words. He pulled the ring out of the box and reached for her hand.

"No," she said, tucking her hands behind her back. "I can't marry you. I love you, David. Believe me, this is hard to say. There's a voice in my head screaming that I can't be doing this. I can't let you go. Except I have to. I'm leaving, and I'm never coming back. It's not just about the job. It's about my life. I can't live it in the shadow of your family."

His smile faded. "You won't marry me because of my mother?"

"In part. Because of her and Rebecca, but mostly because of me. Because of who I am around them. I've wanted to break free a dozen times. This is the only way." She felt tears on her cheeks. "I'm sorry. I do love you."

"Not enough."

She thought about what life would be like with Elizabeth a scant five miles away. With Rebecca's dramatics and Elizabeth's pronouncements.

"Your mother would never let this happen," she continued. "She'd find a way to talk you out of it."

"If you believe that, you don't think very much of me."

"Actually, I do. I think the world of you. I wish you the best."

"Don't start," he said, shoving the ring in his pocket. "Don't tell me to be happy with someone else. That's bullshit."

"No, David. That's loving you."

She raised herself up on tiptoe and kissed his cheek, then walked out. She had a little trouble getting her car door open, probably because she was crying so hard. Then she started the engine and drove away. Back to the real world, where girls like her didn't get the handsome prince, and the glass slipper never really fit.

Twenty

DAVID DROVE BACK TO the office, mostly because there wasn't anywhere else to go. Getting on a plane was the easiest solution. Get on a plane and fly somewhere far and dangerous, and get lost for a few months. Then, when he was better, he would return and face all this.

Except he didn't want to be anywhere else, he just didn't want to be here. Not without Jayne.

He pulled into his underground parking space and took the elevator up to the office level. Dammit all to hell, how could she tell him she loved him, then walk away? Who did that? If she really loved him, she would . . .

The elevator doors opened on the fourth floor, but he didn't get out. They closed again.

If she really loved him, she would change her life for him? Deal with Elizabeth? He knew his mother, and Jayne was right. Elizabeth wouldn't accept the engagement graciously. She would do everything in her power to come between them. While he didn't completely understand Jayne's relationship with his mother, he knew it was complicated and difficult, and he understood that

Jayne's survival was at stake. She wouldn't have uprooted her entire life otherwise.

The elevator stopped in the parking garage again. When the doors opened, Marjorie Danes stepped on, looked at him, and glanced toward the closing doors. As if wondering why he didn't get out.

She was shorter than Elizabeth, and rounder. Not elegant, not expensively dressed. She looked close to her age—something remarkable when one was over forty in Beverly Hills. But there was a kindness in her eyes, and when she smiled, warmth filled the small space.

"Do you hate me?" she asked by way of greeting. "You probably do, and I suppose you should. But I'm hoping we can put a time limit on that. I'd like to get to know you. Blaine can't stop talking about you. He's just so proud." She paused as the elevator began to move. "I never meant to be the other woman."

She shrugged. "I'm not really other-woman material, you know. Blaine and I were friends for years. After my husband died, he helped me with my finances. Helped me to understand them, mostly. I liked him. He's a good man. Funny, which was nice. It sort of evolved after that. Slowly. I knew I was in love with him, but he was married, and I was fine being in the background. Then one night he came to dinner and didn't leave."

David flinched.

She laughed. "Don't worry. I promise not to discuss details. There are few things that can clear a room faster than talk of old-people sex."

They reached the fourth floor. This time David followed her out. She touched his arm.

"I was happy with the affair. But one day Blaine said that he wanted more. That he wanted us to be together always. I'm not saying I don't have responsibility. I do. I'll take all of it. I'm saying we didn't want to hurt anyone." The smile faded. "Isn't that what criminals always say? So that doesn't work. I suppose I want you to know I'm sorry for the pain you and your family are going through. But I can't be sorry I love Blaine. He's a blessing, and at my age, you get pretty excited by blessings."

She paused in the middle of the hallway. "Now I've been doing all the talking. Mostly because I'm nervous. Do you want to say anything? You can call me a bitch if that would help. I won't like it, but I'll understand why."

Marjorie was earnest and sincere, David thought. Excluding Jayne, he couldn't remember the last time he'd observed those two qualities in the same person. Looking at her slightly rumpled appearance, he understood Elizabeth's rage and Rebecca's confusion. But he also understood why Blaine had sought solace in her company. He could see exactly how friendship had blossomed into something more. He also believed that Marjorie would have accepted a long-term affair, but that his father could never treat the woman he loved that way.

Elizabeth was the true victim, he reminded himself. The abandoned wife. While he felt sympathy for her, there was also a part of him that knew she had earned her fate.

He bent down and kissed Marjorie's cheek. "I look forward to getting to know you better."

She bit her lower lip. "That's it? You don't want to take me up on my offer to call me a bitch?"

"Maybe later."

She smiled again, and this time it was bright enough to light the whole building. She practically glowed with happiness. David ignored the stab of envy, the one that told him he wanted what his father had—a chance with the woman he loved.

Marjorie linked arms with him. "Blaine told me you're dating Jayne Scott. She's lovely. I've always enjoying talking to her. I go to the breast center where she works. A few years ago, I had a callback after a mammogram. Talk about frightening. I phoned Jayne, and she was so warm and helpful. She was there for my follow-up. She's very professional, but kind. She made me feel better. It turned out to be nothing, but I've never forgotten how she reassured me."

The sense of emptiness and loss returned. He wanted to go somewhere and lick his wounds in private. He didn't want anyone to know what had happened, yet he found himself saying, "I asked her to marry me."

Marjorie beamed at him. "How wonderful. Such babies you'll have."

"She refused."

Marjorie stopped and faced him. "I find that hard to believe. I've seen her looking at you, David. There's love in her eyes. She watches you like a woman who . . ." She blushed slightly. "Let's just say I know the feeling."

"She's leaving Los Angeles. Mostly because of my family. I understand the reasons, but if she loves me . . ." Back to that again. "I don't know what to do. I can't change my mother."

"Elizabeth would be a problem. Jayne isn't at all the sort of daughter-in-law she had in mind. Now, one of Prince Andrew's daughters might do for her, although they're a little young for you." Marjorie tilted her head. "Is Jayne's largest objection Elizabeth? She doesn't have any problems with you?"

"Not that she said. She told me that she loves me but couldn't live in the shadow of my family."

"Where is she going?"

"Dallas."

"Texas," Marjorie said with a sigh. "I have family there myself. Mostly in Houston, but a few cousins are in the Dallas area."

"She has a new job, and she's sold her condo here."

"She sounds determined," Marjorie said. "Someone who will stand up to you. You need that in a woman."

"It doesn't do me much good if she's twelve hundred miles away," he growled.

"No, it doesn't." She patted his arm. "Have you considered it's not your family that's the problem, but her proximity to them? Part of loving someone is wanting what is best for that other person. I would never have asked Blaine to leave Elizabeth. It wasn't my place. I suspect Jayne would never ask you to change anything about your life for her. But that doesn't mean you can't come up with the idea on your own."

She was right, he thought, the pain easing enough for him to think. The problem was Elizabeth and, in part, Rebecca. Jayne was willing to move halfway across the country to escape his mother. Why couldn't he do the same?

"You're brilliant," he told Marjorie, then kissed her on the cheek again. "I need to talk to my dad."

"Of course you do. I'll go downstairs and amuse myself looking at jewelry. Blaine wants me to pick out something for myself, and I've never found the time. Will an hour do?"

"Yes. Thank you."

"Just invite me to the wedding."

"Promise."

Jayne emptied the last of her towels into the large box, then went hunting for more items to fill it. Packing was a whole lot more work than she'd realized. When she'd moved into her condo, she'd had almost nothing. A dozen boxes and an end table. Her possessions had grown since then.

The movers were coming on Monday. She would get the last of her packing finished, then watch her stuff be loaded Monday morning, including her car. She would fly out first thing Tuesday morning and start her new life in Dallas. Honestly, the move couldn't come soon enough.

Her weekend of packing had started with a call from one of Elizabeth's so-called friends wanting to know if the rumors were true. Had Blaine left Elizabeth for dowdy Marjorie Danes? Jayne had no way of knowing, not that she would have said anything if she had. Still, she couldn't forget the question, and she wondered if it was possible. Marjorie had always been someone Jayne liked, and she had a feeling the other woman could make Blaine happy, but to leave Elizabeth after all these years? She wasn't sure how she felt about that.

After lunch, she tackled the rest of the kitchen. She would live on takeout and use paper plates for the last twenty-four hours. About two o'clock her doorbell rang.

For a second she thought about not answering it. She didn't want to speak to Rebecca again or see Elizabeth. But when the bell rang again, she found herself dutifully walking toward the door and pulling it open.

Her visitor was both better and worse than she'd imagined. Better, because it was impossible to look at David and not feel immediately better about everything, and worse, because there was no way she could be with him.

He looked happy enough as he walked into her condo, leaned in, and kissed her. Then he glanced around.

"You're nearly packed," he said. "I was hoping I could help. I wanted to get here sooner, but there was a lot to do. I should have sent someone over. Talk about being a clod. I'm sorry."

She cleared her throat. "That's okay," she said cautiously. "I didn't expect you to help me leave town."

He looked happy, which was weird. And confident, which was expected. Her lips were still tingling from his kiss. She briefly wondered if he would be open to a farewell night of hot sex. Something for the road, so to speak. Dangerous, yes, but definitely worth it.

"Can we sit down?" he asked.

She motioned to the living room. "Help yourself."

He walked into the small space, but instead of sitting, he walked to the dining area, then back.

"I've been to Dallas. That's where I was most of the week. Blaine went with me. We looked at retail space and office buildings. It's nice. I like it. Marjorie has a lot of family in Texas. Mostly in Houston, but she's been to Dallas a lot. She showed us around. Have you had Tex-Mex? It's great."

He wasn't making any sense, she thought. "Why would you go to Dallas? And with Marjorie?" Oh. The rumors must be true. "Blaine left Elizabeth?"

"Yes, and I think she's the only one who's surprised. It's kind of strange being around my dad right now. He's crazy about Marjorie. But it's good, too. You know? For both of them." He moved toward her. "I thought about what you said. About my family. I get it. You can't stay here and be yourself, and I can't convince you to try. But I still love you and want to be with you."

Talk about perfect and heartbreaking at the same time. "David, I—"

"No. Let me finish. Blaine and I have found space for the offices. And the perfect retail spot opens at the end of the month. We'll need about six months for renovation. And it will take a while for the company to move out, so I'll have to go back and forth at first."

He stepped in front of her and took her hand in his. "Jayne, I love you. I'm not giving you up because of my mother. If you need to live in Dallas, then I'll move there. Worden's can be run from anywhere in the world. Blaine and Marjorie are coming as well, but I didn't think either of them was the problem."

She stared into his eyes, not sure what to think. What to believe. The words made sense individually, but when strung together as a sentence or a thought, they were un-intelligible.

"You're moving the company?" she asked.

He nodded.

"For me?"

"Don't sound so surprised. I love you."

He kissed her then, his mouth warm and firm, yet gentle. It was as if he put all his love into that kiss. Warmth washed over her and through her, heating her from the inside.

"I want to be wherever you are," he said. "It's not about location. It's about you and me. I'd do anything for you, Jayne. Just tell me what you want."

Talk about impossible to refuse, she thought, as she flung herself to him and hung on, vowing never to let go. The enormity of what he was doing stunned her, as did the proof of his love.

"You're the best man I've ever known," she whispered.

"I know."

She laughed, then found herself crying, then kissing him because that made the most sense.

"You'll marry me?" he asked after a few minutes. He was already guiding her back toward the bedroom.

"Yes."

"In Dallas?"

"Anywhere but here."

"Good." He grinned and pulled the diamond engagement ring out of his pocket. "This is for you. But only if you promise to take your clothes off."

She laughed. "I seem unable to tell any Worden no."

"Lucky me."

Rebecca drove around the city until she was lost. As Los Angeles covered hundreds of square miles she'd never explored, that didn't take long. The streets got more narrow, the houses smaller. There were beat-up cars on blocks and graffiti covering houses.

Every few miles she made random turns, not sure where she was going or what she would do when she got there. She only knew she couldn't go home.

Her phone rang again, but she didn't answer it. Only one person called these days. Her mother. Elizabeth wanted them to live together in the Worden house and have part of it converted to a studio where Rebecca could work. Elizabeth wanted to take over her marketing, to run the Rivalsa brand, as she had taken to calling it.

David and her father had left nearly two weeks ago,

for Dallas, of all places. Elizabeth had told her. They were moving the whole company there and settling permanently. Marjorie Danes had gone as well. Blaine had given Elizabeth permission to live in the house in Beverly Hills. He was being financially generous in the divorce, something that made Elizabeth both grateful and bitter.

Neither her father nor her brother had called her, Rebecca thought sadly. Blaine had sent her a brief e-mail telling her that she was no longer a part of the new line of jewelry, but that Worden's would be happy to keep selling her more expensive pieces. Lucky her.

She hadn't heard from Nigel, either. He'd been scared away by whatever threats Blaine and David had delivered. Or perhaps Ariel had been the one to push him into line.

But of all of them, the person she missed most was Jayne. She knew her friend was gone and didn't think there was any way to get her back. She'd lost Jayne because she'd been stupid and selfish and mean. She'd been a horrible friend. Worse, she'd hurt the one person who had always mattered the most.

At the next intersection, she saw a small church off to the right. She noticed it because it was freshly painted in a neighborhood of dull and broken buildings. There were flowers in front, and a sign posted in the grass welcoming everyone to a list of activities.

Between choir practice, Bible study, the women's group, teen challenge, and regular services, the church was a busy place. Impulsively, Rebecca turned into the lot and parked her car.

There was a group of boys playing basketball. They stopped and stared at her for a few minutes, then one of the smaller kids ran inside. Rebecca hoped she hadn't scared him. She just needed a minute to figure out what to do next.

She could go back to Milan. She liked Italy, had always been able to work there. But the thought of creating anything seemed impossible. It was as if all the fire inside of her had burned away. She felt guilty, but she knew she hadn't done anything wrong. She felt alone, and there were people everywhere. It was as if she'd somehow mislaid her life.

Someone tapped on the glass. She looked up into a man's face. His brown eyes were kind.

"Are you all right?" he asked.

She rolled down the window. "Is this your church?"

He smiled. "It's God's church, but I take care of it for Him. Who are you? Are you lost?"

"I think so."

"You're close to the freeway. I-10. Can you find your way from there?"

If she went west, I-10 would take her back to Santa Monica. If she went east, she could drive all the way to Texas.

She nodded.

"Come inside. I'll draw you a map." He straightened. "Don't worry about your car. It will be safe here. On the street, not so much, but in the parking lot, you're fine."

She rolled up the window, then took her purse and followed him.

They didn't go into the main church, but instead went behind it to a tiny house. The building looked old. Inside, the small rooms were filled with worn furniture and books. Hundreds of books were stacked everywhere.

The man, maybe in his forties, wearing jeans and a worn Trinity College sweatshirt, bent over a tiny table, drawing on a lined sheet of paper.

"Two lefts and a right," he said, straightening and handing her the paper. "You'll see the freeway up ahead."

"Thank you."

He studied her. "Are you all right?"

"Sure. I'm great." She looked around at the crowded space. "Do you live here?"

He grinned. "Yeah. Me and an old cat. Just as well. There's no room for anyone else."

"You run programs, preach, help the poor?"

He frowned, as if confused by the question. "Something like that."

"The flowers outside are nice."

"God is into nature." He shrugged. "Sorry. I was kidding. Not everyone gets that."

"Do you accept donations?"

"It's how we survive."

She probably had a few hundred dollars in her purse, but instead, she reached into the front pocket of her designer jeans. The small blue stone slipped out easily, as if it had been waiting to be set free.

The flawless diamond nestled in her palm.

The man took a step back. "What is that? A sapphire or something?"

"A blue diamond. There aren't very many in the world that are natural rather than manufactured. A friend gave this to me. I didn't know what to do with it. I want you to have it."

"I don't think that's a good idea."

"It's not stolen. I swear." She put it on the table. The instant she released the stone, she felt oddly light inside.

He eyed it suspiciously. "Why are you giving it to me?"

Because she didn't want to give it back to Nigel, but she couldn't keep it. Because in the end, a diamond was just a hard rock, and what she'd lost instead was much more heartbreaking. Because she'd never once done anything selfless in her life.

Because of Jayne.

"Because God is into nature," she said.

She returned to her car and glanced at the map. Ten minutes later, she was heading east on I-10. Dallas would take a couple of days, which was probably just long enough for her to figure out how she was supposed to say she was sorry.

There was a lot more she needed to do, but she would start there and somehow find her way back to where she was supposed to be.

THE BEST OF FRIENDS

Book Club Discussion Guide

Dear Reader,

I'm honored that you've chosen *The Best of Friends* as your book club selection. I've provided these questions to help you get the conversation going. Be forewarned, the questions contain spoilers, so I recommend that you not read them until after you've finished the book.

I would love to hear from you and the members of your club. Please write to me via my website, www.susanmallery .com. Or stop by my Facebook page, Facebook.com/SusanMallery, and join the discussion there. I'd be happy to answer any questions you have about Jayne and Rebecca's story. In the meantime…

Happy reading!

Susan Mallery

Questions

1. What are the major turning points of the story?

2. What are the overall themes? How does the title *The Best of Friends* reinforce or contradict the themes? Describe the lessons you take away from this book.

3. Discuss the subplots. How do these subplots support and enrich the major themes?

4. With whom did you empathize most strongly, Jayne, Rebecca, or Elizabeth? Discuss each of these characters in terms of how they are alike and different. How did you come to feel differently about the characters as the story progressed? What did you learn about each that made you consider them in a new light?

5. Do you believe that Rebecca truly loved her friend Jayne? Why or why not? What did she do or not do to support your belief? Do you believe that Jayne truly loved her friend Rebecca? Why or why not? What did she do or not do to support your belief?

6. Everyone in life is the hero/heroine of his/her own story. How do you think the women in *The Best of Friends* perceived themselves differently from the way they were perceived by others?

7. Why does Jayne feel that she has to move? Do you agree that this is the only way for her to reclaim her own life? Why did she make so many sacrifices for the Worden family over the years? Was it out of love or weakness? Would you have done the same if you'd been orphaned and alone in the world? Explain. When did Jayne finally begin to stand up for herself, and how did you react to her actions?

8. In their own way, both David and Rebecca ran away from the family long before Jayne did. Why do you think they left? Why did they come back, and why now? Why did Rebecca take the name Rivalsa when she began to design jewelry?

9. Jayne believes that everyone sees her as "reliable and sensible." Do you agree? Why or why not? What is the one personality trait that stands out most strongly in your mind for each of the following characters?

   a. Jayne
   b. Rebecca
   c. David

d. Elizabeth

e. Blaine

f. Jonathan

What do you think is your strongest personality trait? What do you think are the strongest personality traits of the other members of your book club?

10. Do you believe Jonathan had any lingering feelings for Elizabeth? What did that affair mean to him? What did Elizabeth feel for him at the time and now? How did you feel about Rebecca's behavior toward Jonathan? Do you think he truly had feelings for her? How did you feel about his revenge on her? Was it appropriate retribution for her actions toward him?

11. Discuss the animosity between Rebecca and Elizabeth. Where do you think it started? Do you think their relationship will improve in the future? Why or why not? How is their relationship similar to or different from your relationship with your mother?

12. Why do you think Elizabeth was horrified when she discovered that Jayne was David's mystery woman? How did you feel about David's reaction when Elizabeth confronted him? Why wasn't Rebecca happy for David and Jayne when she realized they were falling in love with each other?

13. Do you think Jayne and David will have a happy relationship? What makes you believe that? Do you think they made the right decision about where to live? What would you have done differently, if anything?

14. Do you think Jayne and Rebecca will ever become friends again? Should they? Why or why not? Is every friendship worth saving? Why or why not? Have you ever experienced or witnessed a toxic friendship? Explain.

15. Did you find the ending to be satisfying? Why or why not? How were the plot and subplots resolved? What questions were left unanswered? Do you think there's hope for Rebecca and, if so, how does she need to change in order to have a happy life?